A Love to Die For
Part 3

Restless Souls

Leigh Oakley

"Secrets, like buried weeds, will one day break the surface"

Chapter 1

Carl's pain was visible as he heard the words fall from his son's mouth. Tommy knew he would be disappointed, but he also knew that he was not about to embark on a lifetime of toil in a backstreet garage to appease his father.

"Psychology? What the hell do you know about psychology?!"

Tommy didn't react. There was a lot he could have said, but he didn't want to turn his father's disappointment into another rift between them. He simply smiled.

Sonya quickly started to collect the empty dishes, to excuse herself from any confrontation. She had kept out of any conflict between father and son since her marriage to Carl several years ago. Sonya had no children of her own and this relentless conflict between father and son was a mystery to her. If this was normal, then she was thankful she had never had any.

They seemed like a hell of a lot more trouble than they were worth. But then, she didn't really know what they were worth. She had never felt the kind of love that rips your heart open and the despair that consumes you when you can't fix everything for them. The insane rage with which you would defend them, to the death if necessary.

Tommy smiled again. Sonya amused him in her housecoat and slippers scurrying away to avoid having to pick a side. As a stepmother she had been almost invisible other than for a constant source of amusement, food and clean clothes. Tommy didn't dislike her, as there was really nothing to like nor dislike. She was just one of those women who wanted nothing more out of life other than to look after her man and be as agreeable as humanly possible.

"So after a wasted year re-sitting your A levels and another on that fad of being a sports coach, not to mention two years bumming round Europe interrupted by Kelly's luxury cruises, you want to train in psychology at a private college!"

Tommy winked at Sonya in acknowledgment of the state his dad was getting into. She looked away worriedly, but Carl hadn't noticed Tommy's frivolity.

"It'll do me good to live away from home for a while."

Carl looked at him in disbelief.

"You're going to be resident?! It's at Ravenscar for Christ's sake, it's less that twenty miles away!"

Sonya placed the desert in front of each of them, giving Tommy the opportunity to thank her and to ignore his father's outburst.

"and I suppose Kelly is going to pay for this fancy new place, is she?"

Tommy rolled his eyes as though Carl was asking the obvious again.

"Well?" Carl snapped.

"Well what?"

"Is Kelly paying for it?"

"Yes," Tommy sighed "Kelly is paying for it and she's also paying for the accommodation before you ask."

"Bloody hell Tommy. Have you seen the place? It's brand new, and private tuition? How much more time and money do you intend to waste?"

He poured the cream onto his sticky toffee pudding and ignored the question. He knew this reaction well. Carl was feeling inferior to Kelly again. It was a familiar road and the best way to defuse the situation was to stop himself from saying anything at all, and right now the pudding was the perfect solution.

"Has she been tinting your bloody eyebrows again?!"

Tommy sighed. They had this confrontation at least once a month.

"I've told you a thousand times dad, anyone who has blonde hair has to tint their eyebrows unless they want to look like an albino!"

He hadn't listened to the answer, he'd heard it before.

"That woman is turning you into a pompous poser -boy!"

Tommy stuffed more pudding into his mouth without responding.

"And what's happened to your mate Adam? He's meant to be starting at the garage next week and I've not heard a peep from him?"

"Oh yes, about that." Tommy said sheepishly.

"He's changed his mind, I suppose, after I offered him a favour?"

"He's ill. I was meant to tell you, but I forgot."

"You two need to wake up," he was becoming more and more agitated, "If someone gives you a message to pass on, make sure you bloody do it and Adam needs to do his own dirty work. What's wrong with him anyway?"

"He got ill as soon as we landed from Thailand. He's got a hell of a fever. No idea what he's got but he's really sick."

Carl's eyes narrowed at his son's cavalier attitude.

"Well that's what you get for sponging off Kelly for the flight. Bet he had no money to spend when he got there. Probably been eating maggot-ridden meat from some slum market or other."

Tommy didn't bother enlightening his father to the fact that they had actually eaten like kings while they were there, thanks to his upgraded credit card. There was no point. It would just end one accusation and trigger a new one.

"Is this about your mother?" Carl blurted abruptly.

"Is what?"

"All this psychology nonsense!"

It was a predictable question and Tommy merely flicked back his heavy blonde fringe confidently and held his silence.

He would have loved to speak his mind, but it wouldn't end well.

Firstly, he would have loved to remind his dad that he didn't regard Sophie as his mother and never would. He also wanted to agree that when the woman who gave birth to you ties a boulder around her foot and throws herself off a cliff in the hope of finding a more agreeable family, then naturally psychology is going to hold some interest, but instead he shovelled in more pudding.

Anyway, these were not the deciding factors that had put Tommy on his chosen path. The truth would have been too painful for his dad to hear.

Kelly's success still stung Carl every day. The little hairdresser who had built her beauty empire into a string of Spa's and fitness centres across the county. Who would have thought that vanity and self-image would suddenly spiral as a lucrative business? More to the point, who would have thought that air-head Kelly would have the determination and focus to capture the market in an untouched area? An area previously ignorant to the status attached to perfect brows, toning, tanning and botox? The power and drive of a woman scorned!

It was obvious that Carl had hoped Tommy would carry on the family business by rolling up his sleeves and delving into the wonders of engine grease and brake fluid but the cruel reality was that he held no admiration for his father's achievements.

He tried never to take sides, but their respective lifestyles spoke for themselves. He had already turned down an attractive offer to join Kelly's company but out of compassion for Carl he had refused. He looked over at Carl's scouring face. If he kept on pushing like this he might just blurt it all out. That he thought his father was an idiot when it came to business. He had trundled along with his nose under one bonnet after another when he should have had it in the air evaluating the changing wind of small garages.

He should have noticed when car insurance companies started to offer breakdown cover for peanuts. When breakdown companies developed networks to improve reaction times, monitored performance, gave digital updates and hit response time targets.

That dealers were offering service plans, using manufacturer's diagnostics machines and providing courtesy cars. That small garages like his were jumping on the bandwagon and buying franchises in specialist services like tyres and exhausts. He should have sold when the tide started to turn or bought a franchise from one of the giants, but he didn't. Carl had simply plodded along while his revenue slid away along with his buying power. As a result, his customers diminished to a handful of elderly couples with cars they had owned for many years. The ones who didn't like change and didn't understand the streamlined approach. The ones who wanted to chat for half an hour at every visit.

Tommy often wondered how different it would have been if he'd managed to hold onto Kelly. Perhaps they would now be the tycoon family of North Yorkshire or perhaps Kelly would never have reached her potential at all, settling for Saturday perms in an equally pathetic backstreet business.

Of course, Kelly was equally disappointed that Tommy didn't want to slip into the position of her protégée, but she also understood how devastating that would be for Carl. Maybe some time in the future he might join forces with Kelly, maybe as a therapist but for now he needed to assume neutral ground. He couldn't deliver that blow to Carl right now any more than he could share his thoughts on the lack of foresight that had left him in the same house they bought when he was a child.

"Well?"

"Well what?" Tommy asked calmly

"Is this about your mother?"

"No dad. It's not. I just think that as I got a good A level grade in psychology, I must have a flair for it that's all."

Tommy had answered without hesitation. He didn't want his father worrying that he might be hoping to drag up their painful family history by trying to find answers to Sophie's madness, even though it was the absolute truth.

The absolute truth was that Tommy wasn't sure what he was hoping to achieve but he knew he had an insatiable obsession with the power of the mind. He had buried the tragedy of Sophie's tortured life admirably, but as the years passed, he had been as fascinated with that ability as with all the other unanswered questions. Did he really orchestrate his mother's death? Were the late-night whisperings something he made up or were they real? Was that question just his inner mind trying to vindicate himself, to relieve him of the guilt?

He was in no doubt that he hadn't liked Sophie, and in no doubt that he wanted her gone, but sometimes when he lay alone in the dark, he would dare to allow himself to remember.

He remembered her sickly smell, her wild eyes accusing him, her bony fingers and frail frame but he also remembered something else. Perhaps he wanted it to be true, perhaps he needed to justify his behaviour or to grasp at some hope of his innocence, but whatever the cause, the feeling was the same.

As he lay alone and allowed himself to remember there was something that he found impossible to deny. In the nights of whispering when he knew Sophie was outside his bedroom door he remembered the feeling of pleasure, he remembered the satisfaction of knowing that what she was hearing would spur her on to leave, he remembered not caring if she lived or died but he also remembered something else.

He remembered the sound of Becky's voice.

"You realise you're going to be a few years older than just about everyone else on the course?" Carl continued.

Tommy picked up the bowl and drank the rest of the cream from the bowl, putting it back on the table revealing the white cream moustache just as he had when he was a child.

He grinned.

Carl grinned.

"So, will you at least come to the open day tomorrow?"

Carl nodded and then rolled his eyes.

Sonya breathed a sigh of relief and Tommy splashed her with washing up water triumphantly on his way out. She flicked him with the tea-towel in retaliation.

Chapter 2

The following morning Carl was looking at Sonya and wishing she had chosen something different to wear. He had taken the time to carefully select his own outfit from the meagre selection of decent clothes he owned, but he knew better than to criticise Sonya, especially when they were about to venture into Kelly's company.

If he paid too much attention to the way they both presented themselves, she would accuse him again of trying to impress his ex-girlfriend, or even worse, of being ashamed of Sonya. He'd already got away with his own exceptional effort and to criticise hers would definitely be pushing it. So, when she stood before him proudly in her hideous outfit he nodded approvingly, grateful that she hadn't made any comments about his gelled hair, special occasion watch, or expensive aftershave.

This didn't stop him however, from gritting his teeth as he walked behind her. He wished she knew more about hair and makeup instead of sticking with the same panda eye- shadow she had splodged on for years and plastering her hair to one side with hairspray. He also wished she would realise that pleated skirts with checks only work on stick thin supermodels. They are far less appealing when the pleats shoot out sideways from the waistband to create a box effect.

He opened the door for her, wishing she would trip down the curb and disappear down the grate. Anything to prevent him having to turn up to meet Kelly with a bad imitation of Barbara

Woodhouse. Alas, her feet found the car and her pleated backside found the seat despite his prayers.

He spotted Kelly and Tommy long before either of them spotted him. Their heads of blonde hair stood out spectacularly in the crowd and he couldn't help thinking how much they looked exactly like mother and son.

Kelly's deerskin trousers followed the pert curve of her buttocks down her perfectly shaped thighs and slid seamlessly into her knee- high boots. Her matching jacket was edged with black trim and fell loosely open at the front revealing a white silk blouse showing the tiniest hint of cleavage. She was literally stunning. Her makeup was its usual work of art perfectly exhibited by an intricate French pleat, held in place by an ivory hair pin.

Heads were turning as they made their way passed the elegant pair.

Carl had to take a moment to catch his breath. He needed a moment to deal with the envy, jealousy, pride, admiration and heartache that were seeping through his body from the sight before him.

He knew how it felt to kiss those lips, to caress those breasts. He couldn't resist torturing himself further as his eyes moved down her body. Oh God, he knew exactly how it felt to cup those buttocks as he pulled them towards him with every wonderful thrust.

"Hi!" Kelly smiled as she cordially kissed Carl's cheek and affectionately hugged Barbara Woodhouse. There was no hint of the superior smugness that he was sure would be rightfully overwhelming her.

Sonya hugged her back enthusiastically. She liked Kelly and she didn't feel threatened. Kelly was now out of Carl's league and she found it hard to believe she had ever lowered herself to the forth division, where Carl clearly sat. She marvelled that someone like Kelly had ever been remotely interested in the small-time grubby mechanic standing beside her.

In reality, Carl was no longer the man Kelly had fallen for all those years ago. He watched her networking tirelessly, even at this college open day. For not one second did her energy or enthusiasm waiver. In contrast, his own existence had been devoid of energy of any kind since the day she stopped being his lover.

On the day she flounced out to return to Jake she left him with nothing. With one slam of the door she took his self-respect, his confidence, his ego, his zest for life, his hope for the future and his fragile heart. What was worse was that he knew she was entitled to do just that. He deserved every bit of it.

There had been a moment, a few days later, when he'd heard that Jake rejected her, that he expected her to come crawling back. Thinking of that day now he still felt disgusted with himself. He was preparing for her return but not with a heart felt apology or with a determination to really appreciate her. He was preparing his terms and conditions for having her back. He was making sure he could continue to treat her as he always had.

He didn't get the chance. She didn't return. It was the final blow for him. She would rather have no-one than to return to him. He was worse than nothing.

After a few weeks he realised that he had to do something. He no longer had anyone to take care of the house or Tommy or him and he was spiralling downwards fast. He met Sonya in the local bank where she worked, and everything was so easy. With Sonya there was no drama or confrontations.

He asked her on a date, and she accepted. They went on a few dates and when he asked her to stay the night she accepted. The sex was textbook biology. Get undressed, get into bed, missionary position and sleep with backs together. She started staying over and helping with the housework, with Tommy and with the cooking. He asked her to marry him and she agreed. Everything was taken care of quietly and systematically and it was exactly what he needed. He didn't have the strength for anything more because he was broken. Life had dealt him blows he hadn't recovered from and Kelly's abandonment had sucked the life out of him. Even now as he looked longingly at the woman he still loved, he knew he no longer had the drive or energy to hold onto her.

Sometimes he wondered if she still had feelings for him and today he needed an ego boost desperately. He made a few attempts to make eye contact with her, but she didn't seem to notice at all. He moved alongside her and allowed his hand to tangle close to hers, hoping she might touch his fingers but she didn't even bother to move her hand away, she was too engrossed in something a lecturer was telling her. He smiled at Sonya and took the brochures from Tommy promising to read them later.

"I'm going to stay at Mum's tonight then"

Carl had long since stopped objecting to Tommy calling her mum.

"You leaving already?" Kelly frowned

"Yes. I think it's a great place Kelly, and I hope Tommy will show his appreciation by getting a qualification" he smiled while making a point of visibly holding Sonya's hand.

"I'm sure he will" She grinned "He's conned me into paying for a night at the adjoining hotel the night before registration too."

"Well that doesn't look cheap either" Carl directed his comment at Tommy.

"They're offering it at half price to encourage the discerning parents to stay the night before" Tommy winked "I'm sure I'll find a companion to join me."

"I'll pretend I didn't hear that" Carl said as he leaned in to kiss Kelly goodbye. He recognised her perfume and wondered if she had worn it purposefully for him tonight. He hoped so, he was sure of it, and it was enough to put him in a good mood on the way home.

Later as he lay awake beside Sonya, trying to concentrate on the brochures in the light of his bedside lamp, he looked around the room. Her supermarket moisturiser stood on her bedside table beside her reading glasses and the coco stained mug she had brought to bed. Her fluffy pink, wifey dressing gown hung forlornly on the back of the bedroom door just as his mother's had, and her mother's, before that.

He imagined what Kelly might be doing right now. She would probably be making some poor guy work hard to hold her interest over a very expensive dinner, only to dismiss him with a polite smile at the end of the evening when she became bored. He didn't know where she got her energy to fuel her lifestyle of late nights, early mornings, supplier meetings, promotional campaigns, and client hospitality weekends alongside her own exercise regimes.

They had both been through hell in those early years and both been totally crushed emotionally yet, Kelly, like some Phoenix, had risen from the ashes and taken on the world, while he had merely curled up in a ball and settled into the ashes thankfully and pathetically embracing the warm and softness of his nest of ash.

He turned off his reading light and draped his arm affectionately around Sonya's chubby belly. He didn't have the drive or motivation for anything more than the life he was living and there was some relief in accepting that, but he knew that sometime before he awoke his imagination would take him somewhere else.

He would be dreaming of the life that might have been. The life where he works alongside Kelly as they build their empire together and how proud he would feel to have Kelly on his arm. Even more compelling was the feeling he remembered well and abused repeatedly. That feeling of knowing without a grain of doubt that he was the only man in the whole world Kelly had ever wanted or would ever want. The feeling that had generated limitless energy in his soul. He knew that if he still had her love, his passion for life and success would surpass anything he was currently envying in Kelly.

He withdrew his hand and turned onto his back to stare into the darkness. Kelly deserved her new life, her admirers, and her money. He had broken the heart of the woman who had wasted half her life loving him with no other agenda other than to share her life with him. She deserved her life and he deserved his, it was that simple.

As the days of the week passed towards the registration day scheduled for the following Monday, Tommy seemed unusually inspired and Kelly was sure he wouldn't prove her wrong this time. He carried the course books back and forth with him, as he split his week between her condo and his dad's house and, on several occasions, he had been buried in one of them, making notes, barely keeping track of the football game on tv.

By the time Sunday arrived he was feeling confident and inspired, and as he packed an overnight case for his night in the hotel he was quite excited.

Yes, that was partly anticipation for his date. The girl who had eagerly accepted a night in a posh hotel but whose name he had carelessly forgotten, but he was also excited about delving into the mystery of his mother's illness. Of the mental disorder that had caused her to drag him up a mountain and then willingly plummet into an icy grave.

He arrived at the hotel early and took a shower before ordering champagne for the room. He then had time to fix himself a gin and tonic and relax for a while before the knock on the door.

He was pleasantly surprised when he opened the door as she was much prettier than he remembered. He was not, however, pleasantly surprised by the amount of effort she had made on her appearance. This was a girl clearly heading for a public appearance in the swanky restaurant of this prestigious five-star hotel. She was not about to settle for a glass of champagne, a couple of room service club sandwiches and a roll on the bed.

He smiled and quickly made an excuse for his jeans and tee-shirt.

"I'm sorry. I'm running late. I ordered champagne so we could chat while I'm getting changed. Hope that's ok?"

She grinned widely confirming that it was definitely ok, as she strode over to the folding balcony doors. The view of the bay was spectacular and as she admired it, he poured her a glass and took it over.

It was obvious that her hair had been styled at a salon. Dark brown curls had been loosely teased into ringlets and pulled to one side to reveal the curve of her neck. He could smell the hair spray through the lighter scent of her perfume. He must remember not to ruffle her hair too much as he knew if it fell down, it would look disastrous, half curls and half scraped flat. Living with Kelly had produced a young man who knew far more than was normal on hair and makeup!

He handed her the drink, noticing that her dress was definitely Karen Millen as he smiled and made his way to the bathroom to reluctantly change into something annoyingly smart and uncomfortable.

He wished he had brought more clothes to choose from, but more importantly, he wished he could remember this girl's damn name.

Over dinner he listened to the same questions most of his previous conquests had asked.

"So, Kelly Palmer is your mother? I mean *the* Kelly Palmer of Kelly Palmer Health and Beauty? Wow!"

He smiled politely and didn't bother to clarify that technically she was not, but she was his godmother and legality meant nothing. Kelly was his mum.

"Yes, that's right. More wine?"

She didn't answer as she wasn't listening. She was checking her reflection in the window beside her while pretending to admire the view. He suspected she was trying to decide which of Kelly's expensive treatments she ought to try to get out of him.

"Your hair is fine" he said curtly, as he poured more wine irrespective of whether she wanted some or not.

"I was just watching that sailboat on the horizon" she lied as she scanned the room, in the hope that someone she knew had seen her out with the son of Kelly Palmer. She was obviously thrilled to be seen drinking expensive wine with this gorgeous blonde local icon, and as he topped up her glass again and finished off his desert, he had a feeling she would be in no rush to get back to the room.

He had been in this situation a number of times before and right now he had reached the point where he considered that further investment was not going to be worth the prize. This was the moment he would play his 'make or break' card.

"Well, I have an early start tomorrow so I'm going to head back to my room"

Her moment of fame, for the time being, was over. Now she had a choice. She could either accept it and leave or she could try to hold onto him a little longer. She had lost all the power here, and she knew it but walking away at this point was something she knew she would live to regret. Her friends would be green with envy if she managed to turn this into something more.

He signalled for the bill and watched her face with amusement.

She was visibly offended. Announcing he was about to desert her for an early night was a significant slap in the face.

He watched again. Now she was feeling worthless, inferior and hurt. Any moment now she would try to recover the situation no matter what the cost.

She flicked her hair haughtily and forced a confident smile.

"Well I could head back with you if you like. I don't snore so I won't keep you awake."

Tommy turned his head away slightly to conceal his grin …back of the net!

Back in the room he took another bottle of wine from the mini bar and poured her a glass. He wasn't going to drink any more as he needed a clear head for his registration day even though he didn't need to be there until midday.

She drank half the glass in one go and curled her hand around his neck as she placed the glass down beside the bed. He purposely allowed her to take the lead knowing that it would vindicate him of any accusations of false promises.

This was a game he knew well. He was an expert.

As she started to unbutton his shirt, she kissed him hard. The wine was starting to take effect and he was in no doubt as to where this was going.

She pushed him backwards onto the bed, temporarily enjoying the power that seemed to have suddenly become hers. Before he had recovered from the fall, she was already astride him, gently biting his neck as her hands fumbled a little drunkenly with his shirt buttons, his belt and finally the button at the waist of his trousers. Her mouth was moving swiftly, following the path her hands had taken, as though she was afraid he might stop her at any moment.

He did nothing. He neither encouraged nor rejected her kisses as they trailed down the centre of his chest and stomach. He waited.

"I expect you have a lot of influence with your mum then?" she whispered.

There it was. Exactly as expected and right on cue! The moment when the bargaining for botox, facials, retinol treatments and brow shaping emerges from the bullshit.

"I guess so"

Tommy was having a pivotal moment on indecision. He had no intention of asking Kelly for any freebies in exchange for getting laid but nor was he completely comfortable with accepting sexual favours under false pretences.

"For girls who are special to you of course?" she breathed between licks.

She hadn't named her price, but her currency was crystal clear and morally he knew he should put her straight. He ought to place his hands either side of her head and gently push her away from the growing bulge that was already straining for release.

He needed a moment to think.

She pulled his trousers down to his hips and gently nuzzled him through his underwear.

He closed his eyes for a moment to allow his conscience to decide his next move. This happened to him all too often, so he placed a hand either side of her head and pulled her fiercely into his groin muttering.

"Ah fuck it."

She eagerly took him into her mouth, she believed the deal had been done.

He groaned as his entire shaft slid into her warm wet mouth, believed she'd got what she deserved.

Half an hour later he was laying alone on the bed, thankful for the peace and quiet her enraged exit had afforded him.

It had been the usual scenario. She asks about her appointment, he pretends he doesn't understand. She calls him a bastard, he calls her a whore. Da dee da dee da. She sits on the bed crying, he lies about calling her tomorrow. She gets dressed and gathers her belongings while he goes into the bathroom to wash the slut off his skin until he hears the door slam.

Great! Now he can watch the late-night match without any babbling in his ear!

Chapter 3

He woke at ten o'clock and headed straight back to the shower. He didn't want to miss breakfast and had less than half an hour to take full advantage of the prestigious buffet.

As he hung the towel on the hook, he had to hold onto the shower door to steady himself. He didn't think he had drunk so much the night before, but he was feeling a little woozy.

As the warm water washed over him, he started to feel a little better but when he took the towel and started to dry himself, he had to sit back on the bed for a moment. The wine must have been much stronger than he thought.

The breakfast buffet was spectacular. The hotel had really gone the extra mile to win the future business of the affluent college parents who were all seated proudly with their spoiled offspring. Tommy looked along the platters of smoked salmon, kippers, cold meats, cheeses, fruit, eggs, bacon and almost every item that had ever been considered suitable for breakfast. He picked up a plate and wandered down the display feeling quite ill. Eventually he settled for two rounds of toast and took it back to the pot of tea already on his table. He felt hot and sweaty. He swigged a mouthful of the sweet tea and ripped off the corner of his toast with his teeth. He put the rest of the slice back on his plate and battled with the urge to vomit. Quicky he left the restaurant for some air.

Once outside he decided to walk along the beach to clear his head. He loved this part of the coast. The small town of Ravenscar had been put on the map by the college and hotel complex which had been built on the headland. The views were spectacular. The construction company had definitely hit on a winning recipe to attract investors. Surrounded by sea on three sides it gave the illusion of being on a private island. The perfect environment to study or to be artistically inspired.

The complex certainly wasn't lacking in attraction for the students with it's five star accommodation, campus pub and music bar, but it also gave a great deal of peace of mind to affluent parents. There wasn't much students could get up to outside of campus in the small retirement town. The population consisted mainly of the over sixties and although there was an element of tourism, it focussed on the sparce weeks when the seal cubs made an appearance on the rocks twice a year. There was definitely little opportunity for students to be distracted by sex, drugs and rock and rock 'n' roll in Ravenscar!

He took a deep breath of the damp salty air. There was still half an hour before the registration for psychology, but the college had been a hive of activity all morning as cars drove in and out of the carpark and, from another direction, droves of parents with their excited offspring walked briskly between hotel and college building.

He took a few more deep breaths of sea air to keep his hangover at bay and made his way to the registration hall, in the hope that his future classmates would now be congregating.

The seating in the hall had been arranged in tables and most were already taken by the expected groups of three. Unlike himself, he assumed most had travelled a considerable distance and therefore unaccompanied students were few. He continued to scan the room and noticed a girl sitting alone on a table for four. Result.

He wasn't exactly in the mood for chatting up girls, but a seat would be nice, so he made his way over to the girl who was filling in her registration form.

"Do you mind if I sit here?"

She looked up and smiled.

"No. I'm grateful for the company to be honest. I thought I was the only one to turn up without parents."

"I'll join you on the orphan table then" he grinned.

"You need to get a form from the desk over there" she pointed to a small queue of people.

"Thanks. Are you registering for Psychology?"

"Yep. You?"

"Certainly am. I'll be back in a minute. Save my seat."

By the time he got to the desk, most had been served with the obligatory form, so he gave his name and waited while smiling back at the girl. She was not the kind of girl who would normally take his eye, but she was attractive in a refreshing way. Her dark hair seemed to have a natural wave to it, falling over her shoulders in shiny product free clumps. Her face showed no sign of makeup at all, just shiny with face cream and dappled with the freckles she hadn't tried to hide. Her natural dark brows and lashes framed her eyes. He was still admiring her when the woman spoke.

"I'm sorry. We don't seem to be able to find any record of you on the system. What's your name again"

"Thomas James Taylor." he repeated without taking his eyes from the girl.

There was silence again causing Tommy to check what the annoying woman was doing. She was frowning over her glasses as she continued to click the mouse repeatedly.

"I'm sorry" she said again "I can't seem to find you or any record of your deposit. What name would the deposit have been in?"

"Kelly Palmer" he said confidently "you know Kelly Palmer, Health and Beauty? She's my mother"

The woman became suddenly flustered.

"I'm sure it's just our system playing up. I'll get my supervisor to sort it out later." She smiled apologetically as she handed him the form.

"Thank you." He smiled sarcastically as he took the form and headed back to the table.

She was still studying the questions on the form while he quickly entered his name, ticked several boxes, scribbled a few words at the end, and then pushed it aside.

She looked up from her carefully part-completed form.

"You have a very casual attitude to this." She frowned.

He was instantly taken aback by her criticism. Girls usually loved that about him. They found it impressive and decisive.

She was still looking at him, waiting for a response like an annoyed school teacher, but for the first time in his life he couldn't think of anything witty to say. He found himself turning red. This was a whole new experience for Tommy, and he didn't like it. He didn't like that she had made him feel inferior and he didn't like that she wasn't backing down, but one thing was certain. He did like her.

He picked his form back up and she smiled.

"I will pay more attention to it." He grinned, feeling even warmer towards her.

"Good!" She nodded her satisfaction as he picked his pen back up.

They went through the questions together and he contributed as much as his distracted mind would allow. He was watching her face, admiring her thought process, and being totally amazed by her.

"So, do I get to know your name classmate?" he asked, when he was finally allowed to consider his form as completed.

"It's Vicky, and yours?"

"Tommy."

"What was the confusion at the desk just now?" she asked a little suspiciously.

"Oh, some computer glitch, I think. They couldn't find me but once I told them my mother was Kelly Palmer, they changed their minds."

He waited for her response. He always threw in Kelly's name when he met girls just to gauge their response. He justified this blatant name-dropping as a way of weeding out gold diggers, but in reality, he just loved the power of it. He liked being someone, and inevitably it got him what he wanted, gold digger or not.

"What did you put for question eight?"

"What?"

She looked up from the form.

"Question eight. The one about intended career path?"

Tommy was off balance again. She hadn't paid any attention to his bombshell pedigree at all. This girl was something else.

"Have you heard of her?"

"Who?"

"Kelly Palmer."

"Oh! Yes, She owns a number of Spa's up here, doesn't she?"

"Yes, it's just that you didn't say anything?"

"You mean I didn't faint from the shock of it?" she laughed, "I prefer to measure someone by what they do, not from the random luck of the particular womb they popped out of!" she tapped her finger on his nose playfully, causing him to close his mouth.

He hadn't realised his mouth was open nor had he realised there were girls out there who were not so easily impressed by his origin. He felt ridiculously inferior. He'd done nothing impressive in the years since he left school and he hadn't even had the good luck to pop out of Kelly's womb anyway. He had popped out of the womb of a mad woman and achieved nothing so far.

He wasn't sure if he was starting to dislike this Vicky. The girl who had pulled him down several pegs with her sweet brutal rebuffs and her condescending smiles.

For once, he didn't have a witty inuendo in his bag of tricks, so he simply smiled politely and pretended to check his form.

She could see she had taken the wind out of his sails and felt annoyed that she had done it so brutally.

"It's not that I have anything against rich boys."

Tommy just shrugged a little dismissively.

"I've just yet to meet one who has the metal to recover from my attempts to put him down. Don't suppose you know anyone like that?" She nudged him with her knee under the table.

Tommy grinned and nudged her back. Vicky was smart and she was entertaining. She had put him in his place, but he knew he'd deserved it. He'd deserved it for a very long time, and as he walked along side her he was thinking that if some girl like her had come along a few years ago he might have actually had a reason to make something of himself.

"Looks like we're about done here then?" he said, noticing that some parents had already started to make their tearful goodbyes to their molly coddled off-spring. .Fearfully abandoning them to the mercy of the metropolis of geriatric Ravenscar, as they embarked on their 'settling in' week.

Tommy wasn't moving in until the actual lectures started the following week. He couldn't see the point of wasting a week of his life just to familiarise himself with the location of the library, canteen and running machines but he was thinking that she maybe had a room here.

His confidence was returning, and it brought along with it a newly repaired ego and a healthy shot of bravado. If she was a resident, he bet himself that he could have her naked before the end of the night!

"Are you a resident from today then?" he asked hopefully.

"No. I'm staying with my grandparents tonight then dad is picking me up tomorrow teatime to take me home. He's bringing me back next Sunday."

Tommy's heart sank a little. Grandparents houses generally were not a great location for a seduction.

"Maybe we could go for a few drinks then?" he was already standing with both forms in his hand, as though the invitation had been accepted.

She frowned again and then peered up at him through her dark lashes.

"Afternoon drinking? Really?"

"Coffee then?"

"Coffee it is." She smiled as she stood up and snatched the forms from his hand.

"I'll hand these in while you find out where the coffee bar is"

As she walked away Tommy interrupted a group of boys standing close by.

"Anyone know which direction the coffee shop is?"

An obese boy with a mop of brown and blonde highlights leaned over.

"Coffee shop? We're heading to the pub mate! You comin?"

Tommy nodded towards Vicky as she stood in line to hand in the forms and the boy rolled his eyes sympathetically.

"Girlfriend not a drinker eh? That'll change when she's been here a week!"

"She's not actually my girlfriend," Tommy shouted above the increasing noise, "only just met her."

The boy leaned in again until he was only inches from Tommy's face and winked.

"Fast mover eh? Good on ya! Well, I'm Jack, we'll be there all night if you get chance."

Another boy, taller and slim with raven black hair flopping over his eyes rolled his eyes in apology for Jack.

"Name's Harry, maybe we'll catch you later. Ignore Jack, he had a morning Vodka or two."

Jack threw his arms around them both as though Tommy had just been enlisted into their inner circle.

"Yeah! Come on! Leave her in the queue and come for a pint."

Tommy gently peeled the boy's arm from around his neck and laughed.

"Thanks. I might just take you up on the offer later."

"Good man!" Jack slapped him hard on the back and then put his finger on his lips as he saw Vicky approaching.

"Shhhh. Mums the word" he smiled tapping the side of his nose before turning back to join the rest of the group.

"Did you find out where it is?"

"Not really, don't think coffee is their thing somehow. It'll be somewhere up the main corridor. We'll find it."

Tommy guided her through the intoxicated rabble back towards the door feeling suddenly protective of her.

"Why would anyone drink before registering?" She shook her head disapprovingly as she pushed through them.

"No idea!" Tommy smiled from behind as he imagined the state he would be in now if he'd met Jack at eleven when the campus pub opened!

As they left the hall, they could hear the clatter of pots and smell the coffee from the door.

"I think it's down here" Tommy shouted.

"You don't say, Sherlock" she shouted back.

It was only meant as light-heated humour, but it was enough to chip at his confidence again. He wasn't used to this kind of girl and he definitely wasn't used to being kept on his toes.

"You find some seats and I'll get the drinks" she said decisively "What would you like?"

"What I would like?" he thought to himself "Is for you to behave like a normal girl and go sit down while I took control" but instead he meekly looked at the board and answered obediently.

"Flat white please."

She didn't acknowledge his response, but he was starting to understand her adversity to unnecessary pleasantries. The coffee would arrive as ordered and he needed to find a table. He'd been given the task and wasn't going to fail, despite the fact that all the tables were already taken. He was back in chartered waters as he offered a group of students twenty pounds to vacate.

By the time Vicky returned with the tray of coffee's and two slices of lemon cake he had dumped the dirty pots on the trolly, and his task was complete.

"I hope you like lemon cake," she sighed, "it was all they had left."

"I love lemon cake."

At last there was some sign of approval as she placed the tray on their table and handed him a fork.

"So, are you going to tell me where exactly your grandparents live?" he loosened his collar as he had another surge of adrenaline.

"That depends." She babbled, through the forkful of cake she had shovelled into her mouth before sitting down.

"On what?"

"On whether you are trying to make small talk or whether you are genuinely desperate to know the whereabouts of my grandparents."

She looked right at him in an almost confrontational way.

Tommy had been caught off guard again. This girl was nothing like the other girls he knew, the girls who would have just answered the question. The girls who would fumble and stutter their response as they tried to impress him, while he relaxed, listened to the meaningless ramblings and watched them turn to putty in his hands.

He needed to return her serve.

"I'd just like to know if I need my car keys or my walking shoes to get you home safely." He smiled.

She narrowed her eyes in acknowledgement of the game he was playing, and then relented.

"They retired here a few years ago. That's the reason my dad wanted me to come to this college. They live, literally over the hill behind us, its less than a two-mile walk."

"Sounds perfect for walking off the calories of that cake then?"

"Guess so."

He nudged her playfully and she grinned through another mouthful of cake.

"So, tell me about your family," he said, more genuinely, "I'm interested, not small talk." He removed his jacket and used the menu as a fan as he suddenly felt nauseous again.

"Nothing much to tell really," she shrugged, "traditional family. Mum, Dad, Sister, house, jobs, no divorces or traumatic events. What about you?"

"Same I suppose. Stepmother, real mother topped herself, godmother who brought me up, live between two houses, tried a few jobs I didn't like, travelled, and now here."

She narrowed her eyes again as she tried to determine if he was winding her up.

He shrugged.

"Really?" she asked.

"Yep."

"Wow!" she seemed to visually mellow towards him.

"I thought you were just a rich kid who's never had a day's worry in his entire life."

"Well you got the first bit right."

She laughed spontaneously and he watched how her nose crinkled up, hiding most of her freckles. He liked this girl. He liked her a lot.

"Grandparents?"

"Well, don't see much of the ones on my dad's side. They bought a villa in Spain when they retired. Bit of a cliché but they seem to like it out there."

"Your mother's side?"

It felt strange that someone was referring to Sophie as his mother. Even his dad had stopped doing that.

"Never met my Grandmother on that side, she died of a brain tumour before I was born but yes, I have a Grandad on that side. Still lives in Filey."

Suddenly Tommy was finding himself articulating his relationship with David.

David still doted on Tommy and was grateful for every moment they spent together. After Christine died and then Sophie, Tommy had become his only blood relative. As he looked over at Vicky, he became overwhelmed with guilt. The kind of guilt that makes you want to run home immediately and make it right.

David had tried so hard. He had frequently tried to bond with Tommy, buying him gifts he could hardly afford on his state pension and trying to arrange camping trips and fun sleepovers, but Tommy had never really engaged with it.

He had politely accepted some of it and politely refused the rest but even when he did accept, he was always holding back, always anxious to get back to Kelly where he could give his affection freely.

Tommy knew he was doing it, but he couldn't help it. More recently he had understood why.

The truth was that it had nothing to do with his love for his Grandad, it had only to do with the fact that he felt like a fraud. He knew that if ever his Grandad found out the part he had played in killing Sophie, killing his only daughter, he would never have bought those gifts, never have made tents in the garden. David would't have given Tommy the shit from his shoe if he knew what he had done.

"Are you alright?" Vicky asked, reminding Tommy how long he had been silent.

"Yes, sorry. Just thinking of my Grandad for a moment."

They chatted for another hour and then ordered more coffee. Eventually she got up to leave.

"My grandma is taking me into Scarborough for tea, so I'll have to be making a move."

"I'll walk you home." Tommy's offer was clearly non-negotiable.

As they left the complex and started up the hill towards the small cluster of houses in the distance, he allowed his hand to slip casually into hers. Instantly she pulled away and stopped walking.

"What?" he smiled.

She tilted her head to one side inferring that he knew the answer to his own question. Her wavy hair was blowing over her face, causing her to keep sweeping it away as she widened her eyes as him. She was the cutest thing he had ever seen and for the first time in the company of an attractive girl, sex was far from his mind.

"Ok. Sorry." He sighed dejectedly walking on ahead with his hands in his pockets, mimicking a disgraced child.

She ran up beside him and linked her arm in his.

"Friends?"

"Absolutely!" He laughed as she skipped along beside him.

She leaned against him gently as they walked and he reached over to the hand she had buried in his elbow and rubbed it reassuringly. He just wished he could stop shivering for a moment.

At the gate of her grandparents' bungalow he took both her hands in his and stood back to look at her again. She did not tick the boxes of a conventional beauty but there was something about her. Probably no more than five feet four with a figure that suggested she didn't live on lettuce leaves, but everything was in proportion, perfectly curved and impressively solid. She was her own version of perfection from her unruly curls, fresh complexion, enormous eyes, lips that gave the appearance of a permanent smile and of course all finished off with sprinkles of freckles.

He sighed.

"What?!" She frowned, biting her bottom lip.

"Nothing." He finally said. "Absolutely nothing."

"Well are you just going to stand there?"

"It depends."

"On what?" she said comically.

"On how long it takes you to give me your number."

She studied his face for a while and then relented.

"Ok, give me your phone."

He clicked onto contacts and typed Vicky into the name space. She took it from him, smiling as she added her number before returning the phone and squeezing his nose playfully.

"See you next Monday then?"

"Yep." He replied waving an arm in the air as he turned to walk away "Monday it is. I'll buy you lunch at the hotel."

"I'd prefer a home-made butty on the beach!" she called back.

He turned and put up both thumbs, grinning like a Cheshire cat.

As he walked back to the college he decided to call in at the pub and see if the lads he had met earlier were still there. He didn't intend to have a drink as he needed to drive home but it would be nice to make a few new friends before next Monday.

As he walked back over the hill, he was still thinking of Vicky. She was the only girl he had ever known who had made him want more from her than sex. He wanted her to like him, to admire him, to respect him and he was going to take all the time in the world to get it.

He reached the college gates and kicked the mud off his shoes on the concrete path. He thought of her again, it was more than that. Sex seemed somehow beneath whatever it was between them.

"I need to get a grip!" He mumbled to himself as he stamped his feet to rid himself of the last of the soil and made his way towards the pub.

He could hear the noise before he had even opened the door. It was like an after-match celebration inside, the bar was heaving with arms in the air waiving money at the flustered bar staff as they tried to remember who was next. Everyone was shouting and the place was humid with body heat. He glanced around but the whole room was a sea of strangers faces and it was going to be impossible to get a drink.

"Tommy!" Came a voice from the front of the bar "You made it!"

There was no mistaking the blonde and brown streaky mop, of the boy who was taking up most of the counter as he spread himself even wider to occupy as much space as possible.

"I'm being served. I'll get you a pint!" He screamed above the noise of the crowd pushing behind him.

He was obviously already drunk. As far away as Tommy was, he could see the sweat on Jack's face as he picked up a tray of several pints and headed off. Tommy followed in the hope that he was heading for a table. He wasn't. He was heading over to Harry who was stood alone in the corner.

"Who's the drinks for?" Tommy shouted as he approached noticing that the tray was swimming with lager spilled from the six pints he had tried to balance through the crowd.

"Two each!" Jack slurred "Oh fuck it! We've only got six hands and I've got six pints and a tray! He swayed precariously in Tommy's direction until his face was only and inch away. "Who's gonna hold the fuckin tray?"

Tommy couldn't help but laugh as he rescued two of the glasses from the moving tray. Harry did the same and Jack looked back to his tray and leaned forward to Tommy again.

"Now what?"

If anything could stop Tommy mooning over Vicky for a few hours, it would definitely be these two! He put his two pints on a shelf and solved Jack's dilemma before trying to make some sort of conversation.

"So, what are you studying Jack?"

Jack frowned for a moment and then his sweaty face returned to Tommy's.

"Athletics!"

They all laughed spontaneously, and the mood was set. After another few hours they were all sitting on the floor singing to whatever was playing. It seemed that the alcohol had managed to cure Tommy's illness, or at least taken his mind off it.

"Are you staying at the college tonight?" Tommy was already wondering how he was going to get home. He had only booked one night in the hotel and there was no way he could drive.

Jack completed the chorus and then replied.

"We're getting a taxi back to Scarborough in a bit. We've got a mate who lives there. Come with us if you want. He won't mind"

"Thanks, but I'm sorted." He lied.

There was no way he was going to spend the night on the floor of some grotty flat with these two and if he mentioned booking the hotel for another night, he knew exactly what would happen. Better get them on their way before they ended up spewing in his hotel bath.

"Come on Jack." Harry slurred as he tried to pull Jack to his feet.

Tommy helped get him up and Harry called a taxi. After half an hour of singing with arms firmly locked around heads, the taxi arrived.

"Here! Give me your phone and I'll put my number in it!" Jack demanded as he pulled it from Tommy's hand.

Jack swayed back and forth squinting and smiling at the phone while the taxi driver tapped his steering wheel impatiently.

"Is the lovely Vicky in here by any chance?" He winked.

"Give it here!" Tommy snapped as he grabbed it back. How long does it take to put a bloody number in? It's not war and peace!

He pushed his phone back in his pocket and bundled them both in.

"These two better not puke in my cab!" The driver shouted to Tommy as though he was responsible for them.

Tommy was used to handling this particular scenario and slipped him a twenty- pound note.

"I don't think they will mate but just in case."

The driver nodded and the taxi disappeared through the college gate. Tommy turned back to the pub as he swayed gently and tried to focus. The pub had already been locked up. The campus was silent, and he was totally alone.

He didn't want to ring his dad or Kelly in this state, so he decided to sleep in his car.

"Good idea Tommy!" He told himself out loud as he walked into the carpark of the hotel. There were still a number of cars parked but he couldn't remember exactly where he had left his. He staggered around and every section was separated by ornamental hedges, they all looked the same. He stopped to take a deep breath and then threw up as he steadied himself against a BMW and put his hand in his pocket for his keys.

"Damn it!" He said out loud. He must have dropped them somewhere.

The wind was blowing the sea mist inland and the temperature was dropping swiftly. Late August days along this coast often turned into very cold evenings and he hadn't brought an overcoat. He decided to book into the hotel for another night.

Before entering reception, he tried to sober himself up, but it was difficult to focus on anything or to form any meaningful words. As he entered the warmth of the brightly lit foyer a middle-aged woman frowned at him over the reception desk.

"Can I book….," he had to stop to take a deep breath "a room please?"

She looked him up and down as though trying to decide if she should reply or get him removed.

"I was here last night. Room 501"

The room number seemed to do the trick, it was one of the few executive suites. She clicked the mouse a few times and then smiled.

"Mr Goodall?"

Tommy looked at her. It was his turn to decide how to proceed. She had obviously looked up the wrong room or he had got the number wrong, but it seemed like a bad move to throw any doubt into the pot, so he just nodded.

"Credit card?"

He reached into his jacket and took out his wallet, but his credit card was not in the slot. He tried to think when he last had it. He had used cash in the pub and the meal at this hotel with the nameless girl had gone on his bill. He was feeling sick again. Perhaps he had left it at home, but he couldn't remember.

"Just a moment." He tried to smile apologetically but he could feel his mouth watering.

He could hardly add it to Mr Goodall's bill without a card.

"I think I got the information wrong." He slurred.

"The room number or your name?" she asked sarcastically.

"Actually both!" He grinned as he tried to steady himself on the counter.

"What name then?" She snapped as he started to slip sideways.

"Tommy James Taylor!" He announced proudly.

She frowned as she interrogated her computer again.

"Nope! No-one in that name."

Tommy tried to remember if Kelly had booked it for him but he was sure he did it himself.

Most of his cash had been spent and as he watched her peering at him over her glasses he started to giggle.

"How many guesses do I get?" he slurred through his own laughter.

"I think you better leave before I call security young man!" she said sternly as she wondered if this was going to be a typical occurrence in this hotel so close to the college.

"It doesn't matter," he slurred, "thank you for your marvellous assistance."

She glowered at him as though daring him to remain in her elegant reception area.

"Ah, fuck it!" He gasped finally, as he rushed back out into the night air and threw up on the flowerbed.

He was feeling woozy again, reeling uncontrollably, as he tried to take the few steps back into the carpark. The scenery was spinning around him and he could no longer keep his balance.

He tried to search for Kelly's number on his phone but he couldn't focus and there seemed to be less numbers in his contacts.

"Bloody Jack!"

He wrapped his thin jacket around him and decided to head for the beach. It would be sheltered there and sleeping out in the cold air would probably help him sober up.

Swaying back and forth with determined exaggerated, lurching steps he made his way toward the sea and finally slumped down into the softness of the knee-high heather that sprawled before him like a purple mattress.

He tried to sleep but the cold was creeping into his bones and making him shiver. He felt ill again. He should go back to the hotel and use Kelly's name. Why didn't he think of that? They could call her and verify who he was! He stood up again and looked around. The hotel lights were still shining brightly as he tried to stand.   He staggered and fell, staggered and fell. Staggered and fell again as he tried to head in the direction of the hotel.

Chapter 4

Before Tommy even opened his eyes, he smelt the fragrance of the Egyptian cotton hotel sheets and the warmth of them around his naked body. The sickly smell of the heather had gone. He had made it back to the hotel but had no recollection of his drunken victory or the conversation he must have had to get himself back into his suite.

As he rose to his feet, he was relieved to see his car keys on the floor. At least he hadn't dropped them in the pub. He was also pleasantly surprised that he felt as well as he did. A little tired, but apart from a minor headache, he had escaped a full-blown hangover!

He went down for breakfast and ate a full English before returning to his room to watch the news with a cup of coffee. He needed to visit Kelly this morning and report on his registration day but obviously he would leave out the binge drinking. One thing he would definitely not leave out would be his encounter with Vicky. His reputation as a playboy had been irreparably damaged and he loved it.

He finished off the complimentary chocolate cookies and headed for the carpark. How easy it was to find the car in daylight and sober.

He threw his overnight bag onto the back seat of his Mini and drove like a maniac out onto the open road in the direction of Kelly's Spa complex.

He swung his bashed up Mini behind her sports car and barged through reception, flinging open her office door without knocking, causing her to drop her phone.

"For Christ's sake Tommy. You nearly gave me a heart attack"

He made a grab for the phone on the floor and looked at it.

"Still stalking Jake, are we?" he laughed as he looked at the Facebook posts of Jake's newest baby.

"I'm not stalking him! Give it back."

"So, when are you going to buy me something nice to replace the rust bucket my dad cobbled together?"

"When you stop driving like an idiot and get rid of your points I guess."

"You're such a meany" he teased.

"You have three bloody points already and you've only been driving six months college boy! Don't forget who's paying the fees for this fancy place you're starting at."

Tommy pulled a sulky face and then smiled. Kelly laughed out loud. He loved to make Kelly laugh and to watch the little lines burst from the corners of her eyes like tiny fireworks. She was still stunning in a sophisticated way. A strong determined woman who power dressed, and delivered direction in her own special way. A polite but ruthless tone of 'don't mess with me'. He loved his mother regardless of the lack of biology or legality to support his claim.

She frowned as he plonked his legs unceremoniously on her desk.

"So, how's your dad?"

"Same."

She smiled and shook her head affectionately.

"And how's your step-mum?"

He rolled his eyes sarcastically.

"Oh the house mouse is still around somewhere. Scurrying along the floors with a mop and hyper ventilating over my muddy footmarks."

"Really Tommy. She seems really nice. You shouldn't give her such a hard time."

"Yeah, I guess. She's nice enough."

Kelly nodded her approval

"In her own boring, pathetic, irritating mousy way."

Kelly threw a ruler at him as he ducked.

"Kelly you've no idea," he laughed "they totter up to the seafront and sit drinking coffee together. When you were around, dad used to run in the sea with his trousers on, and eat ice cream down there. We all used to dance in the living room flashing torches and pretending it was a disco! You used to do that funny dance that dad loved, the one where you spun on your back. Do you remember?"

"We're all a bit older now."

"Well he definitely is! I've even caught them at a garden centre for God's sake! Their idea of a wild night out is half a lager in a beer garden and chips on the way home. Anyway, talking of wild nights out, have you booked our New Year cruise yet?"

"Is that why you're here? Making sure I've booked us in?"

"No, I just wanted to ask if you would like to meet my new girl" He raised his eyebrows several times suggestively as she rolled her eyes.

"I seem to do nothing other than to meet your girls. Perhaps you should wait until you can introduce them without forgetting their names before you rack up my credit card on fancy meals."

Tommy leaned forward as though about to whisper a secret.

"This one is a keeper" he whispered, "I can feel it in my bones."

He shoved a pile of invoices aside and plonked himself down on her desk.

"It could be love." He smiled, giving his eyebrows a few more bounces.

"Yes, and it could be lust, and you're hoping a few glasses of champagne on my card will do the trick."

"Not this time" he said boastfully, "this girl is something else. I spent all afternoon with her yesterday, and guess what?"

Kelly checked her watch again impatiently.

"Go on then. What?"

He smiled that smile that never failed to crack her up. The smile that totally disarmed her no matter what he'd done or said. She was already fighting to keep a straight face when he put his face directly in front of hers and widened his eyes.

"I'm hooked."

She laughed out loud.

"Is that a way of telling me you've maxed out my credit card trying to impress her?"

"Nope! I don't need money to impress this one. You wouldn't understand. This one is happy to sit on the beach with a homemade butty. I think she's the one."

Kelly tugged the invoices from under his buttock and straightened them into a tidy pile.

"The real thing eh? After one date?"

"She could be. She makes my stomach feel like a washing machine. You wouldn't get it."

Kelly smiled. She knew that feeling far too well. It was the feeling she had loved and hated her entire life. That special inner turmoil when she used to live or die with every text from his pathetic indecisive father, as he pulled her back and forth several times a day. The feeling that had dropped her to the ground in public, when he had triumphantly announced the news of his new girlfriend. Stupidly gushing about her as though he had no concept of the bullets he was firing directly into her heart. She marvelled at how she had been so besotted with Carl for so long. The pain he had put her through, the way he rode rough shod over her feelings, the sheer selfishness of him as he spouted about 'doing the right thing.' About feeling guilty towards everyone, everyone except her.

She thanked God that her feelings for him had finally died, as she tried to banish the memory of the washing machine stomach from her thoughts.

"So, what's her name? This girl who's stolen your heart in a single day."

He grinned "Her name is Vicky and she's studying psychology. We're on the same course."

"So where did you meet?"

"At the registration. Where else?"

Kelly's frowned.

"I thought the registration was today?"

"You need to get a grip," He laughed, "registration day was yesterday.

Kelly opened the calendar on her laptop where she had marked the registration in for Monday at 12pm and that was today. She turned her screen towards him.

"Look. I've got it down for today. That's what you told me, and I've never known a college to register on a Sunday!"

"Today's Tuesday!" He said irritably as he took out his phone to check, "Have you finally lost the plot?"

He flicked his screen back and forth as though trying to get it to refresh and reveal that it was Tuesday. It remained on Monday.

He could feel his heart pounding. He looked back to Kelly for reassurance, but she was shaking and staring at him like a rabbit in the headlights. Beads of sweat were appearing on her forehead and upper lip.

"What's going on?" Tommy stuttered, "Mum what is it?"

She rubbed his leg comfortingly as she tried to think of something to say.

"Mum?" His eyes were fixed firmly on hers.

He had seen this marque of terror before. He had seen it in the eyes of a woman crouching over her precious bits of paper on her bedroom floor.

"What's happened? Where the hell did Monday go and where was I?"

"It's ok darling. I just need to make a call. You wait here for a minute."

Tommy sat silently as she left the room. No-one knew enough yet but he was already making an instinctive link between Sophie's madness and the expression of dread on Kelly's face.

He could hear her whispering outside the room, but he couldn't make out the words. He looked at his own hands, they were trembling too.

Quickly he took out his phone and searched for the contacts icon. He couldn't hit the right button, he couldn't think straight, he couldn't keep his hands still. He took a deep breath and started again. He opened the contacts and typed in the letter V. Valeting, Van-hire, Voicemail. That was it. No sign of Vicky but all his other contacts, the ones Jack mischievously deleted, were back!

After a few moments she returned smiling reassuringly.

"Your dad is coming over. Don't worry, we'll sort this out."

Tommy knew she was lying. He knew something terrible was happening, and he knew that there was some connection to Sophie.

He had been only a boy when she awoke from the coma and he had no idea what kind of accident had put her there. All he knew was that she believed she had a different family and had jumped off the Brigg believing she would get back to them.

He looked over at Kelly who was pretending to be unconcerned, as she tried to change the subject.

"Would you like a cup of tea and a few biscuits?"

Tommy took a deep breath and nodded. The last thing he wanted was tea and biscuits, but he wanted to get her out of the room. He needed a few moments alone. He needed to think. He needed to try to remember exactly what happened and the part he had played in it.

Guilt was starting to overtake the feeling of fear. He knew that if Sophie's illness was about to be unearthed then so might many other things. Things like the fact that he had murdered her.

He put his head in his hands and tried to remember the details. The night Sophie's friend Niki had turned up and found the scribblings he'd been hiding. The night she stormed off to the Police station screaming at him while he begged her not to tell. The night she had told him he was lucky that she had no intention of making things worse for his dad by exposing what he had done. She had kept her word until now, but Tommy was no longer a small boy and Carl was no longer a vulnerable wreck and if anything might bring Niki back into the picture it could be this.

If they decided to delve back into the sequence of events that eventually led to Sophie's demise, she would be an obvious source of knowledge. If she was ever going to feel the need to spill the beans, then now would probably be the time.

Both he and Niki knew that it may have been Sophie who committed the final act but, without a doubt, it had been Tommy who passed the sentence.

In those moments alone in that unremarkable office time stood still. Tommy was facing himself for the first time in his life. The burden that he had refused to pick up, the horror of the things he had done, the gravity of his past and the fear of what might lie ahead.

He knew that the day of his reckoning could be fast approaching.

Chapter 5

Tommy heard his father arrive, the speed of his footsteps on the polished laminate of the reception floor. He could feel the panic from behind the closed door of the office as he tried to sip the sweet tea.

The door failed to open, he could tell from the sounds that they had rushed into the adjoining office to talk. Hurried mutterings infiltrated the silence around him. Parts of sentences were more audible than others as their voices rose and fell in exasperation. He was beginning to grasp the seriousness of his parents' dread.

"Why didn't you tell me that before?" It was Carl's voice.

"She was closer to Niki than to me." It was Kelly's voice.

"It doesn't mean it's the same. He was probably just wasted." Carl again.

"Thinks he's in love." Kelly again.

"You're fuckin paranoid!" Carl again.

Then there was silence. Low whispers until he heard a sound he had never heard before. His dad was crying.

"I'm scared Kel."

"Keep your voice down."

The door finally opened but only Kelly entered.

"Your dad will be in shortly. He's just nipped to the toilet." Kelly was an excellent liar. He looked at her face. Not a trace of emotion to give her away. He supposed she had always been good at acting, hiding her feelings, painting on a positive expression and pretending everything was ok. That was the skill she had perfected, the only positive thing she seemed to have gained from the years of her devotion to Carl.

"What's wrong with me mum?" He asked, knowing that Kelly would give him the reassurance he needed. She would fix this. She always fixed whatever was wrong for him.

She smoothed back his heavy blonde fringe from his eyes and smiled.

"There's nothing wrong with you. Nothing that can't be sorted and that's exactly what we are going to do."

Tommy buried his head in her waist as she stood beside his chair and folded his arms around it.

"Is this how it started with Sophie?" He whispered.

Kelly smiled above his head. Not at his question but at the fact that he still called his biological mother by name.

"I'm not sure. She talked to Niki more than to me but even if it did, medicine has moved on a lot since then, and with a bit of medication, you'll be good as new."

"Promise?"

"I promise that I will either get you fixed or die trying." She laughed.

He squeezed her waist tightly as she stroked his hair.

As the door opened and Carl walked in meekly, Tommy looked up. His father was pathetic at acting but he's never needed to put anyone else's feelings before his own. His eyes were red, and he looked as bewildered as Tommy felt. His dad was not about to become a tower of strength. His dad was about to lean on Kelly and make this all about him.

He sat down opposite Tommy and tried to smile.

"Everything's gonna be ok son." He said softly as he looked at Kelly "Isn't it mum?"

"Of course it is." She confirmed, frowning back her disappointment at Carl.

She then gently removed Tommy's arms and handed him one of the cookies he hadn't even tried to eat.

"Here, dunk this before your tea gets cold. I'm making a plan."

She strode back to her desk and woke up her laptop by jiggling the mouse.

"What's the plan then?" Carl looked grateful that she was taking control.

Tommy failed to show any surprise at his father's pathetic behaviour. He had stopped expecting anything useful from his father many years ago.

"I'm checking the electoral register to make sure Niki is still at the same address and then I'm going to track down that other woman."

"What woman?" Tommy asked as he dropped the soggy cookie into his mouth, suddenly comforted by his mother's confidence and determination.

"The one who treated Sophie. What was her name Carl? Was it Mary? or Susan or something?"

"Anne!" Carl blurted out, seemingly proud that he had finally contributed something.

"Anne! That was it and she was the resident psychologist at Scarborough from around 2005 if I remember. She should be easy enough to track down."

Kelly continued clicking her mouse as she shouted through the closed door for more coffee.

"You take Tommy home Carl. I'll work faster on my own."

"I'm meant to be registering at College about now!"

"I'll ring the principal. His wife is a client. It'll be fine."

"Of course, it will." Carl thought to himself.

She always knew someone, and she always made him feel as useless as he did right now, but he could remember a time when he had all the power. When she had been putty in his hands. Grateful for every text he could be bothered to send her.

He hated how completely the tables had turned.

Even now, even as she threw all she had into saving his son, he hated her for the powerful, shrewd and driven woman she had become.

"Well go on then! I'll come over to yours as soon as I have all the information. Where's my bloody coffee?" She strode out of her office to rattle some cages while Carl and Tommy made their way out behind her.

Carl wished he could say something to astound her, to cause her to sit up and take notice. He wished he could mention a match he wanted to see and watch her scurry around to get tickets. He wished he could enjoy the many hours between her text and his eventual reply as he imagined her checking her phone a hundred times. He wished she would send a text in the first place. He wished he hadn't been such an arrogant dick.

Tommy suddenly stopped and turned back.

"Just a minute. I've left my phone. You go dad, I'll follow you. I've got my car outside."

Tommy walked back into the office to get it and as he did so he passed the printer. On a printed page was the address of Niki so he quickly folded it and put it in his pocket on the way out. If anyone was going to talk to Niki, he had to get there first.

Back at Carl's house Sonya was waiting with hot chocolate and a sympathetic ear. It was hardly what they needed but Tommy recognised that at least she had made the effort.

He often felt sorry for Sonya. She seemed to go along with whatever Carl wanted to do, whatever he wanted to buy or wherever he wanted to go. She didn't have the confidence in their relationship to make a stand.

Tommy suspected that she knew she didn't have the bargaining power to demand or insist on anything. She probably knew that she was disposable to Carl. His heart would not break, nor his lifestyle change if she left because she contributed nothing to his life that he could not easily replace.

"Thanks Sonya." He smiled as he took the mug of chocolate from her. The good thing about Sonya was that she was easy to manipulate and she was grateful for any kindness or inclusion Tommy extended to her.

She had never tried to compete with Kelly as his mother, but he often wondered about women like her. There were quite a few of them around, looking after husbands, staying at home and complying. Maybe they were the shrewd ones. Women who were getting exactly what they wanted without having to put in much effort. As he watched Sonya, he realised just how easy her life actually was.

She didn't have to go to work or to worry about money, she didn't have to take responsibility for Tommy or for cars or holidays. Everything was done for her, everything happened without her needing to stress about it. Perhaps these jobless, childless women were not to be pitied but to be admired. They were getting a free ride through life without taking responsibility for anything at all.

He thought of Kelly, frantically tracking people down, sorting out his college registration, pulling strings all over the place and then he looked back at Sonya as she arranged the last of the summer roses in her favourite vase humming to herself.

He spat back a mouthful of his drink. The woman couldn't even make a cup of hot chocolate without lumps!

An hour later, the tranquillity of the house was disrupted by the tornado entrance of Kelly with her folder of papers and frantic jabbering.

"I've tracked down Anne!" she announced triumphantly, "she's retired now but I have her address."

"Has she agreed to see us?" Carl asked as he was suddenly jolted from his depressive daydreaming.

"Don't have her number. Mobiles are harder to find but we can find out when we knock on her door can't we?" It wasn't a question.

"How far away is she?" Tommy asked nervously.

He wasn't ready for all the information that might emerge from his mother's therapist.

"About an hour away. On the road to York." Kelly was consulting her folder as though it were a business meeting.

"I think it would be better if you stayed here with Sonya though," She continued, "Let me and your dad make the first visit."

Tommy didn't need telling twice. He was grateful for the time to track down Niki, and he was pretty sure Anne wouldn't even remember Sophie from so many years ago.

"Fine. I'll hang out with Sonya for a bit. Perhaps we could go to the pub and get spliced?" he was aiming the joke at Sonya, but she took him seriously.

"I'm not really sure that's a good idea Tommy."

"I was joking!"

Even now. Even when he was obviously trying to lighten the mood, she was too uptight to recognise sarcasm.

Carl rolled his eyes at Tommy in response to his wife's stupidity, and then left with Kelly. Tommy watched them get into Kelly's car. They would sort this for him. They were his mum and dad after-all.

Sonya watched them walk down the path towards the red Ferrari. She knew he was still in love with Kelly. He probably always would be, but Kelly would never take him back. It was amusing to watch him try! It didn't matter because she liked her life. She liked the house and her long walks along the beach. She liked the women she met for lunch twice a week and she liked having Carl to talk to and for the occasional sex. Sonya was mundanely but consistently content.

As soon as they had disappeared down the road Tommy jumped up and went upstairs to get changed into his jeans.

"I'm going out for a bit."

Sonya looked mortified. She had been left in charge of Tommy and he was about to escape.

"Where are you going?" She flattened her hair into the nape of her neck with both hands nervously.

Tommy looked at her. Her mousy brown hair was definitely in need of a restyle. Kelly would have loved to get her hands on Sonya, and give her a makeover. Give her some cheekbones for a start and shove some style into her retro wardrobe. However, he also knew that it was not in Kelly's interest to transform Sonya into a woman of the twenty first century. It was probably why she had never offered.

Sonya was still staring at him as though she were about to rugby tackle him into staying put.

"Where are you going Tommy?" she repeated even more desperately.

Tommy considered giving her a reasonable explanation, but the opportunity was too good to resist.

"I thought I'd go throw myself off the Brigg. You know, save everyone a bit of time."

She screamed out loud.

He laughed out loud.

"Calm down. I need to buy another bag for college. I'll be back in an hour."

For a moment she seemed undecided on what to do, but he knew she would do nothing. She always did nothing when given the choice.

As he grabbed his car keys from the hook and made his way down the path, he paused for a moment and considered the possibility that she might ring Carl to alert him, but then he continued towards his car. She didn't like drama or conflict. She wouldn't make the call. She would simply wait it out and hope.

Tommy followed the directions on his phone until he arrived at a semi-detached house a few miles inland. There was a car in the drive, and he could see the flashing reflection of the tv screen through the window. Hopefully, Niki was home.

He was hopeful that he would recognise her when she opened the door, but the young woman who peered around it was certainly not Niki.

He was physically stunned by the beauty of this girl. Flaxen blonde hair and cornflower blue eyes. She smiled politely.

"Can I help you?"

"I'm looking for Niki." He explained without taking his eyes from hers.

"Oh, that's my mum. She's at work at the moment. Won't be back until around five. Can I give her a message?"

Tommy couldn't think of a plausible message he could leave for Niki nor a plausible excuse for knocking on her door randomly on a Monday afternoon.

"No.er I was just in the area and I recognised the house. She used to be friends with my mother years ago."

"Really?"

"Yes. They were best friends at one time. She might have mentioned her. Kelly? Kelly Palmer?"

"Oh my God!" the girl put both hands to her face "You must be the boy who lost his mother! I think my mum was friends with her too. Sophie wasn't it?"

"Yes, that's right. She told you about it then?"

"Oh yes. It must have been awful for you. I've seen photos of the three of them. Why don't you come in for a bit?"

Tommy wasn't sure if it was a great idea or a terrible one, but it seemed a better distraction than sitting watching Sonya polish the ornaments.

"Maybe just for a few minutes then."

"Yes, then I'll give her your number when she gets back. It's Amy by the way." She said as she led him into the lounge.

"Well nice to meet you Amy." He just couldn't stop looking at her face. It was like a perfect painting that was impossible to take your eyes off. Kelly would have been impressed by this perfect canvas.

He knew instantly that her hair was naturally flaxen and that her eyebrows were therefore tinted but apart from that there seemed to be no trace of cosmetic intervention. Her lips were full and dark rose in colour but there was not even a hint of lip liner where they contrasted with her porcelain complexion. He was still studying her when she surprised him with her reply.

"And this is Dean." She announced waiving her hand in the direction of a gangly teenage boy sprawled on the sofa with headphones on and a gaming console in his hands. Tommy hadn't even noticed there was anyone else in the room.

"Don't try talking to him," she laughed "he's in a world of his own."

Her glib remark caused his stomach to tighten as he was reminded of the reason he was here.

"It seems to be an addiction doesn't it?" he said, finally getting a grip of himself, "never really been interested myself."

"Me neither. I don't know about you but I'm starving. Not eaten today and I'm definitely not cooking anything for that lazy bundle of bones. I was about to go and grab a burger down the road if you want to join me?"

"That would be great" Tommy wasn't hungry at all. He was too anxious to eat but he knew it would give him the chance to find out anything Niki had told her about Sophie, or about him.

She pulled on a pair of high heeled ankle boots and tucked her skinny jeans into them before grabbing a leather jacket and shoving a bank card into her pocket.

"Come on, it's starting to rain." She called as she stepped outside while he was still standing in the lounge doorway.

"So, how come you're at home on a Monday?" he asked as they stepped out onto the pavement.

"Oh, I get most Monday's off. I'm a junior buyer for a clothing company so I work a lot of Saturdays. That's the nature of the beast in retail."

"Sounds pretty dull."

She held her coat akimbo as she delivered an indignant stare. "How rude!"

"Oh, I didn't mean…."

She laughed spontaneously, "I'm kidding. It is dull but one day I'm going to work for a serious fashion house and then I'm going to start my own brand. I'm going to be a designer."

She delivered the information as though it was a fact rather than a hopeful prediction, and for that reason alone, he believed her."

They ran up the street in the light rain, and into the burger bar a few hundreds yards up the street. She ordered and paid for her own leaving him to do the same. He liked her direct approach and lack of dithering, it made him feel comfortable.

"So why are you looking for my mum?"

"It's a long story." He sighed, hoping that she would settle for that and pick up the burger that had just been plonked in front of her.

"There has to be a reason to suddenly turn up after all these years!"

"The thing is," he said, suddenly coming up with a viable excuse, "I've just enrolled for a psychology degree and it set me off thinking about my biological mother and what drove her to do what she did."

Amy took a large bite and proceeded to empty her mouth before responding.

"Wow! That's serious shit!"

"Suppose it is. Did your mum say anything about her?"

"Yeah, she said Sophie had some serious issues."

"Did she tell you the detail?"

"Not really" Amy toyed with a bunch of chips she'd trapped between her fingers, "she just said she was having hallucinations. Seeing people who weren't really there and talking to them. Are you hoping to find a cure for her illness or something?"

"Bit late for that!" Tommy laughed.

"Well people do though, don't they? A parent dies of cancer and they become an oncologist, or someone they love dies of a heart attack and they become a heart surgeon." She stuffed the chips into her mouth and continued, "It happens all the time."

"Well let's just say I've found myself wanting to know a bit more shall we? I'm not about to devote my life to whatever she was suffering from."

"If you say so but I think we have a new psychiatric specialist in the making!"

"Shut up!" he laughed, stealing one of her chips.

"Doctor of parallel universes!" She teased.

Tommy felt his heart miss a beat.

"Eat up." She grinned, "Your burgers getting cold"

Chapter 6

Anne was   using a damp cloth to wipe the cat hairs from her velour sofa for the second time that day. She wondered why she had bothered to get a cat at all. It's not like they are particularly good company. A dog would have been a better option. At least you can take them for walks and get a bit of affection in return. Not like with cats who come and go as they please, take advantage of the warmth, and would scratch you as soon as look at you.

She had bought the cat when she lost her husband. She always referred to the event in that way. It felt less humiliating than to say, 'when he walked out'. It was exactly the same when she spoke of her retirement rather than her dismissal. It was much more comforting to be able to talk of the loss of her husband and her retirement than of being dumped and sacked.

Psychology could be a dangerous occupation, she always knew that, and she had been warned several times about becoming too engrossed in one patient or one condition. She had tried to heed the warnings and to keep a balance between her work and home life, but some things were just too compelling to leave alone.

She had started to spend most of her waking hours either at work or on home research. Files and files of research from across the globe, endless dead ends, hundreds of questions without answers. In the end it had all been for nothing and it had cost her her marriage. In hindsight, the cat turned out to be a suitable replacement for her husband. Almost a like for like replacement in fact. Little interaction, minimal affection, zero conversation and a lot of mess to clean up.

She was trying to pick the hairs off her cloth under the tap when the front doorbell rang. She wiped her chubby hands on the tea-towel before attempting to wipe some of the stains from her dirty skirt. She had stopped taking any interest in her appearance long ago, but she did make a quick attempt to tease the clumps of grey hair into separated curls, as she passed the hall mirror before opening the door.

It had been over a decade since she last set eyes on the two faces before her, but she knew them instantly. How could she not when they were at the core of the event that had ruined her life.

"Anne?" Kelly asked

"Come in Kelly" Anne offered calmly, to Kelly's surprise.

"You remember me?"

"I remember both of you. Hello Carl."

Carl was still on the doorstep looking stunned.

"That's remarkable," Kelly went on, "after all these years you remember the relatives of a patient?"

Anne raise her eyebrows.

"She was hardly any old patient, now was she?"

"I guess not." Kelly agreed as she wiped her feet on the mat.

"Tea? Coffee?" Anne offered, already on her way to the kitchen.

"Two coffee's please." Kelly called to her, as she disappeared.

"Might have known," came the voice from the kitchen,

"Used to be tea at one time, now it's coffee, I blame the Americans."

Carl and Kelly looked at each other worriedly but then Kelly shrugged and whispered.

"What have we got to lose?"

Carl nodded and sat down, noticing that the cushion was damp.

A few minutes later Anne emerged with a tray of filter coffee, cream, sugar and coffee cups arranged on a tray.

"So, what brings you here after all this time?"

"It's Tommy" Kelly said gently.

"Ah! The confused little boy. I always felt for him. He thought you were his mother and then suddenly his family got blown apart. How is he?"

"He's not great to be honest," Kelly went on, "we thought you might be able to help"

Anne looked uninterested, bored, or almost resentful.

"It's a bit late to be trying to sort him out now isn't it?"

Carl suddenly felt a need to intervene.

"It's only this week that there's been a problem."

"What kind of problem?"

Carl couldn't bring himself to say the words. He looked at Kelly to continue.

"Tommy turned up at my office believing it was Tuesday today."

"So?"

"Well he thought it was Tuesday because he believed he had already been to college to register yesterday. He remembered a whole day that hadn't yet happened."

Anne was expressionless for several moments.

"Did you hear what I said?"

"Yes, I heard."

"Well isn't that how it started with Sophie? I only remember what Niki told me but I'm sure it was exactly like that."

"Yes."

"Yes what?"

"Yes, it was exactly like that." She was still devoid of emotion.

"So, what are you thinking?" Kelly asked impatiently.

Anne looked down at the floor and closed her eyes tightly, her hands were clenched together so tightly that her knuckles had turned white. She was totally silent as Kelly and Carl exchanged worried glances and then watched in fear. She was silently praying.

Suddenly her dismissal and divorce were of no consequence. Suddenly everything had changed and every moment she had spent destroying her own life had been worth it. Finally, she had been handed another chance. On this unremarkable rainy Monday afternoon, these two people had knocked on her door and placed the possibility of some answers back within her grasp.

Slowly she loosened the grip of her hands and slowly she opened her eyes and raised her head.

"What is it?" Carl asked curtly.

She seemed to want to savour the moment for a while before sharing it.

Kelly felt a chill run up her spine again.

"Anne!" she said firmly, "What?"

Anne had an expression on her face. A blend of excitement and trepidation with a hint of pleasure.

"It's happening again."

Carl wanted to run out of the house. Kelly wanted to shake the stupid woman. Anne just wanted to thank God again, for his intervention.

"What are you talking about?" Kelly snapped "What's happening again? You mean the psychosis or something?"

Anne laughed

"Sophie wasn't suffering from psychosis. She was somehow living two lives!"

"You're insane," Carl bellowed, "come on, we're leaving!"

"Wait a minute," Kelly said putting a hand on his knee to prevent him from standing, "tell us what you know, tell us everything"

Anne looked to Carl for his take on it, but it was Kelly who spoke again.

"Carl, we came here for information. Now I don't care if she's a mad woman or a bloody freak, but I want to hear anything at all that might help us make some sense of this whole fuckin nightmare. So, you can either stay here and listen or you can go sit in the car. Frankly I don't care which!"

Carl put his head in his hands for a moment and then looked up and nodded.

"Ok, I'll listen but you'll not convince me this is anything other than vivid bloody nightmares."

"Fine" Kelly nodded, "Please Anne, tell us what you know."

Anne pulled out a suitcase from a large broom cupboard and snapped it open.

"Before we start, I need to tell you that the information I have is confidential. I could be prosecuted for even having it as I took copies before they dismissed me"

"You were sacked?" Carl shouted. "Bloody marvellous, she's a mad woman with stolen notes!"

"Carl!" Kelly reprimanded.

"Firstly," Anne said quietly, "I can assure you I am not a mad woman. Like you I never have believed in anything other than the power of the mind. That's how I was treating Sophie and that's how I was treating my previous patient."

"I didn't know you had a previous patient like Sophie?" Kelly interjected.

"Oh yes. I told Sophie about her. In fact, I used to use that patient to threaten her into letting go of her fantasy. My other patient was claiming exactly the same thing as Sophie you see. She was trying to get back to her mother, and in the end we had to incarcerate her and put her on suicide watch. I told Sophie the same thing would happen to her if she didn't start to accept that her visions were of her own making".

"So where is she now, this other woman?" Kelly felt hopeful.

"She killed herself." There was no emotion in the revelation.

No-one spoke for a few moments, and so Anne felt compelled to elaborate.

"The truth is that after Sophie died, I spent more time with her. I was trying to establish some connection, some common denominator. Both patients started to experience these vivid dreams in their early twenties, and both lived along the Filey coastline. I looked at everything I possibly could including water supply, environmental factors, upbringing and eventually timing."

She sucked air through her teeth as though despising herself.

"It was the timing that got me."

Carl was desperately trying to get Kelly's attention so they could make their excuses and get out, but she seemed interested in this utter madness.

"The timing?" Kelly asked, "what about the timing?"

"Well my first patient started the symptoms about eleven years before Sophie and there were also eleven years between her first suicide attempt and her final death."

"What possible relevance could that have?!" Carl interjected.

"I had no idea but then I started looking into other things"

"What things?" Carl was getting impatient and annoyed.

"Have you heard of the eleven-year solar cycle?"

Both shook their heads, and it was difficult to tell if the head shaking was purely a negative response, or one of sarcastic disbelief in the question.

"Every decade, between ten and twelve years, the Sun's magnetic fields totally flip, and North becomes South and vice versa. A giant circuit of electrical current comes out from the solar equator into the universe.

"So? what's your point?" Carl was getting agitated with the mumbo jumbo she seemed to be trying to pass off as some startling revelation.

"Well, at first I discarded any connection because you would think that any effect of electrical surges on the brain would be caused at the solar max, wouldn't you?"

She looked at the two blank faces and continued.

"Well yes you would because that's when they are strongest. But then I looked at the timings again and its kind of an awakening, if you get my drift?"

Neither of them were anywhere close to getting her drift.

"The electrical fields, or sunspots, are very active around the flip and then they start to go quiet until they are virtually non-existent at the end of the cycle. Then a new cycle starts, and the activity starts to emerge again. Like an awakening of the sun. These are the timings that match."

Again, no-one spoke. Carl rolled his eyes and Kelly shuffled uncomfortably. She noted their reactions and continued.

"Imagine that when we have all that activity we become used to it. We adapt to it but then when it goes quiet we are not compensating any more. Then suddenly, almost quietly they creep in again and we are so much more sensitive. Imagine that some people have brains so sensitive that it messes up the electrical connections!"

Kelly and Carl were both visibly dumbfounded. Totally speechless.

"I admit that I wanted to find something. I wanted to solve why this had happened three times within a twelve mile stretch of coastline. I got obsessed with it, I guess. Eventually it lost me my job."

She sat down as though defeated and when she looked up her eyes were watery with tears.

"You got the sack for going off on a tangent?" Carl snapped "I'm not surprised. I'd sack you if you started spouting all that nonsense when you were meant to be in charge of the mentally ill!"

"No. It was worse than that," she tried to wipe the tears on her nylon cardigan sleeve.

"How much worse?" Kelly asked suspiciously.

"The woman I told you about, well I left my pen behind after a visit and she used it to open up the artery in her wrist."

"You left it behind on purpose?" Kelly asked.

"No! Of course not!"

Kelly looked at her and cocked her head slightly.

"Well maybe I did. I'm not sure to be honest."

"Fuckin hell!" Carl blurted out, "She's a lunatic Kel. You heard her! Come on, we're leaving!"

Anne put her hand on Carl's arm.

"It wasn't like that. I just hated watching the poor woman suffer. She was in total torment and as time went by, she told me that her visitations to her mother, or whatever they were, started to diminish. I thought the window was closing, and I so wanted her to be reunited, you know? Even if it was just in her head."

This was the first time in years that Anne had found anyone who could offer even a hint of understanding, and the floodgates had literally opened.

Anne's eyes were puffing up, filling her wrinkles with red blotchy flesh but she needed to offload the memory of it.

"They showed me the photos. At my disciplinary hearing they actually showed me the photos! She had picked at her wrist with a broken pen shaft. It must have been excruciating."

Kelly closed her eyes as though trying to block out the image, but Anne needed to talk.

"There was blood pooled beneath her where she had sat hiding behind the door but there was something comforting about it"

"Comforting?!" Carl yelled "You're deranged!"

Anne wasn't listening to Carl, she was too intent on getting Kelly's full attention.

"I mean, to do something that horrific, that painful. Well you have to be sure about something don't you? I might have left the pen behind, but I only gave her a choice. I mean to actually do that means she must have been certain. Absolutely certain, mustn't she?"

Kelly put her hand over Anne's and spoke quietly and calmly.

"Anne, when did this happen? Was it in the same year that Sophie died?"

Anne couldn't speak. She just nodded her head and wiped away more tears.

"I confessed to my husband that I might have left the pen intentionally and he wanted to go to the police. I was already under investigation for negligence, and for my unorthodox notes, so I accepted early retirement and he accepted my offer to let him go with a huge chunk of my pension. I bought his silence. It was a mess."

Carl eventually got Kelly's attention and nodded toward the door. Kelly widened her eyes, reprimanding him for being so obvious.

"I do know how this sounds," Anne sighed again, obviously noticing Carl's expression, "it just all seemed like a huge coincidence and I'm a practical person. I don't believe in coincidences."

"What *do* you believe?" Kelly asked.

"I believe there's a connection that's for sure. Magnetic and electrical fields can affect the mind. We know that. The brain is nothing more than electrical impulses so it's very possible there's a connection."

"But it's not real?"

"It depends on what you consider to be real doesn't it? The mind is, after all, the only thing we really have. It controls everything. What we feel, taste, smell and hear."

Kelly leaned back in the sofa as though reeling from the information overload. She was trying desperately to separate fact from fiction, fantasy from reality and madness from genius. She remained in thought, while the cat rubbed against her legs, leaving white hair on her black mohair trousers.

Anne poured more coffee while Carl fidgeted and looked at his watch several times. Then Anne looked up and asked the question that had been begging to be asked for the last half hour.

"How many years is it since Sophie died?"

The question needed no clarification, any more than the fact that Tommy was in his early twenties and they resided on the same stretch of coastline.

Carl was googling on his phone as he shook his head slowly from side to side to convey his dismay.

He scrolled and then put on his glasses to look more closely at the Solar Cycle table and then looked up at Kelly.

"She's bloody right. It has to be a coincidence. Easy to make things fit if you look hard enough isn't it?"

Anne shrugged. Kelly frowned. Carl could feel the hairs rising on the back of his neck.

Chapter 7

In the burger bar, Tommy was trying to spin out the meal in the hope that Niki would be home by the time they left to walk back to the house. He knew he wouldn't sleep until he'd spoken to her and there was still half an hour to fill.

His phone buzzed, for the forth time.

"Someone is eager to get in touch," Amy said as she strained to look at the name of the latest text.

"Four messages from Sonya!" She teased, "are you supposed to be somewhere else?"

"It's not what you think," Tommy said irritably, "Sonya is my stepmother."

"Oh," she teased again, "Mummy's boy? Or is she the wicked stepmother who hounds you day and night?"

"Neither," he laughed awkwardly, "She'll just be sending me a list of stuff to pick up on the way home."

She widened her eyes at him disbelievingly.

This girl was not one to be fooled and there was something about her that made him suddenly want to blurt out his whole dilemma. He knew it would be disastrous, and he also knew that the urge to do it was a result of the pressure of holding it all inside while he waited to talk to Niki about it. He had to reveal nothing. Once he had spoken to Niki and confirmed her ongoing silence, he would have one less problem to deal with.

Amy's phone rang.

"Hi mum. Well, Dean will want something, but I've already eaten. How far away are you?"

She stopped talking and Tommy could vaguely hear Niki's voice at the other end before Amy spoke again.

"Well actually, I've been having a burger with the son of an old friend of yours. He's called Tommy. He's the son of the girl who killed herself, remember?"

The voice on the other end was speaking more quickly but Tommy couldn't make out the words. Amy blushed and stood up.

"Excuse me, I won't be a minute."

She stepped into the street to continue the conversation and then returned.

"Is everything alright?" He already knew that it clearly wasn't.

"Yes fine," she lied "Mum will be home in five minutes so we should set off back."

This time they walked in silence, each mulling over, in isolation, what had just happened. The air felt thick with unspoken thoughts as they sauntered along, watching one another suspiciously and wondering.

Suddenly Amy looped her arm through his and pulled him close. Tommy had no idea what it meant. Maybe she just couldn't bear the atmosphere or maybe she wanted to comfort him or perhaps she had just mulled over whatever her mother had said and chosen to disobey.

Niki was standing at the front door as they approached the gate and instantly Tommy's stomach turned a somersault. He recognised her immediately. She looked slimmer and taller, but he had been a small boy the last time he saw her. The night she had dragged him upstairs by the wrists while he was still on his knees, her contorted face screaming that he was an evil brat.

Everything was flooding back, and his throat was closing up. He wasn't ready for this. He took his arm from Amy's and was about to make a run for it. To get in his car and drive away. This woman terrified him more than any secret she might spill. He had just taken his arm from Amy's when Niki spoke.

"Hello Tommy. Good to see you. How have you been?"

He was momentarily relieved, he managed to take a breath but mistrust was still tingling through every pore as he followed Amy up the path and back into the house.

"Amy, go and make some tea will you? While I take care of Tommy."

"We've just had two cups of coffee mum. I'm sure he doesn't want another drink!"

Niki glowered at her daughter, and for the first time Tommy saw a flicker of vulnerability in the girl he had been fighting to keep pace with for the last few hours. Submissively she disappeared into the kitchen.

It was more likely that he had got the measure of Niki than that he had misjudged Amy. He wished he had made a run for it on the street.

"What are you doing here?!" Niki whispered harshly as soon as the kitchen door closed.

"I need to talk to you, it's important." Tommy pleaded, still unnerved by the violence he recalled much too vividly.

"What have you said to Amy?"

"Nothing, just that you used to be friends with my mother."

"Well let's keep it that way, shall we?" Her tone was unmistakably a threat.

"Yes ok, I just wanted to ask a few questions that's all."

"Well we can't talk here, can we?"

Tommy didn't see why not so he just shrugged.

"I mean, it's a delicate topic, so why don't you leave me your number and I'll get in touch."

He nodded his agreement, but he felt uneasy about it. Perhaps she wouldn't bother calling and he might never learn about how his mother's illness started or progressed. Perhaps he might never get the reassurance that she intended to keep his secret, if she got a visit from his dad and Kelly.

She slipped into the lounge for a moment, kicking her son's feet off the coffee table as she passed by and returned with a notepad and pen.

Obediently Tommy wrote down his number and placed it on the small table in the hallway as she held open the door for him to leave.

Seconds later Amy emerged with a tray of tea.

"Where's Tommy gone?"

"He's gone home, and like I said on the phone you need to keep away from him. His mother was deranged, and insanity can be hereditary. He's probably as unpredictable and dangerous as she was."

Niki left her standing with the tray and stormed back into the lounge "And get your bloody feet off the table! I won't tell you again!"

"What the hell is everybody shouting about?!" Pete's voice came from the hallway as he pushed the door open, still wearing his coat.

"It's nothing. You go get changed and I'll start tea."

"Nothing?" Amy chipped in, "Mum's just gone off her rocker because I went for a burger with a boy who called in to talk to her!"

"What boy? Why can't she go for a burger?"

Niki shot Amy a reprimanding stare. Amy ignored it and turned back to her father.

"It was Tommy Taylor, do you remember him? His mum killed herself when he was about ten, I think? You all used to be friends he said, and he was looking you up to find out more about his mum."

"So, what's wrong with that?"

Amy needed to report her mother's bad manner to her father.

"I don't know, ask her. She threw him out while I was making a drink and then warned me to stay away from him. She totally lost her shit!"

"Ok Amy, let me talk to your mother and stop swearing!"

"Shit isn't swearing, it's in the dictionary!"

"Yes and so is grounded so go to your room and let me talk to your mother."

"Whatever!" Amy put down the tray of tea she had been carrying around and left the room to make her way upstairs.

"You too Dean!"

"He can't hear you, he's got his bloody headphones on!" Niki snapped.

Pete pulled her out into the kitchen.

"So, what's this about?"

Niki had been quickly making something up while Amy and Pete were arguing.

"I don't want her anywhere near that Tommy, that's all. There's something not right about him!"

"He was a small boy who lost his mother in tragic circumstances Nik. Of course, he was going to get to an age when he wanted to make sense of it all."

"No. You don't know everything!" she spat, "He's not right. Sophie was a headcase and he's exactly the same!"

Pete laughed sarcastically.

"You don't even know the boy! You didn't even know him back then so you sure as hell don't know him now."

"Listen Pete. You remember me going to the police station with the stupid bits of paper Sophie had been collecting?"

"Yes of course I do."

"Well, guess who I got them from? Guess who had been using them to convince Sophie that her fantasies were real?"

"What?"

"I got them from Tommy! He told me everything he'd done! He's made up stories, stories about things he pretended he'd heard from her made-up daughter, but he's got it all from her own collage of madness!"

Pete sat down on a kitchen chair, so Niki pulled out a chair and sat opposite.

"Bloody hell Nik. Why didn't you say anything?"

"Because Carl had been through enough without that."

"Even so."

"Well like you said earlier, he was a child. He probably didn't know what he was doing. He just wanted Kelly back as his mum didn't he? and who could blame him? Sophie didn't exactly throw her arms around him with motherly love, did she?"

"You're right." He patted her hand on the table

"So now you can see why I threw him out."

Pete laughed again.

"I think you went a bit over the top there Nik. He came to ask about his mother, that's all. He was a small boy when all this happened, he probably can't even remember making up those tales and if he does, he probably had no idea what it was doing to Soph!"

"I just think we should all keep away from him. I've seen what he was capable of even then, scheming and acting! Imagine what he'd be capable of now! He could be as disturbed as she was!"

"Now you really are over-reacting! They used to be our friends Niki, remember that and the fact that Tommy came here is quite a gesture. I don't know how we all drifted apart but I think we could have been there for all of them, a bit more than we were."

This was not going in the direction Niki wanted it to.

"Well I would rather leave things as they are, thank you very much and I'm not having my daughter anywhere near that devious disturbed boy!"

Pete got up from the table.

"I'll go speak to Amy."

Niki slammed the dirty mugs into the sink cursing Dean for being a total slob. He was just like his father! Lazy, disinterested, monotonous and a total pushover!

Upstairs, Pete already had his arms around Amy. He was playing the part he loved, being his little girl's saviour. Amy was his favourite, but he knew that parents shouldn't ever admit that, not even to themselves.

Pete had given himself permission to do exactly that many years ago. His daughter was worth ten of his son. It was a fact, not an opinion. She was vibrant, compassionate, bubbly and hungry for life. His son would be content to pass in and out of this world leaving nothing other than his carbon footprint. Achieving nothing more than to have been the lanky, unwashed, living decoration to their sofa.

It wasn't as if Pete hadn't tried.

Throwing the game console out of the window, yanking his headphones from his hairy ears, marching him bodily to the job centre, refusing to feed him and sometimes locking him out of the house had resulted in the same thing. An argument with Niki, a plea from his sister, a resentful submission and the decoration back on the sofa.

"Your mum was just worried, that's all." He assured Amy.

"Tommy isn't dangerous dad, he's not crazy either!"

"I know, I know."

"I really liked him. Mum used to be best friends with his step-mum Kelly, didn't she?"

"Yes, she did and there's certainly a good bit of wealth there!"

Amy dried her tears and laughed.

"Honestly dad! Is that all you think about?"

"I'm just saying you could do worse than get your feet under that table!" he raised his eyebrows comically.

"Well that's not going to happen now is it?"

"You leave your mother to me, and if you want to see this boy in the meantime just make sure she doesn't get so much of a hint, ok?"

"Ok, I love you dad." She held him by the ears and kissed his nose. It had been her way of thanking him since she was four years old and it still made him smile.

"Love you too princess."

Pete made his way back downstairs where Niki was thoughtlessly throwing some random out ready meals into the oven.

As Amy passed back through the hallway she noticed Tommy's number on the sheet of paper and quietly slid her phone from her pocket. She quickly took a photo of it and went into the lounge to sit beside Dean, collecting a cup of tea from the abandoned tray.

Niki followed her in and took one of the other drinks.

"Look, I know you weren't to know but it's best to keep well away from that family love."

Amy nodded and took a gulp of the lukewarm tea.

She had no intention of keeping away. She liked Tommy and he seemed sane enough to her. She had enjoyed his company immensely. She had his phone number and she intended to use it.

After all, he was stunningly good looking, charming, witty, intelligent, confident, and absolutely loaded. There was not a chance in hell that she was staying away.

Niki smiled and patted her hand.

"Good girl."

Amy smiled back and then cast a glance at her father who nodded his approval.

His daughter was more than a match for his wife!

On the A64 Kelly and Carl were on their way home and the conversation was anything but straightforward.

"I don't think she was trying to say that there's some parallel bloody universe in play!" Carl said sarcastically.

"I think that's exactly what she was implying!" Kelly retorted.

"Kelly, she was talking scientifically. Magnetic fields are not paranormal, they are natural."

"There was nothing natural about that conversation I can assure you!" Kelly was becoming as frustrated with Carls interpretation, as he was with hers.

"Like she said," Carl went on "Magnetic fields cause currents to flow through the neutrons and causes it to depolarize. She was trying to say that electrical energy in the brain can be affected."

Kelly thought for a moment.

"Yes, I got all that about magnetic fields penetrating tissue and I would love to rush and tell Tommy that his missing day had been caused by electronic activity in his brain but I think you missed the point"

Carl huffed loudly.

Kelly stopped the car and looked Carl in the face.

"If she truly believed this was all about electricity and hallucinations, and that they were exceptionally strong along our stretch of coastline, then why didn't she just take the poor woman somewhere else?"

Carl frowned as though he didn't understand what Kelly's point was.

"Carl, if she thought there was no parallel existence for this girl to return to, then why the hell would she allow her to open her veins and bleed out on the floor of a secure cell?"

Carl didn't reply. He starred blankly at the windscreen while Kelly restarted the car and pulled back onto the road.

Eventually Carl was the one to break the silence.

"Better not to mention any of this to Tommy." He said gently.

Kelly put her hand on his lap in gratitude and then replied.

"I think we should just tell him we are sure it was just a bad dream and we will take him away somewhere to clear his head."

Carl nodded "Somewhere away from this coastline."

Neither spoke again for the remainder of the journey, until they arrived at Carls front gate.

"For Christ's sake," Carl bellowed "Where the hell has Tommy gone, his car's not here!"

As they entered the house Sonya was waiting in the hallway apologising profusely, even before they had got through the door.

"You were supposed to be keeping a bloody eye on him Sonya!"

" I know, I know," was all she could offer "He went off to buy a new bag, but he's been gone ages." She hated any altercation with Carl, she hated any altercation with anyone.

"Did he say anything else? Anything at all?" Carl asked more calmly.

Sonya hated lying equally as much, but there was no way she was going to confess that she had allowed him to leave after he had said he was going to jump off the Brigg to save time. Her face was white, and she couldn't stop wringing her hands. If anything happened to Tommy, Carl would never forgive her. He would throw her out and she would have to go back to living alone. It had been a miracle that Carl wanted to marry her in the first place, and deep down she knew it had nothing to do with love. The person he truly loved was standing right in front of her.

She paced up and down a few more times wondering if she should speak out and if there might still be time to find him.

Suddenly Carl was knocked forward as the door opened again and a face appeared around it.

"Shall we open a bottle of wine tonight?" Tommy grinned, "It's been one hell of a day!"

Chapter 8

After twenty minutes of awkward bickering between Carl and Sonya Kelly suggested that Tommy went back with her and she would update him on the way home.

Carl didn't put up much of a fight about it, hardly noticing when they left. He was too angry with Sonya and wasn't in the right frame of mind to try to reassure Tommy or to persuade him to get away for a while. Better to leave all that to Kelly.

She was good at finding hotels and places to stay. She could have something booked in seconds. Refining searches, filtering amenities, using her saved credit card details and saving the bookings on her phone. Carl would have to spend half a day on the task! He hated that he had allowed technology to leave him behind when he had always been the technically and mechanically minded one but that wasn't the reason he was in such a mood.

For once, he had given his trust to Sonya in front of Kelly. This had been her chance to show Kelly she was more than a plant-watering robot. He had left her in charge of their son. Kelly's son. He had been hoping that it might sting Kelly a little. That she might have felt just a tiny bit of jealousy that Sonya was staying at home with Tommy as mother and son. That Sonya would be taking care of him as Carl's capable wife. She had totally blown it!

"You had one fuckin' job Sonya!" he said finally as he walked out and slammed the door.

"So, it sounds like I need to stay off the hotel champagne for a while," Tommy laughed   after listening to Kelly's edited account of the visit to Sophie's therapist.

He pulled himself up from the white leather sofa and picked up a bottle of gin as he passed the cocktail bar in the corner of Kelly's lounge.

"Suppose the same goes for this then?"

Kelly nodded.

"The brain is a powerful trickster. I've seen people on drugs who totally believe there's a shark in their bath!"

Tommy cocked his head to one side, inferring that she was exaggerating.

"Sounds like you've been to wilder parties than me!" he teased.

She was amazed at how easily he had accepted the explanation they had given him for his strange day with the girl he now referred to as his dream girl.

Tommy wasn't stupid and she had seen the fear in his eyes yet suddenly he was relaxed and untroubled. She watched him closely for any sign that he was putting on a brave face but there was none. As his mother, she could always tell when he was forcing a smile, but he seemed genuinely fine.

She wondered if he had simply blocked out the incident in the way people block out other traumatic events or if he had been so grateful to get a believable diagnosis that he had sub consciously grasped it, devoured it and declared it a fact.

She watched him as he picked up a dish of nuts and proceeded to throw them in the air one by one and catch them in his mouth. He had done that since he was a child and today, he seemed more like a child than he had in several years. It was this childlike behaviour that caused Kelly to realise what was going on.

It was nothing more than the trust he had for her and for Carl. They were his parents, and just as children continue to believe in Santa Claus and the tooth-fairy long after they should have worked it out, Tommy was going to believe in their explanation for his additional day. It didn't matter that it didn't make sense, or that it seemed as unlikely as Santa travelling the whole world in one night. His parents had said it was true and that was that. It was the truth.

She felt suddenly sickened at the deception and at the way he had regressed to this trusting child, happily catching peanuts, in his moment of terror.

She thought about ringing Carl and suggesting they were more honest, but she didn't want to frighten him again. Not until she had a solution to offer him. It was better they stick to their plan.

She would take Tommy away for a few days on her own and Carl would do what he always did. Stick his head under the bonnet of some clapped out old car grateful that he didn't have to take any time off work and grateful that Kelly would sort out the whole mess.

She also thought that he needed time to fix the rift with Sonya. He had been unreasonably harsh on her since she could hardly have prevented Tommy from leaving but still, he did have a point that she failed to let them know. He was always disgruntled with Sonya, but Kelly couldn't understand why. The woman was pleasant enough. It was best that they were left alone to sort out their differences and allow Tommy some stress-free time with his mum.

Tommy preferred Kelly's luxury condo anyway, with its heated swimming pool but he always made a point of splitting his time equally and of showing equal enthusiasm for each of his homes. Kelly insisted on that above all else.

Now she was busy re-arranging her work diary for the rest of the week. She had already sorted the registration for Tommy but was trying to come up with a plausible reason to re-register him at a different college. A college in a different town. A town far away from the east coast of North Yorkshire. That would have to wait until she had more time to be inventive.

She clicked her mouse back to the search and started to look for somewhere nice to take Tommy on their luxury break.

"New York would be nice." Tommy suggested.

"We are supposed to be finding somewhere you can relax and unwind Tommy. I can't think of a more inappropriate choice than Times Square! Anyway, it would take us as long to fly back and forth as to be there."

Tommy put on his funny sulky face.

"It's not going to work on me this time. I'm finding somewhere quiet and tranquil."

"In that case I better go and pack my hiking boots and fishing rod!" he shouted back as he made his way to the open staircase leading to the gigantic bedrooms on the mezzanine floor.

"You won't sway me Tommy Taylor and you don't own a fishing rod!" she was trying to act as though everything was fine but Anne's words were playing relentlessly in her head and each time she heard them, they took on a different meaning.

Her mind travelled back to the days with Sophie, as she tried to remember anything of relevance in the account Niki had given of Sophie's delusions. She wished she had paid more attention and asked more questions.

She remembered that Sophie suffered from what she called duplicate days and from that she assumed that the same day was being lived through twice, but she didn't know how often it happened or when it happened. She didn't know if this other place Sophie spoke of was totally full of strangers or if some of the people were familiar to her.

She hadn't paid much attention to the actual detail and she knew the reason for that. The characters in Sophie's fantasies were of little consequence. There were only two facts of any consequence and they were that firstly, Sophie was clearly insane and secondly, she was fantasising about another man. Those facts added up to just one thing. Carl would become available at long last.

Over the years, her memory of Sophie had been boxed up and labelled as a girl who always wanted a love she would die for. A girl who got her wish and the opportunity to prove it.

Why would she pay attention to the details of someone else's dream?

It was necessary to box Sophie away. Kelly didn't want to think about her, not then, not now.

She didn't want to face the fact that she'd wanted Sophie's man for herself. That even now, she was haunted by the possibility that her love for Carl could have manifested itself into the delay in calling an ambulance. That bonding with baby Tommy had been mostly born of the fear of Sophie returning to reclaim her family.

That she had set out to steal Sophie's life while she slept. It had felt justifiable until now. Until she could feel the terror

Sophie had tried to describe. See the impact of it in her own stolen son.

She couldn't allow her conscience to be awoken because, if it was, she knew it would consume her. Force her to face her own crimes and destroy the bit of happiness she had managed to carve for herself.

Her obsession with finally winning Carl for herself and her stupidity for mistaking that need for real love. She desired Carl, even now but if it came to actually dying for him, she knew that her feelings were not even close to self- sacrifice. Perhaps things had just changed, perhaps she might have risked her life for him back then, but she doubted it. She couldn't imagine ever loving someone so much that you would value their life over your own. It went against natural instinct. When the chips are down, we all fight to live don't we?

Right now, as she watched the peanuts continue to bounce off Tommy's face and litter her parquet floor, she needed to focus on stopping whatever it was from devouring her son.

It wasn't productive to spend time chastising herself for failing to listen more attentively to Sophie's sequence of events. What started it, how and when it happened and who else existed were, at that time, as irrelevant as the details of someone else's dream.

She was exhausted but she knew one thing. She needed to find a suitable break before she could go to bed and hope to relax enough to grab a few hours sleep.

Tommy was a difficult person to impress. That was also her fault. He was far too accustomed to five-star accommodation with swimming pools and spa baths, limitless Moet and lobster lunches. Nothing she picked out would excite him, but if she didn't find something soon she was in danger of falling asleep on her laptop and waking in the morning with nowhere to go.

Suddenly she smiled. There was a very clear way to surprise Tommy. She clicked away from the luxury breaks and up into the remote west coast of Scotland. A small cottage between two mountains with no cable or tv reception. A half mile walk on foot to reach it, and temperamental electricity. The negative reviews seemed endless but each one was gaining five stars in Kelly's heart.

Three clicks later the confirmation number was on her screen. Perfect.

Tommy pulled out a suitcase and started to throw in socks, underwear and jeans. He didn't know what else to pack as he didn't know what she was likely to book so he pushed it to one side to finish off in the morning.

He always left the arranging to Kelly and he also knew that whatever he neglected to pack could be bought as soon as they arrived at their destination. He had no reason to pay any more attention to the task, so he stripped down to his boxer shorts and jumped on the bed with the remote in hand.

He had put on a brave face all evening. Pretended to go along with the bullshit about hallucinations and vivid dreams but he was terrified. He didn't want to worry Kelly unnecessarily and if she believed there was nothing wrong, then he was going to play along. Contradicting the explanation he'd been offered, would bring his sanity into question and, if he inherited the label Sophie had been given, then his life was practically over.

He had withdrawn into the quiet of his room to think. To go over everything in his mind and to try to come up with a more plausible explanation. He was damn sure it hadn't been a dream and Vicky's freckled face was as vivid in his memory as it had been before his eyes. He had felt so close to her. He had made a friend and that didn't happen very often for him yet, as he agonized over the reality of that day, he found himself doubting his account of it.

There was no third explanation. He was either insane or dreaming and his trepidation at accepting the former convinced him to accept the latter.

Vicky didn't exist any more than the drunken night with Jack and Harry. He tried to backtrack from that morning. The moment he booked into the hotel and waited for his date to arrive. He was staring at the ceiling as he recounted the meal and the way she admired herself in the window, the sex in the room, the argument and her heated departure. Suddenly a smile drifted over his face. Of course! Why hadn't he realised before? He jumped off the bed and ran back downstairs.

"I've got it! I know what happened!"

Kelly almost jumped out of her skin as he clattered down the wooden stairs three at a time.

"What?" was all she could get out, before he landed on the chair beside her.

"The night I was at the hotel!" he was breathless with excitement.

"What about it?"

"I took a girl back to my room! I took a girl back and we were both drinking the wine then we fell out and she left in a temper."

"What did you fall out about?"

"That doesn't matter! The thing is that I left her alone after she called me a...well after she got angry and when I came out, she'd gone!"

"I don't know what you're saying Tommy."

"I'm saying that I left her alone with my drink. She'd already offered me something earlier in the night and I refused. Don't you get it? She must have spiked my drink!"

Kelly watched his face light up with sheer relief, and she couldn't help but share it.

She grasped the explanation as gratefully as he had. An explanation that didn't involve insanity, or Sophie, or some phenomenon about another universe and, for a few minutes the horror melted away. Tommy jumped up and ran back up the stairs.

"I'm going to ring dad!"

Kelly sat for a while, processing what she had just been told and hoping that this really was nothing more than a spiked drink but as she sat alone listening to Tommy gush it all out again the fear began to return. Anne's words were creeping back over her like strangling vines. So many coincidences.

She sighed deeply and then called up to Tommy.

"We are still taking that break."

"If you say so." he called back,

Kelly printed off the details for the cottage and opened a large bag of crisps and as she munched and drank wine she started to relax and to allow herself to consider the more reasonable explanation. To look forward to the few days away with her son even if the reason for it was no longer valid.

Tommy finished delivering the good news to Carl and felt suddenly lighter and full of optimism. He couldn't believe he hadn't joined the dots earlier and as his mood lightened, he felt the urge to tell Kelly about his visit to see Niki.

It wasn't really Niki he wanted to tell her about. He wanted to tell her about the beautiful blonde he had taken to a burger bar and the refreshing way she had insisted in paying her way. He wanted mostly to tell her how he couldn't take his eyes off her perfect face and how her forthright manner had made him feel like he could have told her everything about him, including his fears about his strange day.

He couldn't of course, because if he did, she would ask why he had visited Niki in the first place and that was definitely a topic he needed to stay away from. Niki probably wouldn't call him anyway.

He picked up a bottle of water and lay back on the bed when his phone rang.

"Hello?" he didn't recognise the number.

"Hi. It's Amy. I hope you don't mind me calling. I got your number from the note you left."

"No. Not at all. What's up?"

"I just wanted to apologise for the way my mum acted and for not saying goodbye."

"It's fine. Honestly don't worry about it."

"No, it's not fine, she's being an idiot. She's acting like I might catch something from you and that's awful. It's like she thinks there's something wrong with you because of what your mother did."

Tommy felt relieved he hadn't confided in her after all, as he settled down to turn on the charm.

They chatted for a little while and then it was obvious someone was approaching at her end.

"Sorry, gotta go. Save my number and call me eh?"

"Yep. Deffo. Night."

He smiled widely as he put down his phone and picked up the remote. A few hours ago, he had been like a terrified child and now he was ready to take on the world again. More importantly, he had got his swagger back.

He had barely flicked through a handful of channels when his eyes closed from sheer exhaustion.

In the background he could hear the applause of some talent show and the laughter of the audience as the judges made their comments.

Tomorrow he would be far away from here, sipping cocktails with Kelly just as they did on their cruise breaks. How he loved those cruises. He loved being out on the ocean surrounded by miles of thrashing waves as far as the eye could see.

He loved the smell of it, and the sound of the squabbling seagulls as they fought over the scraps of buffet that passengers hurled into the air. Those cruises were his happy place.

He tried to imagine the sound, imagine the salty smell of the sea and the cool damp air against his face.

He could almost feel the damp mist filling his nostrils, hear the rhythmic crashing of the waves, and the distant squawking of those guls.

He felt comforted by the memory, as he turned onto his side and stretched his arm across the bed. His hand was resting on something cold and damp. He opened and closed his fingers feeling the sand move away as his fingers became engulfed. The pungent scent of heather was heavy in his nostrils as it brushed against his face.

He opened his eyes into the brightness of the morning sun. He was shivering uncontrollably, and the sour, acid taste of stale vomit was rancid in his mouth. His throat ached from sheer dryness. He knew that trying to swallow would deliver extreme pain, but his raging thirst demanded him to try. He closed his eyes tightly to squeeze away the salt and sand, but when he re-opened them, they stung even more. Maybe if he could just lift his head a little? But the effort felt enormous and his brain felt like it was about to explode.

He squinted down his body. His foot came into focus as it partially blocked the line of the horizon. Behind it he could see a boat bobbing about, out on the distant water.

He turned onto his back and gazed up at the sky for moment. Clouds were passing quickly in the wind and gulls were surfing on the gusts. Sweeping across the sky before dropping like stones, only to be swept up again.

He tried to think. He needed to think but watching the birds and clouds was using every bit of his mental capacity. He needed more time. Time to concentrate. If only his body would stop shivering for a moment or his head stop pounding, or the surges of nausea stop rolling over him, perhaps then he could think.

He tried to pull his jacket around him for warmth, but it was a paltry effort with negligible effect. He didn't know anything but there was one thing he did know and that was that unless he got his shaking body up soon, he was going to lose consciousness and die here.

He could hear cars behind him and voices in the distance. He was close to civilisation. He took a deep breath and made a superhuman attempt to roll over. Once on his front he was able to draw up his numb legs until he was on his knees.

He remained in this position for a few seconds, facing into the icy wind, before taking a deep breath and slowly trying to lift up his hanging head.

Through his watering, stinging eyes he peered across the expanse of sand. Only fifty yards away was the college carpark where a few students were walking casually between buildings. He watched them vacuously. His expressionless face stunned by the incredulous sight before him.

His moment of blank meditation was suddenly shattered by a violent pain in his stomach. He felt like his bowel was about to explode. He clutched at his abdomen without even considering the luxury of a toilet. Rocking unsteadily he dug a small hole beside him in the sand, wrestled down his trousers and squatted over it. He was beyond humiliation, beyond disgust and beyond the mortification of what he had been reduced to.

Tommy Taylor, suave, immaculate Tommy Taylor, stinking of yesterday's sweat, tasting of vomit was now shitting in a hole on the beach.

He stood up, dragged up his trousers and fastened his belt.

It wasn't as if he was unaware of his rancid body or disgusting behaviour, nor was he ignorant of the fact that he was stranded on the beach with the hangover from hell and no credit card.

His situation was dire, there was no doubt about that, but none of it, the pounding head, the nausea, the cold, the thirst nor the shit stained pants could compete with the sheer terror that had him firmly in its grasp.

This was the exact spot he had last fallen over in.

As he continued to watch the students walking briskly with their heads bowed against the wind, he knew that this would be Tuesday.

This was the place he had met Vicky.

Chapter 9

Tommy gradually rose to his feet, urinated on the sand, lifted his head into the cold breeze and exhaled. He needed to make it as far as his car where he could get out of the damp air. Slowly he shuffled up the small incline, lifting his feet as best he could over the thick clumps of heather and eventually hitting the flat tarmac with a sigh of relief.

He wandered around the carpark but there was still no sign of his car despite the daylight providing a clear view of all the sections at once. Perhaps it had been towed away as an abandoned vehicle or taken for a joy ride by the pranksters of fresher's week. Either way, it was gone, and he was in no fit state to go into the hotel and have the debate.

He went through his pockets. He had thirty-six pounds in cash. He could get a taxi to Kelly's Spa. He took out his phone but before he searched for a taxi firm he quickly searched under the letter V again. Valeting, Van-hire, Vicky, Voicemail. Vicky's number was back in its rightful place. It was a meagre comfort but a comfort non the less, as he dialled the first taxi number he found on his phone search.

For the first time in his life he didn't give the driver a generous tip. For the first time in his life he had a limited funds at his disposal and if Kelly was at one of her other Spa's with her phone turned off, he might need it. He could at least use the showers and get himself some breakfast.

He stood at the Spa entrance and tried to tidy his hair in the reflection of the full length windows before taking another breath and breezing into the reception area. The girl on the desk was new and he liked that. It gave him the opportunity to startle her as he breezed by without signing in.

"Excuse me, excuse me!"

"I'm here to see Kelly love, is she in? I'm her son"

The girl frowned "Really? I had no idea. She's in the gym. Down the corridor, second left."

As he forced a smile and swallowed hard, he walked slowly but purposefully though the doors and onto the corridor. Twice he had to put an arm against the wall to steady himself. He wondered if they had moved onto shots last night.

Kelly seemed to be assessing a new running machine with the man who was part way through installing it.

"Thank God you're here!" he called out "Seeing Kelly's friendly face felt like an approaching lifeboat. Everything would be fine now.

She looked up and smiled warmly.

"Are you lost?" Her greeting was unnervingly formal.

"Lost? No, I think my car has been stolen. Why would I be lost."

"Sorry, I thought you were looking for the changing rooms," she smiled again, "if your car has been stolen the receptionist will check the cameras for you."

"Mum!"

Kelly looked confused and worried. She continued to smile but whispered something to a girl who was putting away some dumb bells.

"Why don't you come with me and I'll get someone to make you a cup of tea young man?"

"Young man! Why are you calling me young man?! Mum, it's me. It's Tommy!"

Before she could respond, a large hand rested gently on his shoulder. He looked up into the familiar face of the man he used to play-fight with many years ago. It was Jake.

"Jake?"

"Yes, it is. How do you know my name?"

Tommy couldn't think. He noticed a wedding ring on Jake's finger and quickly checked Kelly's. She also wore a ring.

It was too much to process. His mind was reeling and so was his body. He leant against the wall for support and slowly started to slide down it until he landed with a bump on the polished floor.

 Had Kelly married Jake? Was this really a different version of the same life? Was he now living the hell his mother had lived? Was Sophie really sane? As sane as he was right now? Or was he as mad as her?

His heart was pounding, and his stomach was churning, his mouth was watering again, he was about to throw up.

"It's ok." Jake said sympathetically, as a projection of vomit hit the polished floor. " Laura! Go fetch a cleaner."

Tommy tried to breathe. In and out, in and out as he evaluated his situation, but he didn't have the mental agility nor the physical strength. As he sat breathing and processing, he heard the voice of a small child.

"What's going on daddy? Is the man sick?"

Tommy lifted his head slightly as a small boy came into view. A mop of black curly hair with coffee coloured skin. Despite being well-aware that Kelly wouldn't understand, he still glared at her accusingly for clarification.

"Freddie, come here to mummy a moment."

Tommy couldn't bear it. Kelly had a son. A replacement for him. The betrayal was excruciating.

"I think you need to get to a hospital," Jake said calmly, "come on, I'll call an ambulance."

"An ambulance?" Kelly interjected, "You think he needs an ambulance?"

"Yes, I do," Jake said firmly, "He's clearly confused. He might have had a knock on the head or something. Perhaps this stolen car of his is somewhere in a ditch."

Tommy knew he needed to get out of here before any ambulance arrived but for now, the comfort of Jake and Kelly's voices were too overwhelming reassuring. He would stay for a cup of tea and then make a run for it.

The sirens of the ambulance could be heard in the distance, as Tommy made his way along the coast road in the direction of Filey town, the direction of his dad's garage. He wondered if Kelly would be talking about him with Jake tonight. If there might be some spark of recognition when she recalled the image of his face later. Probably not.

He turned the corner and sitting there, between the corner shop and the day nursery, the place his dad's garage had stood, was a coffee shop.

He slid to the floor again and put his head in his hands. It was as if life had carried on here without him. From what he had heard about Sophie, she had seemed to slip in and out of this place seamlessly yet for him, it wasn't like that at all. No-one knew him here. It was as though he had never existed.

An old man threw fifty pence into his lap as he passed by.

He got up from his feet and marched out of the small backstreet, along the seafront and then turned inland towards the new housing estate. He was going to find his dad no matter what.

He tried to stay positive. He had to believe his dad would be home and welcome him with open arms. That his room would be exactly as he left it, apart from his strewn clothes which would have been dutifully collected and washed by Sonya. Oh! what would he give now for a glimpse of that stupid fluffy dressing gown through the window.

He tried desperately to keep faith. Even when an inadvertent glance had revealed a different car on the driveway from a hundred yards away. He kept his head down to delay any further revelations. It was probably just the car of a visiting friend. He knew his dad didn't have the kind of friends who stayed over or visited on a Tuesday morning but still, he kept his eyes down, and continued undeterred, on his journey home.

He stopped outside the gate. The black iron gate that had replaced the wooden one. He looked up the path to the brick porch that hadn't been there yesterday, and to the plain silver curtains, which had replaced the chintzy flowers of the day before.

This wasn't Tommy's home and he didn't want to knock on the door to confirm what he already knew.

He turned to walk away but inside he was still holding onto a thread of hope. Perhaps this was his dad's house, but some things were just different. Maybe he married someone less old fashioned than Sonya.

He turned around and knocked on the door.

A tall, skinny, spotty young man wearing headphones answered.

"What's up mate?" He pulled off one side of the headphones for Tommy's reply.

"I'm trying to track down an old friend. Does anyone called Carl live here?"

"Never 'eard of 'im mate. Sorry."

The headphone snapped back into place and the door closed.

He walked back down the street for a few paces and then set off running as fast as he could. He still felt desperately ill but the anger and frustration whipped up a frenzy inside him that shot down to his legs and carried him at breakneck speed up and down the familiar roads to his grandads house.

He knew his grandad would be there no matter what. He stayed in the same house while Sophie was in her coma even though memories of his late wife surrounded him and added to his misery. His grandad had visited the hospital with him most weeks and he had clung to Tommy after Sophie's death. If one person here would recognise him it would be the old man he felt too guilty to love back.

He arrived at the gate breathless. He bent over to catch his breath back and vomited several times before taking some deep breaths through his nose and trying to blink his watery eyes back to normal.

He then ran his hand through his hair, braced himself and walked calmly down the path.

Even before the door opened, he recognised the silhouette through the glass panel. He closed his eyes to thank God and allowed his body to relax a little.

He fiddled with the keys for several seconds, cursed and then cautiously opened the door.

Tommy smiled and his Grandad smiled back before speaking.

"Can I help you, young man? I hope you're not trying to sell me anything."

Tommy's heart sank.

"Grandad!"

His Grandad put his hand to his ear and then shook his head irritably.

"I don't hear very well. Just a minute. I'll get the wife. Christine! Christine!"

Tommy was already backing away shaking his head as if trying to refuse the image before him.

He backed into the gate and tumbled out onto the street without taking his eyes from the couple who were staring at him from the open door.

Quickly they closed the door as he got up and made his way back to the seafront where he sat on a bench trying to decide on his next move.

Whatever plan he had, he knew it would have to include Jack, Harry or Vicky as these seemed to be the only people here who would recognise him, let alone help him. College didn't start for another six days and he didn't have either of the boys numbers so he opened his contacts again and, with his thumb hovering over the call button he tried to come up with something plausible.

"Hi, it's Tommy."

He held his breath for some indication that she remembered him.

"Oh hi, how's it going?"

He breathed a sigh of relief. At last he had some sort of friend in this hostile place.

"Not so well actually."

"Oh! What's happened?"

"It's ridiculous I know, and I shouldn't be bothering you because we've only just met but I'm in a bit of a fix."

"It's fine. What's wrong?"

"I should have gone home last night but I got a bit drunk with some college boys and ended up sleeping on the beach."

"Oh my God! You could have been mugged or anything!"

"No, I'm fine but I forgot to bring my key for my mum's condo as I was expecting to go home, and she's away on business for the rest of the week. My dad is on a cruise right now so I'm trying to come up with a plan that doesn't involve breaking in."

It was the best pack of lies Tommy could come up with to explain why he had no access to a house of any kind.

She went silent for quite a while. Eventually Tommy spoke again.

"Look. I'm sorry I bothered you. It was the last thing I wanted to do. Don't worry, I'll think of something."

"No. I was just trying to process some options. Why don't you come to my grandma's for lunch and we'll try to think of something?"

Tommy wanted to kiss the phone.

"Are you sure?"

"Yes, absolutely. I mean, you're the son of Kelly Palmer after all, and you're enrolled at my college so it's not like you aren't known around here."

He ignored the irony that felt like some sick joke, closed his eyes and thanked God.

"If you're sure. I'll be there early afternoon?"

"Yes, that's fine."

As he ended the call, he closed his eyes again. This time he was not thanking God but begging him that she didn't check his relationship to Kelly or his registration at the college which he now knew would be quickly rejected.

He had given himself a few hours to get back to Ravenscar as he knew he didn't have enough money left for another taxi. He would need to get the service bus, and although the buses travelled on the hour to Scarborough, he would need to catch another for the onward journey, which only ran twice a day.

He checked his pockets again for money and then the price of the bus trip on his phone. He had only three pounds fifty to spare so he nipped into a corner shop and bought some wet wipes, a can of de-odorant, and some chewing gum. As he handed over the full amount of his worldly wealth, he noted that without the fifty pence from the old man, his breath would have still been stinking like a sewer when he saw Vicky again.

In the bus station toilets while he waited for the connecting bus, he tried to make the most of himself with tap water, hand-soap, wet wipes, deodorant and gum. It was a sorry affair but at least it was an improvement of his earlier state.

By the time he arrived at Ravenscar station the late summer sun had disappeared behind the descending clouds and the air was turning cold again. He wrapped his cotton jacket around him and held the lapels together with his hand as he walked the mile to Vicky's grandparents, anticipating the warmth and the meal he so desperately needed. He hoped desperately that he would not need to spend another night on the beach.

The door opened and Vicky greeted him with a huge smile.

"Come in. You look frozen to death."

"Yep, that's what a night on the beach does for you."

Her grandparents were exactly as he expected. A homely couple sitting in their cosy living room with the TV playing loudly.

"This is Tommy Nan", Vicky announced as her grandmother got up to meet him.

"I've been keeping lunch warm for you, young man," she said as she patted him on the shoulder, "I hear you've had a bit of a time of it."

"Yes, I have rather. Thank you for letting me visit Mrs..?"

"Oh! just call me Nan, everybody does," she said warmly, "Loves to save the day does our Vicky. A sucker for waifs and strays she is. Not that I'm saying you're a waif of course but you know what I mean?"

"Yes, I do. She's certainly saved my day, that's for sure."

As her Nan scurried off to rescue the meal she had been keeping warm Vicky started the interrogation that he had anticipated.

"So why can't you go to your mum's Spa or back to the hotel? I'm sure they'll just put it on her bill for you?"

Tommy sighed.

"Yes, you're right but the truth is that I'm not exactly in my parents good books at the moment."

"Oh! How come?"

"Well let's say it's not the first time I've had a few drinks too many and got myself stranded without keys. I've turned up at the Spa and embarrassed her a few times too many I think."

She shook her head as though reprimanding him.

"I know, I know," he agreed, "it's all my own fault and I really wanted to do this college course but she may just pull me out altogether if I have to admit I got drunk when I was meant to be driving and I left my keys behind because I'd forgotten they both had other plans."

She was frowning, he had to carry on.

"Look it's just that if I now land her with a huge hotel bill again or turn up at her spa looking like this I think she will cancel my course to teach me a lesson.

Vicky smiled widely as though she had just forgiven all his ridiculous crimes.

"You go and eat your dinner while I make a call."

Tommy sat at the table and tried to eat slowly but instinct was taking over and soon he was shovelling the hot food into his mouth. He didn't particularly like sausages, and certainly not the budget supermarket ones in front of him, but today it was the most delicious meal he had ever tasted. The buttery mash, salty gravy and thick chewy sausages with thick stringy skins tasted like pure heaven.

He was washing them down with a glass of orange squash when Vicky appeared at the kitchen door.

"It's all sorted. I've spoken to my dad and he says you can come back with us tonight."

"Really?"

"Yes really. I told him who you were and what had happened. My mum uses a few of Kelly's products as it happens but anyway, he says that since you are at the same college it'll be fine. I think, to be honest, he was quite excited about having Kelly Palmer's son as a guest."

"I don't know where I'd go tomorrow though?" It wasn't so much a question as a need for clarity about how long he could stay.

"Oh! dad says he could bring us both back on Sunday as long as you are sure your mum would be ok with it?"

"Yes of course. I'll call her later, but I'll be sure to leave out the reason for my visit I think!"

Her Nan cleared the plate and squinted at the kitchen clock.

"You'd better get your things together young lady, your dad should be here shortly."

"He's says he's still an hour away Nan. We'll go in the living room for a bit.

Tommy followed Vicky into the cosy living room and sat beside her on the sofa. The softness and warmth of that sofa seemed to hug every inch of his aching body and he allowed himself to sink into its folds he just wished everyone would leave and let him sleep for at least a couple of days.

Vicky continued to chat and he continued to nod smile, as he tried to share his brain between active participation and blissful moments of semi-conscious slumber, until he heard the front door open and a man's voice calling.

"Come on! I want to get back on the road before the traffic gets too bad. I'm just nipping to the toilet first."

"Ok dad," she called back before nudging Tommy, "come on, I'll just get my case, wait in the hall."

Tommy tore himself from the comfort of the sofa and followed her out into the hallway with Nan following close behind.

"Now you look after yourself young man and call in here for a cup of tea anytime when you are up at the college."

Her grandfather rolled his eyes, but she spotted him.

"Don't you be rolling those eyes at me old man!" she snapped, "This is a fine young man here and our granddaughter could do with someone to look after her at that place. Colleges are full of drugs and rapists you know!"

Tommy smiled and then thought back to his theory about being drugged by the girl who failed to get her Botox in exchange for a blow job. His heart sank. There wasn't a drug in the world that he knew of, that could induce hallucinations that went on for two days.

He looked at himself in the hall mirror while he waited. He looked a terrible shade of grey, more like a corpse than a living person.

Vicky clattered back down the stairs pulling the case on wheels clumsily behind her.

"Pick that damn thing up!" her father bellowed, hot on her heels, "You'll dig holes in the carpet!"

He then briefly acknowledged his additional passenger, as he hurried by in his quest to get back on the road before the dreaded rush hour.

"Nice to meet you Tommy. Tell your mum to get a key safe. Saves so much hassle. Wouldn't be without ours."

Tommy relieved Vicky of the cantankerous case on wheels and followed him down the path to his car.

Her father was a couple of inches shorter than Tommy, probably around six feet and he was also bigger built with a definite middle-aged spread around the waist. That dashed Tommy's hope of borrowing any clothes for the next few days. Perhaps she had a brother. He couldn't remember her mentioning any siblings.

The car was still warm from his journey up to Yorkshire.

Tommy knew she lived quite a way south and was grateful for the opportunity to rest on the journey.

As they started to put the miles between them and his tired run-down hometown, he had an overwhelming feeling that he was escaping to safety. Away from the damp sea fret and the horrifying trickery this town was capable of.

"How long will it take?" He asked politely.

"This time of day, we'll be lucky to do it in four and a half I think. That's if we don't have to stop for anything."

Tommy felt relieved at the long journey time. The further away the better and with Vicky in the front and the radio playing he had the perfect excuse not to engage in a lengthy conversation.

After a few exchanges of pleasantries with Tommy, father and daughter became engaged in a conversation of their own. They seemed relaxed and happy with each other's company. It felt similar to his relationship with Kelly.

His stomach churned again as he remembered Kelly's expression when he implied that he was her son. He swallowed hard. That wasn't his Kelly, that was the Kelly who had married Jake and had a son of her own. A real son. Her own flesh and blood. A new wave of jealousy and betrayal crashed over him. Unbelievable as it was, this feeling of betrayal felt more devastating than the fear of being left in a world he didn't understand.

He was too tired to make any sense of anything. He watched through the window and listened to the music with a totally blank mind until dusk turned the landscape from green to grey.

He pulled the shoulder strap of his seatbelt down to his waist allowing him to lay sideways across the large back seat and rest his head. The sounds in the car were like a lullaby. Soft voices, music in the background, the hum of the engine against his ear on the seat and the gentle rocking of the undulating road. As he started to drift into much needed sleep, at last his mind could rest from the relentless questions without answers.

He had no idea how long he had slept for, he thought he could see daylight behind his eyelids.

"Come on, we've got a long drive ahead."

It was Kelly's voice!

Tommy opened his eyes and there she was, smiling at him, recognising him and she looked exactly as she should.

He threw his arms around her and kissed her several times. The sheer joy of that moment rendered him speechless, as she reeled from his outburst.

"What's going on?" was all she could force out from the neck he was almost choking.

"You're here! Oh my God, you're here!"

"Of course, I'm here. Where else would I be?" she laughed as she peeled his arms from her bruised jaw.

He looked at her again. Her face, her arms, her hands as though checking that everything was in its rightful place.

"Tommy?" she asked more quietly, "What's going on?"

Tommy was still smiling from ear to ear but on hearing her question his euphoria at being reunited started to melt away as it was replaced with the acknowledgement that there had been a separation to cause it.

The realisation that he had been torn away in the first place filled him with more terror than the reunification could even start to dilute.

He knew it could happen again at any moment and started to scan the room as though something was approaching.

"Tommy?" she asked again.

He stared at her as though the words wouldn't come. His mouth made several attempts to form a word, but he was sweating profusely yet trembling with cold.

"Tommy, you're scaring me. What is it?"

He took a breath and then lifted his terrified eyes to meet hers.

"It happened again."

Chapter 10

On the road to Scotland, with bags of warm outdoor clothing in the boot, Kelly tried to lighten the mood with some of the silly journey games she had played with Tommy as a child.

He tried to enter into the spirit of it but he knew what she was trying to do and it may have worked to distract a five year old from his urgent need for chocolate but it wasn't going to distract a full grown man from the possibility that he was clinically insane. The atmosphere in the car was dense with anxiety.

Kelly had spoken at length to Carl again in private after Tommy's revelation and again, they had agreed to keep Anne's ridiculous theories to themselves. Tommy was clearly already overwhelmed by numerous theories of his own and the last thing he needed was to add some questionable theory about the coastline and some magnetic surges that happened to coincide with the fateful events in his history.

They had however, agreed that Kelly should get him as far away from their home town as possible, and consequently she had bundled him in the car the moment he had swallowed the last of his toast.

She had tried to reassure him that this was nothing like what happened to Sophie. She told him that Sophie used to pop in and out of her fantasies and everyone knew her. Not like his experience of going to a place where his dad wasn't where he should be or that Kelly had married someone else.

She managed at least to demonstrate some reassuring differences and to convince him that he had invented a scenario that had probably been triggered by her disappointment that he didn't want to join her growing empire.

"I don't get it!" he said irritably.

"I just meant that maybe you thought I was disappointed in you as my son and heir, so to speak. So in your own mind you imagined that I would replace you with a son of my own."

"Yeah I guess it kinda' makes sense but why would I marry you off to Jake?"

"I really can't imagine! I mean, me, married to Jake?" she laughed, "Like that was ever going to happen!"

Tommy knew exactly why he would have married her off to Jake! Jake treated her well and he was excellent father material. Unlike his own father who managed to constantly disappoint on both counts.

Tommy wanted desperately to accept her take on all of this but she hadn't been there. She hadn't spoken to Vicky or walked her home, got drunk with Jack and Harry, spewed on the beach or been half frozen to death. More significantly, she hadn't felt the physical pain of being rejected by her own mother and visibly witnessed herself, being replaced by a new child. Nothing had ever felt more real or more devastating. It was no dream!

He watched her as she continued to sing along as though everything was fine. His heart went out to her. To the effort she was making to comfort him. He would play along for now and getting away to somewhere new felt like a sensible way to break any pattern. There were just two things he was sure of. He wasn't going to let her out of his sight for a single moment and he was not going to go to sleep.

As he sat in the passenger seat and watched the landscape change from the mild undulation of Yorkshire, into the mountainous hills of the Scottish borders, he got a text message from Amy.

"Hi, hope you're ok. My mum has been acting weird since your visit! She thinks you're all crazy!" She added a few comical emojis of crazy faces.

Tommy smiled for a second but then he thought perhaps Niki had a point. Before he could reply she sent another.

"I wondered if you wanted to meet up today?"

"Sorry I can't, gone to Scotland for a few days with mum."

"Oh, that's a shame." She added a sad face.

"I promise I'll call you as soon as I get back."

"Good because my life is a bit lacking in fun right now and you don't seem particularly dull."

He was a little taken aback by her forthright manner again.

"Easy tiger!" he added a grin face

"Well aren't we blondes supposed to have more fun?"

He hadn't realised that they were matching blondes until she spelled it out.

"Yes apparently. You trying to prove the theory?"

"Maybe. Two specimens will give a more reliable result."

"Ok, you're on! Speak soon xx"

He didn't usually add kisses to his texts but for Amy he made and exception.

"Ok. Speak soon x"

He knew she had purposely left him one kiss less. She was a player just like him and he liked her.

Scotland was even colder than Filey, it felt like winter had made an early appearance. September was usually much warmer with the autumn leaves just beginning to fall and dusky evenings that didn't need a coat. Tommy helped unload the car and then hung as many bags around him as he could to make the long walk form the road to the tiny cottage nestled between two hills.

"Did you have your specs on when you booked this?" Tommy called back to her as he struggled with the swinging bags as he tripped and staggered over molehills and clumps of course mountain grass. "It looks more like a sheep pen!"

"It'll do us both good to slum it for a few days!" she called back "We'll have to make another trip for the groceries on the back seat!"

She had brought groceries! Kelly never took groceries anywhere because she would either eat out or order in but today, they had groceries.

She retrieved the key from the plant-pot while Tommy grumbled and then returned for the food. But as he filled the tiny fridge and the pantry with its stone slab, he felt comforted and safe. Whatever this thing was that was hounding him, he felt sure that it couldn't find him here.

Gradually the fear started to evaporate as he looked up to the mountains that seemed to be protecting them from both sides. Instead came alluring visions of cosy nights with an open fire and home cooking, walks in the hills and marshmallows over a garden bonfire. He knew this was a safe place, a happy place but he also knew something else. He knew that they were on the run.

Kelly could feel his unspoken thoughts. She knew he was afraid to sleep and she knew it was her job to protect him from whatever this was, the invisible enemy.

She was totally fifty-fifty on the two possible faces of this thing, madness or science. At least if it was the latter, she had got him away from what seemed to be the epicentre of the phenomenon.

A third option was not on her radar. There was no third option. The paranormal belonged on the bookshelf alongside Alice in Wonderland and the Gruffalo!

"Shall we bring our mattresses down here tonight, and sleep in front of the fire?" she asked with the same excited tone she used to use when suggesting they made a tent from the clotheshorse and bedsheets.

"Good idea!" Tommy smiled. He thought anything that kept them close and awake was a good idea.

Kelly was determined to protect her son as she doggedly dragged the heavy mattresses down the narrow staircase into the tiny lounge. She was going to watch Tommy like a hawk, and if that meant nudging him every ten minutes throughout the night, then that's exactly what she would do.

"Do you have a phone signal mum?"

"Nope, tried a few times but it's what you might call glitchy around here."

"I'm gong to take a walk up the hill to see if I can get a signal to text dad" he lied.

"I'll come with you."

Kelly took his hand in hers.

"Mum, I can walk up the hill on my own. I'm not going to get beamed up by a bloody spaceship!"

"Yes I know but.."

"You can watch me from here. Start peeling the potatoes, you do know how to peel potatoes do you?" he laughed.

"Of course I do! Do I cut them first or peel them first?" she joked as he grabbed his coat and opened the door.

"I love you mum." Tommy was as surprised as Kelly as the words spilled involuntarily from his mouth.

"Love you too, son."

As he walked up the hill checking the signal on his phone, he found a spot that gave him three bars and stood for a moment listening to the pinging on incoming text messages and calls. Three texts from his dad, two from Amy and a voice message from an unknown number.

He clicked on the unknown number first.

"Hi. It's Niki. I've been thinking, and I've decided I will meet with you and tell you what I know. I'd rather forget the whole thing and I'm sure you know I'm not your greatest fan but I have to acknowledge that you were only a child, and probably didn't realise what you were doing. I'm available on Thursday morning. Let me know and I'll come up with a place to meet."

Tommy couldn't work out how he felt about meeting Niki now. He would give it some thought later, but in the meantime, he wanted to read the texts from Amy. He clicked on the ones from his dad first and replied to the predictable questions, yes arrived safe, yes, it's lovely, speak soon. He then moved onto the ones from Amy, saving the best for last.

"Hi. I am now officially your stalker, I think. Just wanted to say goodnight and to ask where you are. I forgot earlier."

He opened the second text.

"Mum just mentioned you again. Tried to make me promise to stay away from you. She doesn't know I have your number!" she added a laughing face.

Tommy replied instantly.

"I'm in Scotland, so I think your mum would be happy with the distance. She's just trying to protect you from the madman! Night night." He added a similar laughing face.

As he walked back towards the cottage, he could see Kelly at the sink, peeling potatoes. It was a welcoming sight. A sight he wanted to remember forever.

After dinner, night began to fall. The little cottage felt warm and cosy against the eerie barren mountains that seemed to cradle it.

"Let's go for a walk along the stream!" Tommy was terrified of drifting off to sleep beside the log fire.

The large glass of red wine in his hand and the absence of a television seemed like a recipe for imminent snoring.

"It looks cold, dark and spooky out there!" Kelly replied as she pulled a throw over her knees and curled up more tightly on her chair.

"Come on!" he teased, suddenly taking hold of the throw, and whisking it away.

Reluctantly she put down her wine and followed him to the door. She put on her quilted ski jacket over the expensive tracksuit she used as pyjamas and handed him the thickest of his hoodies from the hook.

As Tommy led them down to the little brook and started to follow it along the back of the cottage, he cleared his throat to speak but kept his face forward.

"Do you think I've gone mad mum? Like Sophie did?" he was startled by the extent to which his voice broke with emotion as he asked the question.

Immediately Kelly caught him by the hand and turned him to face her. It was the same frightened face she had comforted a thousand times. The face she had reassured against the threat of monsters and ghosts, witches and spaceships. The face she had managed to change back to a happy relieved smile but today she had no magic remedy. No words of wisdom to comfort those troubled blue eyes.

"Listen Tommy. You are not mad. I don't know exactly what is going on, but I do know that. I also know that there's a logical explanation for all of this and you can bet your life I'm going to find it."

Tommy always trusted that Kelly would deliver a promise, and now was no time to doubt her but he had to accept that even his mum might not be able to fix everything.

She could see the doubt and gave him a gentle shake.

"Hey, when you doubt yourself you need to remember whose son you are and straighten your damn crown!"

She used to say that often as he was growing up and it used to fill him with determination but today, although he acted as though it had given him strength, it wasn't helping. He knew exactly whose son he was. The mad woman of Filey.

Kelly slipped her arm around her son and he slipped his around her waist. They continued their stroll along the side of the brook in silence, as the moonlight danced on the water, the questions swirled in his head, and the fear of dread gripped her stomach.

Tommy was thinking about Niki's message, and her offer to meet up on Thursday. He wouldn't be back by Thursday, but he was reluctant to try to rearrange in case it caused her to change her mind. He knew Kelly was working hard to get to the bottom of whatever this was, but Kelly didn't know everything. He had to be alone when he met Niki. He didn't want his mum hearing about the fiasco with the bits of paper Sophie had been keeping. He smiled at her as they walked along, hoping she couldn't read his thoughts through their bodily contact.

Kelly and his dad both loved him dearly, but he knew that might change in an instant if they learned of what he had done to Sophie. He tried again to remember how much of what he did was false, but time had merged his lies with reality and the facts could no longer be disentangled from the things he had made up.

He remembered his dislike for Sophie and his determination to get her out of his life. He remembered going through her notes and picking some out to tease and torment her with. The half and half meals. He shuddered.

"Are you cold?" Kelly asked.

"Yes, a bit. Let's go back now."

He also remembered hearing her outside his door as she tried to catch him whispering with her precious Becky. He remembered smiling when he heard her pathetic feet shuffling about outside on the landing carpet. He remembered making a point of whispering more loudly, to be sure she could hear. He knew he had done a bad thing, a very bad thing but there was something else.

Whenever he forced himself to go back there, to revisit his terrible crime, there was always a small glimmer of redemption lurking in the background.

Perhaps he had invented it to alleviate his guilt, but it seemed real and it was a constant part of his recollection.

Whenever he recalled the whisperings it was as though he wasn't doing it alone. As though someone was there with him sharing the prank. Perhaps he was not in his right mind even then.

Later that night, after the bottle of wine had been drained and Tommy had taken most of her cash in a game of cards, they settled down on the mattresses to sleep.

Tommy was trying to keep his eyes open and Kelly was watching him by the light of the diminishing fire. She wanted to make sure he was asleep before she dared to take her eyes off him.

Finally, his eyes closed, and his breathing changed just as it had when he was a toddler. It was that change in his breathing that used to give her the signal that it was safe to creep out of his room. She shuffled closer and put her hand over his. He wasn't going anywhere without her tonight.

Chapter 11

Kelly shivered as she awoke. The room felt cold and damp as she opened her eyes. Daylight was pouring through the thin living room curtain and her head felt thick from the wine.

Tommy was still snoring soundly beside her but that didn't mean anything, as yet.

She wouldn't know until he woke up if he had slept with or without the terrible dreams but either way, she wanted him back with her as soon as possible so she gave him a hefty push.

"Tommy? Are you awake?"

He stirred a little but didn't get up.

"Tommy, are you awake?"

"Well I bloody am now if I wasn't!"

She smiled to herself. There was no trepidation in his voice. He had slept here without his nightmares. She got up and turned on the electric heating. Log fires are great if you have the time but not today.

She left Tommy on the floor and went out to make some tea. Through the window sheep were grazing on the hillside on both sides of the tiny cottage's little nook. Hidden from the world. She poured the water onto the teabags and sighed with relief. She had done the right thing in bringing him here. He was safe here.

Wednesday passed without incident as Kelly drove to the village and returned with milk, newspapers and fish for dinner. They went on a hike, had coffee at a small village and talked. It was clear to Kelly that Tommy was still intent on going to the college in Ravenscar and for now, she was going along with it.

She couldn't tell him he was safer away from their home coastline without frightening him with the sci fi ramblings of Anne.

For now, she would go along with it but she was secretly hatching a plan of her own to get him away, even though she knew she was acting irrationally. She wasn't a psychologist any more than she was a scientist, but this was her son, and she was taking no chances.

She had recently opened a small spa on the outskirts of Harrogate. It wasn't much, but she had been hoping to grow it, as Harrogate was an affluent town homing an abundance of ladies with time on their hands.

At the moment, it was just ticking along but her long term plan had been to develop the building and start promoting it as her next project. She had installed one of her junior managers to keep it ticking over for the time being, but she had always hoped that eventually Tommy would be her real protégé.

Even before she had finished booking the cottage, she had already started to put things in place to hand the project over to Tommy. She knew it would put Carl's nose out of joint, but this was their son's lifeline, and it was non-negotiable.

She knew Tommy was excited about college but she also knew he was a bit of a power junkie and as soon as she told him she was going to gift it to him, she was sure he would rise to the challenge.

As they made their way back over the hill towards the cottage, she decided to sound him out.

"Perhaps you need a change?"

"A change?"

"Instead of college I mean."

Tommy didn't reply. Kelly was always trying to drag him into the world of facials and eyebrow shaping, so the shutters were going up before she had the chance to make him the offer again of trainee.

"I know what you're thinking," she went on "you don't realise how my business has changed though?"

Tommy did realise it, but he had become unreasonably stubborn about it. He knew that she now employed as many men as women and that fitness, weights and massage had become as prominent as hair, makeup and Botox. He was probably being unreasonably unfair.

"College is fine," she went on "but wouldn't you rather be building an empire than studying for years?"

He wanted to go to college but over the last few days the whole thing had become much less attractive. The only college experience so far had been a literal nightmare and the girl he had met seemed to be some trick of his imagination, so he had to admit that college had definitely lost some of its attraction.

"What did you have in mind?"

"Gifting you a small Spa in Harrogate with a budget to develop it?"

"Maybe" he said finally.

Kelly swung him around excitedly. "Maybe? Is my son actually considering joining forces with me at last?"

Tommy cracked a smile.

"I just said maybe that's all."

"I'll take that as a yes then!"

"You'll do no such thing!" he laughed as he shoved her face out of his, but Kelly was already dancing her victory dance in front of him.

"Fuck off." He said playfully as she pulled him into a headlock.

After dinner, as Kelly opened another bottle of wine, Tommy took his phone back up the hill.

"Are you missing me yet?" Amy had sent a photo of herself making a sad face.

Tommy laughed out loud when he saw it and then wished she were here. He saved the photo to his phone and then re-opened it and zoomed in. Even though she was being comical it didn't disguise the beauty of that perfect face. Her blonde hair had been casually scrunched up on top of her head leaving sexy strands escaping onto her face. He stoked her cheek with his finger and suddenly felt the need to speak to her and dialled her number.

"Hi, did you like my photo?"

"Love it," he replied "I've saved it on my phone"

"Shut up! It's awful."

"Not to me. I'm going to make it my screen saver"

"Don't you dare!"

"Well if you want to delete it, you'll have to do it in person."

He was flirting and she was loving it.

"Well I might just do that. When are you back?"

"Saturday. Want to get another burger? I know you're a junk food girl"

"I am not! and for your cheek you can take me somewhere for a salad!"

"Steady on! Let's settle for something in between. I'll pick you up Saturday at seven?"

"Don't be late" she put the phone down immediately causing him to laugh out loud.

He opened his text messages with a more serious expression.

"Hi, It's Tommy. Tomorrow is fine. Just let me know where and when."

He waited, but there was no reply, and Kelly was at the window, so he returned to the cottage.

"Everything ok with your dad?"

"Yes" he lied. He had totally forgotten to call his dad!

That night they returned the mattresses to their rightful place, and went to their respective rooms after another game of poker in which Kelly had recuperated some of her cash.

Tommy waited until he was sure she would be asleep and then he sneaked back downstairs, pulled his coat on over his boxers, slipped on his hiking boots and headed back up the hill.

As soon as his phone reached the spot it lit up several times. He clicked on the message from Niki.

"I can meet you at ten tomorrow morning. The café at the garden centre. No-one I know goes there."

Tommy tried to calculate the timing. It was six hours away and it was already one thirty. He needed to be away by three thirty but there was little point in going to sleep and risking his phone alarm waking Kelly. He needed to get away while he still had the chance.

The other messages were his dad and a friend asking why he wasn't in the pub. He didn't answer any of them and made his way back to the house.

He needed to limit his number of trips up the creaky stairs so he made a mental note of the clothes he needed that he could stuff into a rucksack. First, he needed to find Kelly's car keys.

He hated the idea of leaving her stranded here, but he would come straight back after seeing Niki, and still be in time for dinner. He hadn't yet made his mind up what he would tell Kelly but that depended heavily on what Niki had to say.

Momentarily he considered texting back and asking if they could just talk on the phone instead, but he knew that wouldn't be enough. He needed to see her face, watch her emotions, look her in the eye and decide if she was telling him the truth and more importantly, if he could trust her permanently with his secret.

As he searched through Kelly's handbag for her car key, he pulled out Anne's business card and smiled. Who retires and keeps their old business card? The phone number had been scored out in ink and a new one written in and on the back was Anne's address.

Perhaps Kelly had taken it out of politeness, as most of her contact details were online anyway, he'd seen her profile and her phone number, qualifications, career history etc perhaps she just wanted a record of the new address. He stuffed it back as he pulled out the keys and placed them on the tiny table at the back door.

A few minutes later, he picked them up again and crept out of the door onto the lane, thankful that the car was parked away from the house. He had cursed the walk down the narrow track when they arrived but today it was a godsend.

Before he started the engine, he sent Kelly a quick text, knowing that it wouldn't reach her phone until she walked up the hill when she woke up.

"Don't worry. I've had to go back home to see a desperate friend. I'll be back tomorrow. Didn't want to wake you xxx"

He started the engine and pulled quietly onto the country lane. It was time to face Niki, time to face his past and time to face up to the murder of his mother.

He arrived back at Filey just before eight. He parked in the garden centre but had two hours to kill so he set his alarm for nine fifty and got into the back seat for a nap.

Two hundred miles away Kelly had just woken up to find Tommy missing. She had gone into a blind panic and rushed up the hill to call Carl when the text arrived. Disappointed, but relieved that he was alright, she started to make her way back to finish the cup of coffee she had been drinking before she'd gone up to wake him.

She took a few sips and then dropped the cup on the table. Grabbing her phone again she raced up the hill and called Carl.

"Hi. At last. Why hasn't Tommy replied to anything I sent."

"I thought he spoke to you last night?"

"No, he didn't. Not heard a word from either of you, and I was worried!" Carl sounded angry and frustrated.

"I'm sorry. He said he had,"

She was not in the mood for his sulking, and the question of why he lied about speaking to his father also seemed irrelevant,

"I rang because there's a problem."

"What problem?"

"He's gone!"

"Gone where? For god's sake, have you had a fight?"

"No, of course not!" Kelly was angry that he would ever suggest that! "He left in the night sometime. He left me a message saying he's gone to see some friend or other, and he'll be back later today."

Carl laughed.

"What's wrong with that? Are you upset that he dumped you up there? Feeling left out are we? that he wanted to see a friend instead of you? Well, now you know how I feel most of the time don't you!"

"Carl?"

"What?"

"You don't get it do you? He's not here with me anymore. He's headed back home. Back to that stretch of coastline!"

Chapter 12

Tommy's cheek was stuck to the backseat of the car when he awoke. He wiped the dribble from the edge of his mouth and gradually opened his eyes.

"Wake up sleepy head, we've stopped for a toilet break and a cuppa!" Vicky was peering over at him from the front seat in the semi darkness.

He stared blankly at her beaming face and then sat up sharply. Vicky jumped back in alarm "What is it?!"

Tommy stayed completely still, bolt upright as he tried to control his behaviour.

"Nothing. It's nothing," he said with a false smile, "Just a bad dream I think."

The truth was that he didn't think anything at all. His mind had been paralysed. He could do nothing other than to follow the instruction to get out of the car.

He followed Vicky through the parked cars into the service station.

"I need the loo first." She announced as she disappeared in the direction of the ladies.

"Come on. Let's see if we can get a sandwich and a drink," her father yawned, "I've been almost falling asleep at the wheel"

Tommy followed. He followed into the queue, picked up a sandwich and followed to the tea machine, took the tea, and followed to the table. He didn't speak a word.

"Are you alright?" her father said eventually as he sat down with his own tray on which he had included Vicky's food.

"Yes, thank you, I'm just not feeling so good that's all. Probably shouldn't have had the sleep." Tommy said quietly, thinking that it was the truest remark he had made in a long time.

"Another hour and we'll be home!" Vicky said cheerily as she sat down beside him and plonked her sandwich and drink in front of her.

Tommy stared at them. He knew he was behaving like a mindless zombie, but his brain was still numb. It was crowded with fear and trepidation. There was no room for questions, answers or conscious thought. Fear was taking up every available space in his head.

He watched their mouths moving, smiling. Their eyes narrowing and widening, frowning and blinking. They looked real. He couldn't hear what they were saying because his ears could no longer make sense of the sounds but these people before him looked real!

Vicky placed her hand on his arm in concern.

"Tommy, you need to eat something."

He looked up at her. She felt real. She had touched him, and her flesh was soft and warm. She felt real.

He had to get a grip.

"I'm going to the toilet," he said softly without having touched his food, "I'll be back in a minute."

As he got up to leave, he saw the look Vicky received from her father. He didn't blame him. If he wasn't careful he would lose his bed for the night.

In the toilet he splashed his face with water and looked at himself in the mirror. He seemed to have turned grey again. In the cottage he had been his usual peachy colour and the Scottish air had put roses on his cheeks but now he was grey. He was the same sickly grey he had been when he'd looked at himself in the window of the Spa. The Spa that belonged to the mother who didn't know him.

He took several deep breaths and ran his wet fingers through his hair. He could do this. He had to do this.

He walked back to the table and sat down with a smile.

"Sorry about that, I feel much better now."

They both smiled at him simultaneously.

"I'd like to say you'll learn but I suspect you won't," her father laughed, "It'll take a few more hundred hangovers first I suspect."

Tommy drank his tea and picked up his sandwich to eat in the car and within a few more minutes they were back on the road.

Vicky flicked through the radio channels and turned up the volume and Tommy settled with his head on the window, watching the lights of the oncoming traffic while he nibbled on his ham sandwich and wished he could fall asleep again and leave this place.

He tried to listen to the humming of the tyres on the road and allow himself to be rocked by the vibrating window but he remained awake until eventually the car slowed down and turned between two large pillars onto a tree-lined entrance lane.

The car swept round a circular driveway and drew to a halt outside a huge arched front door.

The house was a substantial brick built family home situated in huge grounds and sprawling over most of the width of the plot. He opened the door and followed Vicky up the stone steps. Several other cars were parked around the circular lawn.

He stepped into an impressive reception hall where a huge chandelier hung from the ceiling, casting light onto a beautiful, polished piano.

Tommy was used to affluence, but this was not anything like Kelly's condo, there was something classy and subtle about this house, a sort of historical elegance.

"What time is it?" He asked as he followed her inside.

"Almost eight thirty," she replied, "mum has been keeping dinner warm so we can eat right away. I'll show you to your room where you can freshen up.

Tommy followed obediently up the sweeping staircase to a tastefully decorated guest room. Fresh towels and what appeared to be her father's joggers and sweatshirt were on the bed. He thanked her, barely noticing her cute freckles, her seductive expression or her overly sexy walk. He was beyond seduction, beyond conversation and beyond reason.

He showered and wrapped himself in the huge towel for a few minutes.

He picked up his boxers and socks from the corner and attempted to wash them in the basin with hand soap. The socks smelled of stale vomit and his boxers were even worse.

He frantically rubbed them all together as he tried to erase the memory of his night on the beach. Of vomiting on his own feet and of shitting in a hole and dragging up his pants without even wiping his arse. He was disgusting and he intended to eradicate the humiliating memory with this tiny block of scented soap.

He had done as much as he could but there was still an acidic scent to his socks and stains on his boxers. He hung them on the radiator with the stain to the back knowing that they would all smell musty and sickly in the morning.

Vicky's voice interrupted his despair.

"How long will you be?"

"I'm coming now!" he called back as he pulled on the joggers and drew them in several inches with the cord. The sweatshirt was several inches too wide and the sleeves several inches too short, but it didn't matter. Nothing mattered.

He made his way downstairs past the dining room where the table had been set.

"We are in here!" Vicky called excitedly.

He entered the drawing room where her father was finishing off the last mouthful from a whisky glass.

Vicky was walking up and down in anticipation of his entrance, and over in the corner a woman was sitting in an armchair reading. She was at an angle but mostly facing away so he could see only part of her profile.

He stopped breathing. He knew the contours of that face, the colour of her hair, the shape of her lips. Before she even turned around, terror froze every molecule of his body.

She turned to smile. It was Sophie!

Chapter 13

Tommy finally let the air out of his lungs as the woman stood up and started to walk towards him.

His instinctive reaction was to run. To make a dash for the door and disappear into the countryside before she could make the final few feet.

"Tori has told us all about you." She said as she stood up and moved closer. There was not a hint of recognition on her face.

"Tori?" was all he could utter.

"Oh, she always calls me that," Vicky said irritably, "It's Victoria but I prefer Vicky."

Tommy remembered that name. He could still picture the disfigured letters on a scrap of paper. He knew it well. It was the square of paper she had torn at an angle. The one that fitted together with the one with the word Becky on.

"This is my mum Sophie and you already know my dad of course."

"I don't think we have been formally introduced though." He grinned as he reached over to shake Tommy's hand. "It's John."

Muttering quietly to himself, Tommy was guided to the table like a stunned animal. He sat. He heard voices. He heard his own voice responding but he didn't know what about. He was somewhere else inside his own mind.

Sophie was eating happily, and he assumed that, like Kelly, he was a stranger to her. He tried to force down the fried chicken and the buttered potatoes, but he couldn't concentrate on anything other than the motion of his fork and the extreme effort of chewing and swallowing.

The serving dishes were passed back and forth amidst the chatter and then suddenly something changed.

Sophie was sat directly opposite and suddenly stopped mid-sentence. She fell deadly silent.

Tommy watched her face as it drained to ghostly white and then to blood red as fear was replaced by adrenaline. She fixed her eyes on his. Nothing was said and nothing needed to be said. She recognised him.

It was Tommy's turn to be stunned into silence, as he held her stare.

She dropped her fork into her dinner and attempted to pick it up again, with a shaking hand.

Tommy looked down at his meal. It was too much to bear to engage with her. The last time he looked into those eyes he had told her that her daughter missed her. His lies had sent her to her icy grave.

He lifted his eyes and focussed on the wall behind her. There was a bookcase full of well-worn books, and a china cabinet containing some crystal wine glasses and a few bits of pottery, assumingly made by her children. It was diverting attention from the moment at least. He continued to pretend to be admiring it. Anything to avoid the chilling eye contact. A dance trophy and a Christmas bell. It was dispelling the terror, and then suddenly, it did anything but! In the centre, taking pride of place was a tarnished, weathered pepper pot. He gasped for the second time in as many minutes.

Vicky's father continued the conversation, asking him questions about college and he could tell by the expressions around the table, that he must have been responding coherently, even though his brain was neither processing nor retaining any of it.

Suddenly her father stood up and picked up a walking stick from the corner of the room. He raised it above his head and banged three times on the ceiling and then returned it and sat back down.

Tommy felt startled.

"Some people need a rude reminder to get to dinner on time!" he smiled

"Oh, I see." Tommy returned the smile as he heard footsteps plonking reluctantly on the stairs.

The door opened and a skinny red-headed girl entered the room.

"You're late again!" her father scolded as though she were six years old.

She moved towards the spare place beside Tommy.

"I was busy." She announced without apology.

"Excuse my daughter's manners," John continued, "She's studying for a master's degree in Astrophysics and it's clearly more interesting than her family."

She didn't dignify his rebuff with a reply, and as she pulled back the chair to sit down, Tommy looked up at her.

Her face was drawn and her features sharp. She was nothing like Vicky. Her shirt was drab and ill-fitting, hanging off her like it was bought for someone twice her size. Her wiry flame red hair stood out from her head in tight straggly ringlets and her face was covered in brown freckles, which had none of the attraction of her sisters.

As she took her seat she nodded politely.

"Tommy."

"Becky." he replied with equal cordiality.

It was a monumental moment. Tommy could feel the magnitude of their greeting. The power of the force between them.

"I didn't know I'd told you my sister's name?" Vicky frowned.

"I think you must have mentioned it the other day." Tommy lied.

She frowned and then gave him a flirtatious wink across the table. Tommy smiled back but didn't return the gesture. If this girl existed at all, she was his damn sister!

As soon as the meal was over, he made his excuses to go to bed.

"Oh yes, I hear you slept rough last night!" John laughed, "I used to do that a lot when I was young. Not as much fun as it sounds is it?"

"No, it isn't." Tommy agreed.

"Bit of bad luck getting locked out like that. You should get a keysafe."

"Dad you already told him that!" Vicky snapped irritably.

John frowned his displeasure at being corrected and then continued, "Would you like me to call your mother and let her know where you are?"

"No. It's fine. I've already text her.

Tommy wished that was true. He would give anything right now to be able to text his mum. For the number on his phone to be the right number. Not for a second did he register the fact that his mother was actually sitting directly opposite.

John smiled wryly.

"I used to text my parents all kinds of rubbish. I'm sure she will feel more at ease if I speak to her directly. If you give me her number, I'll put her mind at rest."

"No really. Thank you but she's fine. She knows where I am."

"Well I hope we get to meet her in person next week when we take you back. I hear she is quite an entrepreneur up north?"

Tommy nodded without using the opportunity to boast about Kelly. The last thing he wanted was for John to show an interest in Kelly or to take it on himself to call her.

He imagined how that conversation would go if he rang her spa and rambled on about a boy who was now lodging with him who claimed to be her son. A boy matching the description of the one who had barged into her office stinking like a cesspit and vomited on her floor only this morning. A boy who was now about two hundred miles away bothering another family with his tall tales.

"Well if you're sure?"

"I'm absolutely sure. I'll call her tomorrow and if she needs to talk to you, I'll pass her over."

John seemed satisfied, and Tommy breathed a sigh of relief. He then changed the subject back to Becky's obsession with Astrophysics and her determination to get a PHD in the subject.

"Do you know how long that takes?" he said as he poured himself another glass of whisky, "She'll be getting a pension before she even gets a wage!"

"Leave her alone, John." Sophie interjected, "You should be proud of her."

It was the first time Tommy had heard her voice. It was shockingly familiar. Instantly resurrecting memories from his childhood. The confrontation in the restaurant. The altercation at the bonfire and the way she had dragged him by the arm. The way she had frightened him with her wasted body and skeletal face. She looked nothing like that now.

Her hair had a healthy shine, and her face was pink with full cheeks and lips. Her body was a curvy size twelve and her arms were slender but muscular. She was nothing like the woman he had feared yet just the sound of her voice filled him with the same dread as it had all those years ago.

"I'll say goodnight then." He said as he rose to his feet to prevent any further intervention.

"Yes. Goodnight." John said cheerily and, to Tommy's relief, Sophie simply nodded.

"Night Tommy." Vicky called in a sing-song voice.

Becky didn't bother to respond, so he made his way back to his room.

He opened his phone and looked for his dad's number. It wasn't there. It had disappeared in the same way Vicky's number had disappeared back home. He should have been shocked, but he wasn't. He just put his phone down with numb acceptance.

The memory of that morning on the beach still played in his mind and, awful as it was, he found himself wishing he was back there. Anywhere had to be better than this house of horrors.

As he climbed into bed, he recalled how he had been longing for a warm shower, clean towels, fresh linen sheets and a memory foam mattress. He looked around the room and as he lay down and sank into the huge bed, he acknowledged that given the choice right now, he would take the damp sand, vomit, shit and the icy mist.

He wasn't at all tired, he had slept the entire journey, but he needed an excuse to get away from the minefield downstairs. He lay awake listening cautiously for any activity from this house of ghosts.

After an hour or so, he thought he heard footsteps outside his room so quietly he crept to the door and opened it to peer out.

Sophie was standing directly in front of him.

He felt shocked and angry at the same time. He was tired of being afraid, sick of feeling threatened and exasperated by these mind tricks.

"You made it back then?" he said with far more confidence than he was feeling.

"Yes, I did," she said softly, "thanks to you."

He hadn't realised until that moment that she would consider him her saviour, not her murderer.

"You also found the pepper pot."

"Yes, I did. You might say that you and I we were looking in the wrong place."

She extended her hand, and he shook it firmly.

"You're welcome." He said politely. She nodded, and he quietly closed the door.

As he got back into bed, the guilt he had carried with him for half of his life had been lifted, but in its place was the horror of knowing the horrific path his mother had walked.

He knew the torture she had endured and the loneliness of it. He knew how it felt to be looked at as though you have lost your mind. He had added to that pain with his childish pranks but at least she never knew that, and his mischief had returned her home.

There was, of course another possibility and if this was just more than another hallucination then his guilt would return tenfold.

Right now, he was praying that it was the latter. He would rather be a murderer than for any of this to be reality.

He lay awake, fuelled by adrenaline and dread. He was also feeling quite ill. He tried to sit up but felt light-headed, so he lay back down again. The hours crept by as he tried to force himself to relax until he was at least able to doze a little. He could hear the wind outside, but it had faded into the background as his mind, at last, was letting go of conscious thought.

As he lay enjoying the respite from his manic thoughts, he imagined he could feel the warm softness of someone beside him. Silky skin gently moulding to his. Subconsciously he smiled as he felt a familiar sensation. The sensation he had felt a hundred times or more of a woman's breasts dangling onto his chest with erect nipples teasing his skin.

Gently the weight of her easing on top of him as her breasts spread against his chest and settled there. A hand stroking his face and guiding it to her lips. Soft moist lips on his, the tip of her tongue sliding between his lips as she gently massaged them with her kiss. He could feel his loins reacting, his erection growing until it was straining up against her, stroking the flesh behind her buttocks as she moved rhythmically on top of him.

Urgently, he kissed her back. Raking his hand into her hair he opened his eyes to focus on a cheeky freckled face.

"Good God Vicky! What are you doing?!"

"I'm flying a bloody kite! What does it look like?"

He had never heard her swear before or seen her angry. He took her wrists in his hand and gently but firmly rolled her off of him.

"What's your problem?" she snapped as she tried to stop her bottom lip from giving away her despair.

"Look, I'm sorry," Tommy said more gently, "I can see you're upset."

"Upset? Do you have any idea how it feels to be pushed off someone like that? Someone you really care about?"

"Yes, I do, and I'm sorry. You're a beautiful, attractive, wonderful girl, and any man would feel flattered and thrilled by what you just did."

"But not you, apparently?"

Tommy pulled up the sheet to hide the erection that had failed to subside, despite the abrupt exchange. He reached for the robe she had discarded by his bed and hung it sympathetically around her shoulders.

"You shocked me. We are in your parent's house Vicky!"

"So?"

"So anyone could have walked in. I'm a guest here and if I were your father, I'd have thrown me out on my ear!"

She drew the robe around her looked up at him through those long curled black lashes.

"That's all it was?"

"Yes, of course that's all it was," he lied, "If I get thrown out, I don't have anywhere else to go now do I?"

"Guess not. I wasn't thinking"

"No you bloody weren't," he made an attempt at a laugh but all he wanted, was for her to leave his room as quickly as possible, "So go on, go back to your room before we are both in trouble and I'm back on the beach."

Finally, she stood up and he breathed a sigh of relief.

"I'll excuse your behaviour this time," she managed to raise a smile, "but don't you be thinking you'll get away with it once we're at college!"

"I can't wait!" He grinned.

She walked sexily to the door and finally disappeared.

Tommy had just buried his head in his pillow, when the door opened again.

"What the fuck?" he whispered to himself.

"By the way, you have a great body!" she teased.

He smiled and at last she was gone.

He lay on the bed staring at the ceiling in the dim light of the outside lamp.

He had almost slept with his sister! It was a sobering thought. He turned onto his stomach and wrapped the pillow around his head. As if he didn't have enough problems and now this. He couldn't stay here but he was totally out of options.

He sat up again. There was no way he was going to get any sleep now, so he flicked on the tv.

"At least something was the same." He thought as he flicked through the channels eventually settling for the comfort and levity of 'family guy'.

As the comedy ended and he flicked from chat shows to documentaries and finally the early morning news he was astonished that everything seemed exactly the same. He could just as easily have been watching from his mum's condo or from his dad's house.

Outside he could hear voices, as the house started to awaken. He tried to get out of bed again, but his head was pounding, and the dizziness caused him to lay back down again.

"Are you coming down for breakfast?" Vicky was outside his bedroom door again. If he told her he was ill, she'd be inside his room in a shot.

"Yep. Be down in a minute!"

He heard her walk back down the corridor and clatter down the stairs. He had to get up.

Slowly he raised to a sitting position and hooked the oversized joggers onto his toe. Keeping his head up and looking straight ahead he managed to joggle them onto his legs and up as far as his knees. He took a breath and reached for the sweatshirt. Once his arms were in, he managed to pull it down and attempt to stand.

He used the bed to support himself as he rose and then took a deep breath. He felt sick and his eyes were struggling to focus. Perhaps he just needed something to eat or a sugary drink? He carefully pulled up the joggers and tied them tight before making his way to the door. His shoes lay on the floor, but they were too big a challenge right now, so he made his way downstairs in bare feet.

"Breakfast is ready!" Vicky was standing over the stove peering into a pan of poaching eggs. Toast and coffee were already on the table. There was no-one else to be seen.

"Where is everyone?" Tommy asked anxiously.

"Dad's gone to work, mum's out on a run and Becky is studying in her room. It is after nine you know. You must have needed the sleep."

Tommy slumped down in front of his plate of toast as he imagined what a night of sleep actually felt like.

She placed two perfectly poached eggs on top of his toast and smiled suggestively.

He smiled back. This was going to be a difficult morning.

Suddenly the front door opened, and he could hear the heavy breaths of a returning runner.

Relief swept over his face as quickly as disparity swept over Vicky's.

Sophie entered the kitchen and got herself a glass of water, still breathing heavily.

"How is everyone this morning?"

"I'm not feeling too good," Tommy replied as he poked one of his eggs in the nipple with a knife.

"You didn't say anything to me!" Vicky interjected.

"Yes, I know. I thought I was alright a moment ago, but I feel quite ill now."

"Tori's cooking, I expect." Sophie joked, but Tommy could see she was anxious and uncomfortable. She wanted him gone and who could blame her?

"He hasn't even tried it yet!" Vicky said sulkily.

Tommy looked at Vicky as she continued her game, oblivious to the trepidation of those around her. It wasn't her fault, he knew that but, this once attractive, amusing girl who had captured his heart on that walk over the hill from college had suddenly degenerated in his mind to a silly, superficial annoyance.

"Tori, nip up the chemist for Tommy will you while I make him some herbal tea?"

"It'll be quicker if you go in the car." It was obvious she didn't want to go.

"Tori!"

"Ok, I'll go, what am I to get?"

Sophie took a notepad from the drawer and listed a few items then handed it over with her bank card. A few minutes later Tommy and Sophie were alone.

Tommy was the first to speak.

"Does John know who I am?"

Sophie shook her head.

"Why not? He does know about how you came to be here?"

She shook her head again.

He was expecting her to take the lead in this conversation. To explain everything, to know everything and to solve everything. To be his mother!

She disappointed just as she always had. She sat across the table staring blankly at the wall behind him as though she were as desolate and confused as he was.

Tommy tried again. He didn't know how long Vicky would take but this might be the only chance he got to speak to her alone.

"Becky? What does Becky know?"

At last he got a reaction. She took another sip of her water and engaged with him.

"Becky knows. Becky knows everything."

Tommy slammed his hands down on the table in order to make a dramatic rise to his feet, but he fell back down before his legs had the chance to take his weight.

"Jesus Christ! She's been keeping this secret since she was what? Nine years old?"

"Something like that. I'm not proud of it but I had no choice."

"Of course you had a choice! You could have at least told her father, so she had someone else to lean on! Someone who wasn't as unhinged as us!

"Unhinged? Is that what you think this is? That I've somehow infected you and Becky with some madness?"

"I don't know what this is!" he banged his fists again, "I don't know what the fuck is going on but I know that a couple of weeks ago you were a distant memory. My life was fine and then wham! Suddenly the whole fuckin' nightmare is back again with you right bang in the middle of it all."

Sophie put her hand gently over his clenched fist. It was the first time Tommy had felt any affection from his biological mother. The first time, the last time, the only time.

"I'm sorry. I didn't want this. Any of it. I didn't even know you existed until you were already half grown. You had another mother already. It was too late for us, far too late.

Tommy's momentary solace turned back to anger.

"It wasn't too late! It wouldn't have been if you hadn't been hell bent on getting back to your other kids would it? Away from my dad and back to John! Dumping the guy who had dragged me every week, every fuckin week to your bedside, telling me how wonderful you were. Telling me how fantastic my life would be when you came back to us! It was all bullshit! He thought you loved him but you didn't did you?"

She didn't answer.

"Did you?!"

She shook her head

"No Tommy, I didn't. I'm sorry."

"You're unbelievable do you know that?"

"Yes, I do" she smiled, acknowledging the irony of his accusation.

"So why is John still blissfully in the dark while the rest of us deal with this shit?"

"I don't know."

"Yes, you do! I'll tell you why. It's because you didn't want to spoil the pretty picture he has of his life, did you? You didn't want him to see even a hint of imperfection in you? You were afraid he might not stand by you or love you the same. You thought he might fall out of love with you!"

"That's not true."

"Yes it is! You were terrified he would feel the same about you as you did about my dad. Trapped with someone he didn't love any more. Yearning to be somewhere else, with someone else."

"Stop it Tommy! Just stop it!"

Tommy was not going to stop. This woman couldn't help him, he had no use for her, so he was going to unleash two decades of frustration right here in this kitchen of god knows where.

"So, you forced Becky to hide what was happening to her? Your own child! Tormented and terrified, and unable to talk to anyone let alone get help? You forced her to lie to her father, to make up stories and excuses! You're a monster not a mother! To both of us!

"Becky is fine!" She retorted.

"Fine? Have you seen her? She's like a fuckin skeleton! She looks like she hasn't slept for a century! She must be almost my age and she's living her life up in her room studying like there's nothing else out there."

Tommy took a breath and then thought again about Becky.

"Oh! I get in now. She's obsessed with studying just as you were obsessed with your scraps of paper! So, is she really studying to get a qualification to give herself a nice life or is she searching for something? Trying to solve some mystery up there?"

"Tommy please stop! I can't take any more! Tori will be back soon"

"Oh of course, Tori who is going to fix my problem with a cup of Lemsip and a paracetamol. Well let's see how that works out shall we?"

Sophie got up to wash her face in the sink as she heard the front door open.

She put the bag on the worktop and took out a bottle of Lemsip, an indigestion remedy and pain killers.

Tommy smiled and shook his head.

"Thank you, Vicky" he said sarcastically, "I'll take these to my room and have a lie down."

He took a bit of the toast and a swig of coffee before pulling himself to his feet and staggering back up the hallway toward the stairs.

He lay on the bed listening to the dulcet tones of the conversation downstairs. Sophie was a good actress. He had to give her that. Mother and daughter seemed to be chatting happily. He assumed Sophie didn't work. She probably hadn't needed to after she left a car mechanic for an affluent executive. She had probably spent her life organising dinner parties and lunching with the ladies from the bridge club.

He sighed again. He didn't have a plan. He was totally at the mercy of the universe and of the people in this household. A man who was oblivious to everything around him, a mother who hated the bones of him, a disturbed girl frantically trying to make sense of it and a sister who was trying to fuck him every chance she got.

He laughed out loud. He laughed and laughed until the door opened, and a pale face framed in red wiry hair peered around it.

"Are you alright?"

Tommy raised his hand to his head.

"I'm probably hysterically delirious" he announced firmly.

She sat down on his bed and folded her cardigan defensively around her flat chest.

"I heard you've not been feeling very well?"

"Yeah, you could say that." He replied, feeling suddenly inferior to this matronly-like wirey girl.

"So exactly what's wrong and how long has it been like this?"

Tommy felt strangely reassured by her manner. She seemed confident and in control and, if there was one thing he needed right now, it was someone with a bit of control over something!

"I feel nauseous constantly and I'm light-headed when I stand. It's like being drunk but without the slurred jokes."

His attempt at humour fell on stony ground.

He knew she wasn't a doctor, he knew she was only his age but still he felt comforted by her, today, regardless of her lack of medical training, she was the doctor he needed and he needed her desperately.

"Tommy?" her voice was firm and authoritative.

"What?"

"Listen to me."

He was listening. Oh God was he listening but still she felt the need to emphasise the importance of what she was about to say.

"You need to get out of here."

"You don't say!" his attempt at humour was again met with indignation so he carried on, "I'm sorry, what are you saying?"

"I'm saying that you don't belong here."

"I know I don't but neither does anyone else from what I can see!"

"You don't understand, we are all fine here, but you don't belong. You have to leave."

Tommy knew what she was saying and he knew that being here was making him ill, but he didn't know why she was telling him. It wasn't as if he was here by choice."

"You know something don't you? You know what's going on with me, with all of us!"

She huffed as though reprimanding a wilful child.

"What is it? What aren't you telling me?"

She handed him a glass of water and five tablets.

"What are these?"

She looked at him disdainfully, as though she resented the question.

"Sleeping pills. I don't even know if they will work but you need to take them."

Tommy glared at her mistrustfully.

"You're burning up. You need to go Tommy and you need to go right away" She nodded reassuringly.

"Right now, Tommy! Right now!"

She pushed them into his mouth and held the glass to his lips.

He was out of options. He had nothing left to lose so he swallowed and then lay his head back on the pillow to sleep.

In his semi-conscious state, he felt like he had been bumped onto the floor and was being dragged along on some sort of blanket.

He was beyond worrying about where he was going, of how he would get there, or what might be waiting if he ever woke up. He just needed some sleep.

Chapter 14

Carl had taken the day off work after Kelly's call. He wanted to be free to track down Tommy when he arrived. He had been flitting back and forth between his own house, Kelly's condo, the Spa and the college for the last hour. The text message Kelly picked up had a timestamp of 1.58 so he calculated that Tommy would have made Filey any time from 8 am. At 9.30 he called Kelly again.

"I'm going to hire a car and come back." She blurted as though Carl was making a bad job of locating their son.

"No. You stay there. He said he's going back tonight so in a few hours he'll be back on his way up there. You need to be there when he does."

"Ok" Kelly had been standing on the hill for over an hour waiting for news from Carl.

"You go back in the house Kel, I'll text you as soon as I know anything. Just check every half hour or something."

"Ok." She spoke the words, but she had no intention of moving from the spot until she knew her son was safe.

"Carl?"

"Yes."

"Does this remind you of anything."

"Yes. I know."

Neither of them needed to spell it out. The horror of the night they had last been searching for Tommy when his desperate text messages had compelled them to join forces in pursuit of their son.

"At least this time we know Sophie's not got him!" Carl said hoping his humour was reassuring.

"Yep. Thank God for small mercies eh?" she replied

"I'm going back to your place now to check again. I'll speak to you soon." Carl assured.

Kelly returned to the house to make a mug of coffee and then returned to the hill with a kitchen chair and a rug for her knees. She sat down and sipped her coffee. She wasn't going anywhere!

Tommy could hear voices in the background.

"Hold the damn thing steady woman! It's going to fall!" a man's voice bellowed as he opened his eyes. He had woken up on the backseat of a car twice in as many days.

Slowly he raised his head to the level of the window. Outside an elderly couple were wrestling with a potted tree as they tried to lift it from the flatbed trolly into their tiny car.

In the background he could see the familiar doorway of the garden centre. He was back home. He closed his eyes tightly to thank God as tears flowed out of sheer relief and gratitude.

Gratitude to God, to the universe, to Becky and to the manufacturer of the sleeping pills that had delivered him safely back to his former life. Back to his mother and every other person who would look at him and know exactly who he was.

As he peered out again, he caught his reflection in the window noticing that his blond hair stood bolt upright giving him the appearance of Bart Simpson.

He looked at his phone. It was 9.45. He still had time to freshen up in the toilets before meeting Niki in the café, so he grabbed his hair gel and deodorant from his rucksack and pushed them into his ski jacket pocket along with twenty pounds cash from his poker winnings with Kelly.

By 9.55 he was seated at a table with two cups of coffee watching Niki make her way over the carpark. His stomach was churning but not nearly as much as it had been the last time he went to meet her. In comparison to his last few days, a meeting with Niki was hardly an ordeal.

"Hi" he said as he rose to greet her, "thank you for meeting me."

They both sat down.

"Do you take sugar?"

"No." she replied

"Good." He smiled, taking her two sachets and tipping them into his cup.

She smiled back and the ice was broken, at least for now.

"So, what is it you want to know?" She asked quite formally.

"Anything you can remember about Sophie's ..er my mother's illness, before she died. Anything she might have told you about the family she thought she had and what triggered her fantasies."

He paused for a moment and then added, "Also, what brought her out of them?"

"It was so long ago, Tommy. Sophie said all sorts of random things. She was a very disturbed woman and most of the time she seemed to be scared shitless."

"When did it all start then? Can you remember that?"

"Yes. She turned up at work one day thinking it was Tuesday and it was actually only Monday. Like she had lived another day in between. It was weird."

Tommy felt his palms becoming clammy as he continued to listen.

" She thought she'd met some guy there and she just wouldn't leave it alone."

"In her fantasies did she ever mention no-one knowing her there?"

"No, I don't think so," Niki thought for a moment, "No, definitely everyone did because she made a comment that I had given her the same advice in one world as in the other! It was all very un-nerving. She was my friend, but she was acting like I ought to believe all this crazy stuff she was coming out with."

"What was the advice you gave her?"

"To go to the doctor, of course."

Tommy could feel he wasn't getting anything out of this. She wasn't telling him anything he didn't already know. Niki watched him for a moment and tried to think of something that might help.

"She did say that it always happened when she was asleep. That's the reason I knew it was all just dreams. She was always asleep and then waking up. They were all just dreams Tommy, vivid dreams."

"I've got a feeling you didn't just come here to ask about your mother's dreams?"

"No. You're right." Tommy admitted.

"So?"

"Mum and Dad have recently taken a new interest in Sophie's death. I think they might start digging around and going over things you know?"

She knew exactly where this was heading.

"And you are worried that they might ask me about why I think she did it and I might tell them about your little plot?"

"Something like that," he whispered humbly, "Will you?"

She patted his hand condescendingly.

"Like I said before. I have no desire to put your dad or Kelly through any more heartache. I think you were a devious little shit, but you were a child. I also think she would have met the same end, with or without your help."

"Thank you." He whispered again, as gratefully as he could.

" So, why are Carl and Kelly suddenly going over old ground on this?"

"Oh, I don't know," he lied, "think someone they know has a daughter with similar problems or something."

"You're lying." Her abrupt response took him by surprise.

"Why would I lie?"

"I have no idea, but I have two teenagers and I know an ill practised lie when I see one. What's really going on?"

"Ok," Tommy sighed, "It's me. I've been having the same hallucinations or dreams or whatever you want to call them."

"Are you sure it's the same thing?"

"I am now!" he said almost comically, "I started with the exact same experience. Had a full day that hadn't yet happened. You happy now?"

"No, of course not."

"But you'll still stay quiet?"

"Yes I will, but I do want something in return."

"What?"

"I want you to stay away from Amy."

"Amy? What makes you think I'm interested in Amy?"

"I'm not stupid," she went on, "you stay away from Amy and your secret is safe. You understand?"

"Yes." He agreed with a frown.

"I don't want her anywhere near this madness, you hear me?"

"Yes, I hear you."

"I'm sorry you are going through this Tommy. I really am, it must be quite harrowing for you."

"It's bloody terrifying," he continued, "It's probably just my imagination running riot. I mean, everything I saw could have come from my imagination, I know that. I mean, I had already seen Sophie in real life, hadn't I? I knew she thought she had two daughters, didn't I? I knew she thought she'd run off with some bloke called John."

"You dreamt you met all these people?"

"Yeah I did. Everything looked just as it does now. The beach, the new college, the new pub and all of that."

"Perhaps an over-active imagination is hereditary then?" Niki laughed hoping he would shut up now she'd got what she needed.

"Maybe. There was just something really strange though. Something that was different there."

Niki looked at her watch.

"Really?" she said politely.

"Yeah. I couldn't seem to locate my dad. His garage wasn't there, and neither was he."

Niki fidgeted uncomfortably.

"I know this sounds even more ridiculous because, like you said, it's all just in my own head but no-one knew me. It was like I didn't exist or something."

Niki turned ghostly white.

"What's the matter?" Tommy asked as he leaned over to take a closer look at her. "Why do you look like you've just been struck by lightning?"

"No reason. I think it's just bringing it all back to me that's all"

"Yeah, well now I'm sure you definitely want me to stay away from Amy eh?"

She nodded and stood up to leave as though she couldn't wait to get away.

"You'll still not say anything though?"

"No, I won't, it wouldn't look great for me anyway would it? If I suddenly came up with some vital evidence after all these years! Not to your dad or the police?"

"I guess not." She could hear the relief in his voice.

She patted his hand again, picked up her coat and left.

Tommy looked again at his phone. It wasn't even eleven yet. He was starving so he ordered a full English and more coffee.

As he shovelled it into his mouth, he realised that the nausea and dizziness had completely vanished. If he got back on the road in the next half hour, he could be back at the cottage this afternoon.

Back in Scotland Kelly had made a five-mile hike to a pub which she discovered had a reasonable phone signal. She had taken up residence by the window where she had spent over two hours ordering a variety of drinks and snacks to justify her occupation of the table by the fire.

It was now close to three pm and she had already read the menu a dozen times, browsed through all the tourist leaflets in the huge slotted display unit, and completed the crossword of an abandoned newspaper from the next table.

Every text from Carl was a further confirmation that there had been no sighting of Tommy.

Eventually she made her way back to the cottage and started to prepare dinner in the hope that Tommy would keep his word and return in the evening.

Tommy had every intention of getting back to Kelly before six but before he had finished his coffee, he got a text from Amy.

"Do you know what time on Saturday you'll be back yet?"

He could never resist a good surprise.

"Well actually, what would you say if I told you I was just around the corner from your house?"

"I'd say it's a windup and even if it isn't then it's a shame as I'm just leaving the dentist"

"On your way back to work now then?"

"That depends."

"On what?"

"On if you are really here, and why."

"Maybe I just needed to see you." He teased.

"I don't believe you! I can hear bagpipes" she joked.

"If I really was in Filey would you come and see me?"

"I might do," she said playfully, "I mean my tooth is really hurting"

"Is it?"

"No but it would get me out of going back into work."

"Well why don't you come to the garden centre and see for yourself?"

He clicked her off and watched the entrance to the carpark. He loved to surprise people like this! He couldn't help himself, and it didn't matter that he had no plausible excuse for being there. He liked to be a man of mystery.

He was beginning to lose hope, when he caught a glimpse of some long blonde hair cascading from the grip of a bobble hat. She strode towards the door in her skinny jeans, knee high boots and pink ski jacket.

He stood up to draw her attention and she beamed at him.

"I thought it was a wind up!"

"Well you came anyway?"

"Of course, I did. I like a good mystery!"

"What can I get you?"

"Hot chocolate please."

Tommy stood up to go over to the counter taking the empty coffee cups with him, one of which had the mark of her mother's lipstick on it.

Momentarily he worried that he might be playing with fire but as soon as he paid and returned with two fresh drinks, her smile filled him with a new confidence.

It's not like she was going to tell Niki and even if they got caught what could she do? Like she said herself, she could hardly come forward with new evidence after all this time, and if she did it would look like sour grapes for his disobedience.

"So how come you're back here again?"

"Would you believe me if I said I just couldn't bear to be away from you?"

"Nope," she smiled taking a small sip of the hot liquid through froth.

"Am I wrong?"

"Nope," he smiled, suddenly feeling the need to be honest with her, "I actually came to see your mum. She just left before you arrived."

"Shut up!" she said, flicking the froth at him.

"No really! You know I wanted to speak with her about my mother, well she agreed to meet me, so I came back?"

"Why didn't you just tell her to meet you next week? And why all the secrecy?"

He looked across the table at those huge blue eyes and suddenly realised why everyone always commented on his own. There's something about that shade of cornflower blue that is quite captivating.

"I think she didn't want to talk in front of you about my family madness!" he said raising his hands at her like a pair of claws, "I also think she wants to keep me away from you in case you catch it!"

"That's ridiculous!"

"Well maybe she's afraid you might fall instantly in love with me, get married and breed lots of little mad imps."

She blushed. He hadn't noticed her instant acknowledgement of the implication.

"Not that you would of course."

"Naturally," she said, "You do have a bit of a reputation according to her."

"Do I indeed?"

"Yes, actually she said you treat women like meat."

He grinned as he imagined the amount of effort Niki had put into her quest to keep them apart.

"Well maybe that's because most of the women who throw themselves at me have the same IQ and conversational skills as a side of pork!"

She pressed her lips together to control the grin that might otherwise have been interpreted as a green light.

He watched her with interest. He could tell that she was warming to him and he wanted to play along. The events of the previous day were starting to lose credibility in his own mind. Of course, it had to be a dream. What else could it be?

"Well I'm not about to throw myself at you, and that's a fact." She announced as she straightened her bobble hat.

"Well thank god we've got that off the table," Tommy continued, "I've got a long drive back to think about."

"I would like to be your friend though. If you'd like me to be?"

Tommy had an array of smart one-liners when a girl said that but today, he allowed the idea to penetrate his bravado. He liked her. She wasn't a girl, so much as a person. A person like Adam or Kelly. He could talk to her and he liked the idea of having someone he could talk to without keeping his eye on his bedpost score.

"I would like that. Very much in fact."

Suddenly the atmosphere relaxed, and the game ended. There was no score, but he felt that today there were two winners.

"So why does she think you're mad? Just because your mum was?"

"We are friends, right?"

"Yes," she said, "didn't we just say so?"

He put both elbows on the table and rested his chin on his hands.

"You really want to know?"

"Yep."

"Well, the other day when I came to ask about my mother it was because I'd had a nightmare and I thought she might have started in the same way."

"We all have nightmares!"

"I mean, really vivid ones, but now I'm pretty sure it was just a symptom of something else?" As he said the word symptom, he remembered the fever Adam was suffering from. He was discovering a new possibility as the words left his mouth.

"I've just come back from Thailand you see, and my friend had a terrible fever, so I think maybe I had the same thing."

"Oh. Is it infectious do you think?"

"I doubt it, but I'm a lot better now anyway" The reply aimed at reassuring her, was reassuring him tenfold, and as he started to feel the relief, his eyes began to water.

"Are you alright?"

He was too choked to speak.

"Come on," she said decisively, "Let's get out of here and go somewhere more private."

Out in the carpark it had started to rain.

They sat in Kelly's car for a moment and then Tommy made a suggestion.

"We could book into a hotel for the afternoon if you want?"

Amy glared at him.

"I just mean so we have somewhere private and warm to sit and talk. With somewhere to make some tea and maybe complimentary cookies?"

"Cookies?" she raised her eyebrows, "If there's cookies what are we waiting for?"

Tommy opened his phone and with a couple of scrolls and a series of clicks he slipped it back into his pocket. Come on, we're off to Scarborough for an hour or so.

Amy was less than a year younger but she didn't have a credit card or a hotel booking app on her phone. It was a little un-nerving yet strangely exciting.

As soon as she entered the room on the third floor, she knew this was not a standard room. There was a large queen-sized bed on the left which was adorned with several velvet cushions and to the right was a sofa, an armchair and a small dining suite.

She pretended not to be surprised and he pretended not to notice how badly she had disguised that surprise.

"Hot drink or cold?" Tommy asked cockily

"Cold please, I'm thirsty after the hot chocolate"

He flipped open the mini bar and took out several bottles of soft drinks, a few packets of crisps and nuts and a few bars of chocolate. Amy knew the extortionate prices of snacks from the mini bar. She was never allowed to touch one in a hotel.

"That should keep us going for a while."

She noted that his previous vulnerability had been replaced by behaviour almost bordering on arrogance, so she said nothing as he threw his wares onto the table. She simply watched him.

"What?" he said finally.

Still she remained silent as she looked at his face, almost confrontationally.

"What?" he asked again. He was clearly thrown off balance a little.

"Come here and sit down."

He wasn't used to a girl taking over the reins.

She pulled a chair up to the table and selected a cold drink then pushed the other chair out with her foot, as though instructing him to join her.

Tommy sat down with far less confidence than the person who had breezed into this room a few moments ago.

"So, tell me about these dreams and why they don't seem normal"

"Oh that? Like I said before, I think I just had a fever or something."

She opened a packet of crisps, pushed one into her mouth and chomped.

"You're such a damn liar."

"I'm not lying. It just gave me a bit of a scare, you know, with what happened to my mother. I'm over it now, it was just paranoia I guess."

"Tommy," she said firmly as she reached over the table and took his hand, "You were close to tears an hour ago and I don't really know you, but I don't think you're the kind of person to burst into tears easily."

Tommy could feel the emotion rising up again. He hated that this girl could read him so easily.

"Ok," he relented, "I'll tell you why I got upset and why it felt so real but then let's talk about something else."

"Deal!" she smiled, stuffing a bunch of crisps into her mouth again.

Tommy thought for a moment. He wanted to share some of this with Amy. She was a neutral person, and he knew she would be honest with him, but he didn't want to scare her off. He needed to filter the bits he didn't want her to know, censor some of the events, temper some of his despair.

"Well? I'm waiting."

She pulled off her bobble hat and raked her fingers through her hair and then pulled off her jacket and hung it behind her. There was nothing threatening about her at all. She didn't look like the kind of person who would be easily rattled, and she definitely felt like someone he could trust.

She wiped the salt from her lips with the back of her hand, took a swig of orange juice and then gave him her full attention.

Her hand was back on his, her eyes were searching his face in anticipation.

He might never get a chance like this again. He took a deep breath and started from the beginning while she listened intently to every word. The day he thought he had registered at college and even when he got to parts that he knew were nothing short of shocking he continued.

He watched for changes in her expression. For her to look at her phone for an excuse to leave or to give him the patronising reassurance of someone who wants to appease him so she could make it to the door. There was none of it.

The empathy he could see in her eyes was real, she was imagining his experience and living it with him. She was believing every word he spoke and the relief of telling his awful story felt like the lifting of an enormous weight. He finished with his meeting with her mother a couple of hours earlier.

"Wow!" She said finally.

"Yes, wow indeed," he sighed, "so this is the part when you call your mother and tell her you need rescuing from the mad man!"

Her face remained solemn.

"I don't need rescuing from you, we agreed to be friends remember?"

"Yes, I remember."

"The thing is though," she went on, "I just don't know how to help or what I can do."

"You're already helping, just by being here. I just need you to be here."

She stood up then knelt down in front of him with her arms outstretched, and as he moved towards her and her arms folded around him, the emotion soared to the surface.

He was never like this with girls, he was the one in control, the one with all the bravado and smart remarks but with Amy, he didn't want any of that, he just wanted to be held.

"Shall we just lay together for a while?" she whispered.

Tommy nodded, "I'd like that."

They laid down on the bed with arms around each other. Neither spoke a word. Seconds turned to minutes and as the minutes passed by, they clung together in the silent embrace as though they were feeding from it. As though it was nourishing their souls and cementing a bond between them that might never be severed.

She stroked his hair to comfort him and he squeezed her hand in acknowledgment. Her gentleness had stripped away his armour, but he no longer felt vulnerable, all he could feel was an indescribable relief. He pulled her closer and she held him tighter and the moment went on. He could feel the trust between them growing with every moment as the silent embrace continued. It was almost tangible. He could feel it and touch it.

She smoothed back his hair again and softly brushed her lips against his. Seamlessly and silently they sank to a deeper level of intimacy as she slid her hand under his tee-shirt and he responded by gently stroking the curve of her back. There was no urgency to the caresses, nature was simply guiding them through the levels of unification, exactly how they were meant to be. Each touch made a deeper promise, and each kiss formed another connection that would fuse them together for life.

Even as he peeled off her clothes and eased her naked body closer to his, neither spoke a word. They were melting together in a moment of purity and words did not belong there. Even as his body entered hers there was no sound other than the barely audible breaths of pleasure as they moved rhythmically in unison. His hands firmly grasped hers and held them above their heads as his eyes found hers. It was crystal clear that here, in these moments of sexual pleasure, something sacred was happening.

The silent embrace continued long after the sweat had evaporated from their naked bodies.

Eventually Tommy took a breath to speak but she put her finger over his lips.

"Shhh"

She rose from the bed and put her clothes back on and then looked at him for a few moments.

Tommy wanted to say a thousand things, but he didn't know what or how to put them in order. He did know that he needed to drive her home, but she simply stood at the door and smiled, blew him a kiss and she was gone.

He wanted to run after her. He wanted to explain so many things, reassure her, blurt out everything he was feeling but he didn't. He didn't because something perfect had just happened and anything other than parting in that perfect unstained silence would have ruined it. He knew that as distinctly as she had.

He also knew something else.

He knew he had fallen in love.

Amy took the lift back to the foyer and made her way to the bus stop. As she sat on the bus and headed home, she smiled. She didn't care if Tommy wanted to see her again or not, she didn't care if he turned out to be everything her mother had warned her about.

She had something no-one could ever take away from her. She had lost her virginity in an afternoon of sheer perfection.

Tommy picked up his phone and saw scores of missed calls from Kelly and from his dad. He had put it on silent to avoid interruptions, but now he felt guilty, as he slipped it back into his pocket and tried to decide what he should tell them about his impromptu trip. He needed more time to come up with something, so he got on the road and headed back north. He would call Kelly when he got nearer.

Kelly was back on the hill with her chair and blanket. She read the news on her phone and then flicked through her bank account to distract her from the torturous wait.

She suddenly jumped to her feet and the blanket fell to the ground.

"Carl, It's me. He used my credit card in Scarborough this afternoon to book a hotel room and again in Newcastle half an hour ago to fuel up. He's on his way back here!"

"Thank God." Was all Carl could say, "Thank God."

"He should reach Arbroath in about three hours. I'll text you when he arrives!"

Carl's relief had turned swiftly to rage.

"He's been with some girl, that's what this is! He's been having sex in a hotel while we've been going out of our minds!"

"He's safe Carl."

"He won't be when I get my hands on him. This is down to you this is! You encourage this despicable behaviour with your platinum credit cards. You're not doing him any favours!"

"Bye Carl." She clicked him off.

She wasn't in the mood for his lectures. Tommy was on his way back and she needed to get dinner started.

Carl heard her click him off and threw his phone across the lounge.

Sonya looked up from her paper. She had tried to make a special effort today. She had put her hair up in the way Kelly often did and she had put in some earrings now that her ears were on view. She had also changed her makeup. The bright blue had been replaced by subtle autumn shades of browns and beige. Her usually garish lipstick had been thrown in the bin and her lips now bore the shine of subtle peach.

Carl was still staring at his phone with his fists clenched.

She quietly folded her paper and walked over to him.

He was instantly startled by her approach. She looked different somehow, but he couldn't put his finger on it.

"It will always be you and Kelly, won't it?" she asked, almost casually.

"What?!" he was irritated by the interruption.

"It will always be you and Kelly. It doesn't matter where she lives or who she sleeps with, you will always be a couple Carl."

He had more important things to worry about than Sonya's stupid questions right now, so he just shook his head dismissively and picked up his phone.

"I've tried. Really, I have but she's always there, wherever I turn"

"She's Tommy's mother, for Christ's sake!"

"Well that's just it, isn't it? She's not his mother, is she? Any more than I am?"

Carl thought about it for a second. She was probably right. He had been with Sonya as long as he had been with Kelly, yet he had never regarded Sonya as Tommy's mother. Kelly had always held that position.

"Are you giving me an ultimatum here?" he scowled.

"I wouldn't be that stupid as to give you the chance to humiliate me, but you do know that Kelly will never take you back, don't you?"

"Well that hardly matters does it? Because I don't want her back! Do you know how many men she's slept with since we broke up?"

"Ah!" Sonya smiled, "So now we're getting to the point. You can't let her go but your pride would never let you take her back! You're jealous of all the wild sex she's been getting! That's it, isn't it?"

Carl was losing patience fast.

"Sonya, just go and finish your crossword or make the bed or something, I need to think."

"You need to think? Well, maybe you should think about this? I'm leaving you."

He stared at her as though she had suddenly burst into flames.

She walked calmly out to the hallway where a small case was already packed.

"I've decided that I'm moving on."

The classic euphemism for 'fuck you!"

His expression changed from surprise to amusement.

"Whatever!"

The classic euphemism for "Fuck you back!"

The door closed quietly as Carl swiftly kicked the sofa.

Damn it! now he would have to find someone else!

Chapter 15

Niki had left Tommy in the garden centre and driven home where she poured herself a large glass of red wine.

This was the last thing she needed, that stupid boy suddenly crawling out of the woodwork. At the time she left him she felt confident that she had dealt with it effectively but now she was having doubts.

She picked up her phone to call him but put it back down again. She couldn't think of anything more to say to him other than to try to reiterate her threats. It sounded desperate. It might make him more curious. Better to leave it.

She swigged the wine and poured another.

It had taken years and years before she had finally allowed herself to relax about the matter of Amy's parentage, and now this! She was probably blowing it all out of proportion. Tommy seemed desperate to guarantee her silence, and like he said, he hadn't shown any real interest in Amy anyway. He believed he had more to lose than she did.

She sat down and took another gulp of wine.

There had been times, many years ago, when she'd wanted desperately to leave Pete. That would have given her the inner peace she craved. It wouldn't have been such a big deal then, if the truth came out.

She might even have managed to win Carl! She'd stayed away from him all these years, but she'd seen him from time to time and she'd heard about his yoyo relationship with Kelly. He obviously craved a real family and a woman who could handle him. Niki could offer both. She had thought about it a lot, the actual moment of revelation, and it always gave her goosebumps.

She would have blurted it all out in a blaze of glory. Got rid of Pete and the burden of her secret in one wonderful, empowering moment.

Many times, she had played it out in her head. The moment she would declare Amy as Carl's daughter! The shockwaves she would cause, the looks of sheer amazement, that she had captured Carl's desire while his precious Sophie lay fighting for her life.

She put her feet up on the couch and recalled the many resulting scenarios she had once gone through in her head. It would certainly have thrown a spanner in the works for Kelly! Poor Kelly who was already competing with one mother of Carl's child, without another one turning up!

She relished the opportunity, but she wasn't that brave. Niki wasn't a gambler when it came to relationships.

There was a chance she might lose both Pete and Carl. Even if Carl chose her and Amy, over Kelly, she would still be competing with Sophie just as Kelly had.

Niki had decided to stick with the hand she'd been dealt and to make the most of it. She wasn't going to take the risk of being discarded by anyone and that didn't mean she had abandonment issues!

She finished off the second glass, slammed the glass down on the coffee table and refilled it, the bottle was almost empty.

Just because she had been dropped off at the school gate one morning by a mother who never returned, people ignorantly slapped that label on her. Abandonment issues! As if!

She had been thirteen, and apart from the blur of a few disjointed events, like a tearful conversation with the school cleaners at eight pm, the return of the headmistress and the nice lady from social services, she had been fundamentally unscathed.

After being settled in at Nan and Grandad's house in Hull, she started a new school and things went along pretty much as normal.

She had little interest in why her mother had done that. Some weird do-gooder said she was blocking it out but that was ridiculous. Her mother had chosen to go on tour with some bloke in a rock band, without looking back and that was that.

It wasn't the first time she had put a new boyfriend first. She was used to it. She was also used to the relationship process. A few weeks of locked doors, giggling and grunting followed by a few weeks of slammed doors, raised voices and then the eventual exit. Finito!

Her mother didn't believe in second chances, compromises, or apologies. When it was over, it was over. It seemed she applied the same principle to motherhood.

She had a difficult time after her Grandad died and she and nan had to downsize and move to Filey, but it wasn't as if her Grandad had abandoned her for God's sake! He had died so she didn't know why people kept on saying she had abandonment issues.

Yes, she was exceptionally tolerant of friends and yes, they sometimes took advantage but that was just her nature, it didn't mean she was afraid of losing them.

She also admitted that there had been times when she had tried to hold onto a boy longer than she should and had definitely made a fool of herself, but doesn't every teenager do that at some point?

She poured the dregs of the bottle into her glass.

Ok, so there might also have been a couple of times when she had allowed a 'kiss and tell' boy to go further than the relationship warranted and consequently suffered the name calling from the entire neighbourhood, but all girls make that mistake too!

In fact, it had been one such mistake that led her to the best friends she had ever had.

She was eighteen at the time and was avoiding her normal local pub after Kevin 'something or other' had spread the news of her liberal sexual attitude.

She saw two girls sitting at the bar who she had seen around the town quite a bit. They seemed quite popular and fun, but a little above her normal crowd when it came to class.

They were at the bar with three boys. Sophie was draped around Carl, Kelly was being chatted up by a tall geeky looking boy and Pete was standing alone.

Niki got up from her seat in the corner and walked over to the bar beside Pete. He instantly offered to buy her a drink and her fate was sealed. It was the moment in which she couldn't believe her luck. She had gained two new girlfriends in as many minutes and Pete became her steady boyfriend from that moment. She loved being in a relationship and she loved being part of a group of coupled friends.

Kelly's geeky boy was regularly substituted with various types, but the dynamic of the main players was never interrupted. They were a group of five friends with a flexible sixth position and that became an accepted constant. The new arrivals added extra entertainment as Kelly introduced, toyed with, and discarded each one in turn.

Carl had been a different person back then. He had a real zest for life and was by far the most intelligent of the group. He had a passion for mechanics far beyond his job. The garage he rented behind his flat was always full of junk he had bought at car-boot sales to repair. Vacuum cleaners, washing machines, clocks, car radios and basically anything he could take apart.

He was also a talented football player and could probably have made a career out of it, if he hadn't been in such a rush to settle down with Sophie.

Niki envied Sophie. It wasn't that she particularly wanted Carl (although he was much more impulsive and exciting than Pete) but she envied the way Carl treated her. The romantic gestures, the imaginative silly gifts, the way he held her coat and pulled out her chair. Carl was besotted and he made a point of showing it.

Pete was passably comfortable to be in a relationship with Niki, and that was equally obvious from his behaviour. He might have lacked imagination, but he also lacked the desire to impress women, her included.

She drained the last of the wine into her mouth and nodded drunkenly to herself. Staying with Pete had been the right thing to do. He was never going to run off with anyone!

Once she had reaffirmed her choices, she allowed herself to examine her one single mistake. The night with Carl.

She knew that it had been nothing more than her curiosity. She loved the way he attentively cared for Sophie's every need and she just wanted to know what that actually felt like.

She didn't see the risk, even though she and Pete had stopped paying much attention to birth control at Christmas. They were settled with the deposit for their first house, so they'd decided to let fate decide.

Everything would have been perfect if Carl hadn't turned up at the flat in a bit of a state while Pete was on a late shift.

"Can I come in for a minute?"

"Of course, but if you're wanting Pete, he won't be home for a couple of hours."

"No, it's you I need to talk to."

He looked like a dog who had just been beaten and thrown into the street. She let him in.

"What's wrong?" It was a stupid question.

He sat down while she filled the kettle.

"Do you have anything stronger?"

She opened the cupboard and took out a bottle of brandy with two glasses.

"It just doesn't make sense Niki."

"I know it doesn't."

"I mean, if you don't want to marry someone, you just tell them, don't you? If you don't want to be with someone, you just leave? That's what normal people do."

"I guess so."

"You don't take pills into the shed and try to kill yourself. There must be something I'm missing here."

Niki poured the brandy.

"Niki?"

"What?"

"She talked to you. More than to Kelly, I know that. She trusted you."

Niki took a sip without speaking.

Carl looked at her expectantly.

"She must have said something! Anything? Do you think it was about her mother's tumour?"

She handed him the other glass. There was plenty she could have told him but none of it would have helped. She could see he needed to place the blame somewhere and was hoping to lay it at the door of her mother's illness.

"Maybe. I was as shocked as you Carl."

She could have told him about the fantasy lover, the man she wanted to leave him for, but what good would it do? Sophie might wake up any day and realise she was just having some psychotic episode. This was not her secret to tell.

Carl drained the glass in one go and then poured himself another and did the same.

"I think I need some lemonade in mine." She said as she stood up and squeezed behind his chair.

As she passed behind him, he caught her by the hand. He was on his feet in a second and hugging her close. She could hardly breathe. He turned his head from her neck and kissed her hard on the lips and although she started to writhe herself free, his grip on her remained.

"Carl!"

"You could have any man you want Niki. You do know that, right?" His grip was loosening as his voice softened "I don't know why you're with someone like Pete. I mean, he's a good mate but really?"

As his arms relaxed from their grip, she could feel him moving away. His body was leaving hers and it might never return. He was leaving her, abandoning the exciting moment he'd created and suddenly she wanted him to stay.

She kissed him back.

It was stupid. It was a mistake. It was unforgiveable, but it was irresistible. She needed this.

He tugged open her shirt as she pulled back the strap of his belt. They were still kissing but there was nothing tender about it. As they pulled and dragged at each other's clothes their lips were locked, writhing and bruising clumsily as they fell to the floor.

In seconds he was on top of her. She wasn't ready. He tried to enter her several times until she gasped with the pain and burning sensation as he finally forced his way inside.

The pain, the burning, the pounding, his contorted face inches from hers, his rough hands kneading her breasts. It was unlike anything she'd experienced before, but she didn't fight it. Despite the pain and the urgency and the absence of any physical pleasure, she wanted this. She wanted him to enjoy her body because this was Carl, and he hadn't turned away.

The moment he collapsed on top of her, his senses seemed to return as he quickly rolled away and jumped to his feet.

"I'm sorry. I'm so sorry!" he was trying to get dressed while she still lay bruised on the floor.

"I don't know where that came from. I'm sorry, I'm sorry!"

He knelt back on the floor, put his head in his hands and cried like a baby.

"It's alright." Was all she could say as she stroked his back reassuringly, and then dressed herself as best she could with several missing buttons.

"I think you need to go now."

He nodded and rose to his feet as he tried to cover his flaccid penis with one hand as he grappled for his underwear with the other.

She turned away, partly out of politeness but mostly out of distaste for the vision before her.

As he quickly made his exist, among more pleas for forgiveness, she closed the door, sat down and drank the rest of her brandy.

He hadn't pulled out her chair or held her coat. He hadn't treated her the way he treated Sophie at all.

In that moment, as she gulped the fiery brandy that never got to be diluted with lemonade she knew exactly what this had been.

She had been his revenge fuck on Sophie!

That was the afternoon everything changed.

Carl lost his confidant, Niki lost her self-respect, and they both lost a friend.

That was the afternoon two desperate angry people made Amy.

At the end of the month her period was late. She told herself that a single incident with Carl was hardly likely to be the cause, but when the pregnancy test proved positive, she tried to recall the last time she'd had sex with Pete.

He had been away on a fishing trip that month and he had also worked a lot of late shifts. There had been the night they rented a film and drank a bottle of wine, but he'd fallen asleep. She tried to think of another occasion but couldn't. After a full hour, staring at her diary, the answer was still the same.

Fortunately, by the time she broke the news to Pete, they'd had sex a few times, and he didn't question it.

"I hope it doesn't have buck teeth!" he'd said excitedly when he looked at her first scan, "did I tell you I had buck teeth as a child?"

Niki looked ashamedly at his beaming face.

"It won't have buck teeth." She replied, almost without thinking.

"Oh, it might!" He teased.

She wanted to slap him for his stupidity and hug him for his trust all at once. Instead she just smiled and wished with all her heart that this baby inherited buck teeth from Pete's pathetic mutant genes.

Throughout the pregnancy she managed to hold onto some hope that her calculations had been wrong, but any such hope was dashed the moment Amy was placed in her arms.

She looked down into the face of that beautiful pink skinned, blonde little girl with the huge blue eyes and button nose and her heart missed a beat. It was like looking directly into the pram Kelly was proudly pushing around the neighbourhood! The two babies were clones of one another.

From that moment on, she knew she needed to break all ties with Carl and Kelly. If Pete ever saw these babies, side by side he would know.

And, so started, her quest to disentangle them immediately which was far easier than she expected. Kelly was busy being a mother and Carl was steering clear of the whole situation out of guilt and fear.

For a couple of years, she felt she had got away with it but then Dean came along, and the difference between the two children was startling. Dark hair with sharp features. He was nothing like Amy. He had Pete's wide set eyes and his square jaw, with Niki's raven hair.

Pete didn't once comment, even though their personalities were poles apart and only one of them had to have his buck teeth straightened as a child. Dean was lazy, in both thought and action. He didn't like sport or anything outdoors. He didn't read, and his schoolwork was well below average.

Amy, however, had Carls zest for sport. She played hockey for the school and ran whenever she could. She also had his logical inquisitive mind but not so much for mechanical objects as for the unexplained.

Her bedroom was cluttered with photos of UFO sightings, paranormal orbs and ghostly images, captured on camera.

The books beside her bed were of unexplained co-incidences, or children who suddenly started speaking another language. She was totally fascinated with unexplainable mysteries of any kind.

After she finished school she became totally obsessed with the paranormal and Niki was relieved when she finally got a job as a fashion buyer for a company in Malton. She got to travel a bit, and it gave her less time to sit in her room absorbed in this unhealthy, weird preoccupation.

On the whole, Niki considered that her own life so far, had been alright. It wasn't as if Pete was an abusive monster any more than he was an adoring sex God, but their years together, had been stable and safe.

The only real unnerving disruption had been Sophie recovering from her coma and dragging her back into the whole mess, but she had managed to do her duty after Sophie's death and escaped unscathed. She wasn't even sure Tommy would remember any of it.

Now here he was again! Dragging up things that were better left buried. Infiltrating her life with his smarmy smiles, fat wallet and sickening charm.

She threw the wine bottle in the bin and took another from the rack.

She was not going to let this damn boy back into their lives with his insanity, nor was he going to get anywhere near Amy with his matching hair, matching eyes, and idle meddling. She had put him in his place once before, and she would do it again!

Chapter 16

By the time Tommy pulled up into the parking spot on the lane and started his walk to the cottage it was well after 9 pm. He had sent the obligatory text to apologise to Kelly for his lateness, but she hadn't seen it. She'd returned to the cottage to make dinner and not tried to access her phone since, she knew everything she needed to know.

Any frustration or anger she had been harbouring had evaporated as she reminded herself that Tommy knew nothing of the bizarre dangers Anne had tried to convince them of.

Tommy walked along the grassy track towards the light of the kitchen window with his phone in his hand. It had been in and out of his hand for most of the journey. He was desperate to text Amy, but nothing he thought of seemed appropriate.

"How the fuck do you follow something like that?" he had asked himself out loud as he threw his phone on the seat again after deleting the last of several previously deleted messages.

He was beginning to feel like a frustrated poet searching for the one line that might define him. She hadn't text either, but he knew she wasn't sat agonising over the perfect response to what had just happened. She was waiting for him to do that. She was testing him, measuring him, assessing him.

He took out his phone again. He knew that his silence wasn't earning him any points. He had almost reached the door and any second now Kelly would be bombarding him with questions. He stroked the phone gently with his thumb and then turned swiftly in the direction of the hill as he opened up Amy's contact.

With a few frantic clicks he pressed the send button before he could change his mind and slipped it back in his pocket before running back down the hill and pushing open the heavy wooden door.

Amy was sitting on the bed reading through her notes for the supplier meeting the next day when her phone announced a message.

She picked it up and opened the long-awaited message from the boy who had just taken her virginity, and most of her heart.

"I love you"

She nodded approvingly. Not bad for a spoilt philanderer, even so, she would make him wait for a response. She put her phone down and continued with her list of complaints for the supplier she was about to dump.

Up in Scotland Tommy was sitting in front of a beef stew being grilled about the girl he had travelled half-way up the country to meet.

He smiled as he devoured the meal. It was delicious, but then he hadn't eaten for several hours.

"So, what's her name, where did you meet and what was so urgent that you had to sneak out in the night and go to a hotel?"

"You know about the hotel?"

"Credit card!" Kelly reminded.

"You've been tracking me?"

"We were worried!"

"We?"

"I called your dad, I'm sorry, I was just worried."

"It doesn't matter. He already thinks I'm out of control."

"So, who is she?" Kelly wasn't giving up.

Tommy thought for a moment. There was no harm in telling Kelly. Kelly was good at keeping his secrets.

"Well actually, I think you know her mother. You used to be old friends."

Kelly frowned. She'd had lots of casual friends over the years, women who pretended to be friends while they were getting cut-price treatments anyway.

"Your old friend Niki?"

Kelly was stunned. She hadn't seen Niki for years apart from a few sightings in the shops now and then. She had never made the effort to go over and speak but she didn't really know why.

There was a sort of unspoken hostility between them that had never been repaired since the stressful night in the police station. She had always felt there was something awful. Something Niki hadn't told her and something deep inside her, had caused her to stay away from it.

"Niki? God I've not spoken to her for years. Do you even remember her?"

Tommy's stomach turned a somersault.

"Vaguely." He lied as he remembered the terror of being dragged up the stairs by one arm.

"I knew she had two kids," Kelly said thoughtfully, "don't think I ever knew their names though. Did she have two girls?"

"No, a girl and a boy. Amy and Dean."

"Do you know what? It might be nice to see Niki again," she grinned, "Maybe we'll be mothers of the happy couple at some point."

"Mum really!"

Kelly stood up and collected his empty plate and ruffled his hair just as she used to when he was a child.

"Just saying! I mean if a boy leaves in the middle of the night and drives for six hours, books the executive suite of a fancy hotel and then drives back another six hours? Just saying!"

Tommy watched her filling up the tiny sink humming happily to herself.

How wonderful would this moment be if things were different! If Niki wasn't obsessed with Tommy's potential madness, if she hadn't witnessed his devious, evil behaviour, if he hadn't just had another episode, if the image of Sophie's face wasn't still haunting him and filling him with dread every time he allowed himself to think. He needed to speak to Adam.

"I'm just going up the hill for a moment."

"Well don't be long, I'm putting out the jam roly-poly."

Kelly was feeling suddenly light-hearted. Her son had found himself a girl he seemed to care about, and he had been free of these hallucinations since she brought him away to de-stress. Things were heading in the right direction.

As she wiped away the drip of custard from the stove with a cloth, she watched him striding purposefully up the hill. He was desperate to talk to his new girl and already Kelly was imagining herself and Niki reunited, maybe choosing outfits for their children's wedding even, or maybe, one day, even sharing grandchildren!

Tommy was already opening Adam's contact detail in readiness, before he reached the top of the hill.

"Adam?"

"Tommy?"

"Yeah, you ok?"

"For fuck's sake Tommy, do you know what time it is?"

"Yeah, sorry mate, just wanted to check how you were?"

"Tell your dad I'll be coming in on Monday if that's what you want to know."

"Not exactly. It's just that I think I've got what you had so I wanted to check."

"You should have checked earlier! You know, when I was almost dying, shitting through the eye of a needle, and throwing my guts up!"

"So, what did the doctor say it was?"

"Something called Campylobacter. Fancy name for dodgy egg eh?"

"Sorry mate. Sounds awful. Did you have fever?"

"I had it all! Stomach cramps, fever, the lot!"

"Fever's not good is it? Makes you hallucinate sometimes if it's bad enough."

"Yeah it does."

"Were you hallucinating then?"

"Yeah I must have been because I thought my mate had come to visit to see how I was!"

"Very funny! No real ones then?"

"A real hallucination! What the fuck is that? What's this about Tommy?"

"Did you have them or not Adam?"

"No, I didn't. Can I go to sleep now?"

"Yep, sorry mate."

Tommy looked back at the window where Kelly was still watching. He waived cheerily and then opened the text from Amy.

He smiled. He wished he could talk to her. He wished he was sure of his sanity, he wished he hadn't tried to kill Sophie and he wished more than anything that it was Amy at the window waiting for him.

He was thankful that tomorrow would be the last day up here as he tried to sleep. He had his date with Amy on Saturday night, but he was worried she hadn't replied to his message.

He wished he hadn't sent it now. It was too much, and he knew it. He wondered if she had read it and replied, but he wouldn't know util the morning when he got a signal. He tried to sleep.

Half an hour later he was creeping back down the stairs, grabbing his coat and heading out the door and back up the hill.

Several text messages arrived at once. He ignored the ones from his dad, quickly read the one from Adam which simply said. "Are you alright mate?" his call to Adam must have sounded more weird than he thought, he then opened the message from Amy which had been sent only a few minutes earlier.

"Impressive move college boy" she added a smiley face.

He punched the air. He wanted so badly to reply but he resisted. It was one thing to be texting at two am but only a total weirdo would respond immediately to a text at two am!

He went back to his room and tried again to sleep but his mind was spinning with theories and questions.

He thought of Sophie in her house with John, Vicky and Becky. The thought relieved him of the feeling of guilt for a few seconds. Perhaps he hadn't killed Sophie at all but sent her home to the man she loved.

He quickly decided again that none of it was real, and as the fear started to fade away, the guilt returned.

He thought of his conversation with Adam. There had been no hallucinations but maybe a fever affects everyone differently.

He recalled his conversation with Niki and the warning she'd given him and finally he recalled his afternoon with Amy.

None of it made sense and he was exhausted with the same questions spinning round and round and round. He needed sleep desperately, but he knew only too well, the horrors that sleep could bring.

Gently he knocked on his mother's door.

"Tommy?" She called from her bed. She'd been asleep but now she was wide awake. Tommy hadn't knocked on her bedroom door since he was a small child worrying about monsters in his toybox.

Tommy opened the door and entered sheepishly.

"What is it?"

"I don't know."

"What do you mean, you don't know? It must be something!"

Tommy sat down on the bottom of his mum's bed, put his head in his hands and sobbed.

Kelly felt the blood drain from her face. This was serious.

"What is it Tommy? You're scaring me."

She peeled his hands away from his face and placed hers directly in front of him. His eyes were red and puffy but that wasn't the thing that caused Kelly's heart to start pounding or her hands to turn clammy. His eyes were no longer a beautiful blue but totally black. His pupils had dilated to the extent that they had completely pushed away the colour. Tommy was terrified!

He buried his head back into his hands.

"Tommy! Look at me!"

Slowly he raised his face back up to Kelly's.

"I saw her."

Kelly felt a shiver of nerves rise from her legs, directly up her spine and into her mouth. His terror had ripped through her body like a tidal wave. She didn't ask who, she didn't need to, she knew who.

They held each-other's eyes for several seconds as though any motion from either might unleash some external force.

"Where?"

"I don't know" Tommy took his eyes from hers and held his head as though trying to remove it from his body. "It happened again, this morning."

Kelly tried to think of something comforting to do or to say but she was already realising that this changed everything. She had to be sure.

"But you went there and back in one day! You didn't sleep there, Tommy?"

"I fell asleep in the car," he said softly, "When I was wating for, er.. Amy"

Kelly felt a little less helpless. Sleep seemed to be the trigger and the fact that he'd been back in Filey reinforced the other theory. The theory that was almost laughably ludicrous, but the theory that was still compelling the mother in her to keep him away from there.

"Why aren't you saying anything?" he said, causing Kelly to realise how long she'd spent going through her thought process.

"It's a lot to take in Tommy." She sighed.

"Do you think it's me? Is this all coming from inside me?"

"I don't know but if it is darling, that doesn't make it any less real."

"Of course it does! I've just told you I spent yesterday with my dead mother and her whole fuckin' family! I didn't dream it. I was there! I'm telling you! I was there!"

Kelly felt another surge of electricity up her spine as she saw the honesty in her son's face and for the first time, she allowed herself to consider the possibility that he had actually seen Sophie.

"Did she look as you remembered her?" It wasn't meant to be a trick question, but she thought if it was just imagination then, to him, she would be the same.

"Nothing like it," he said defensively, "she looked healthy, fit and happy."

"So, what made you think it was her?"

"You don't believe me, do you? You're trying to catch me out! Make me believe it was just a childhood memory, well it wasn't!"

"I was just…"

"I know what you were doing but this isn't an imaginary monster you can chase away mum! It was her! I met her kids for Christ's sake, and I met John."

"You saw John?"

"Yep. Fat guy in a suit. Don't know why she'd want him over dad but there you go."

She could feel the sarcasm as he tried to provoke her into taking his side again. She was always on his side and she needed him to know that.

"I believe you Tommy. I don't know what this is but never doubt that I believe you."

He hugged her again as she whispered into his ear.

"And never doubt that I am going to protect you. Your mum is going to fix this Tommy, even if it kills me."

Tommy stood up to leave but Kelly held onto his hand.

"Bring your mattress in here tonight, I'm going to keep an eye on you, nothing is going to happen tonight"

Kelly felt confident. They were miles away from danger here. Tommy smiled. He didn't know why, but he totally believed her.

While Tommy returned to his room to drag in the mattress Kelly nipped back downstairs.

"I won't be a moment. I'm just going to make a call." She grabbed her phone and coat and headed up the hill.

"Carl, I don't have long so don't talk, just listen."

Carl listened and then put his phone back down and stared at the wall. He got out of bed and went downstairs, poured himself a whisky and sat down at the table.

He told himself it was all some elaborate fantasy. Hallucinations brought on by his son's over-active imagination or even by the weird magnetic interruption Anne had ranted about. Even so, his stomach was churning, and his tee-shirt was stuck to his back with sweat.

Tommy had seen Sophie!

Despite the gripping fear and shock. His heart skipped a beat.

Tommy had seen Sophie.

The following morning Tommy was feeling more positive. He got up before Kelly and went down to make breakfast. He poached some eggs, made coffee and popped bread into the toaster. He'd just made it to the bottom of the stairs with a tray when Kelly appeared at the top, already dressed in walking pants with hair tied up and makeup done.

"You always do that!" he snapped.

"That's because you always make enough noise to wake the dead when you're doing anything!" She said, in the same rhythmic voice she had said it since he was ten years old.

It was a great day for hiking. Cool and sunny with no wind. As he walked along the mountain ridges and looked down on the valley below, he felt better than he had for quite some time.

His lungs were full of the clean Scottish air and Kelly was by his side. If it hadn't been for his longing for Amy, he could have stayed in this place, but she infiltrated his thoughts constantly.

They were in the middle of something and he needed to see her. He needed to feel her in his arms again. He had never felt this kind of ache before and it frightened him as powerfully as it excited him.

When they stopped at a pub for a warm, a sandwich and a hot drink he was instantly texting.

"I'll be home tomorrow afternoon. Is our date still on?"

He waited with his phone on the table while they ate, hoping she would respond before they headed away from the wifi and back into the barren hills.

Kelly saw him constantly watching it.

"You got something going on?"

"Might have." He smiled, "maybe a date tomorrow night."

Kelly's face changed.

"What's wrong with that?" he frowned.

"I was just thinking it would be nice to stay here a bit longer?"

"Longer? Come on mum, it's been great and all that but really?"

"I thought it was doing you good, and you haven't had any of the weird dreams since we've been here. Maybe another week and you'll be back to your old self?"

Tommy hated to disappoint Kelly, but he had no intention of staying here for another week. Whatever it was that was causing these nightmares was getting worse not better and staying here in the middle of nowhere was not going to cure him of anything.

His phone lit up.

He opened the message and smiled at Kelly.

"Too late, I've got a date tomorrow night, let's go back and start packing."

As they walked back along the ridge Kelly was frantically trying to think of some reason to keep him away from Filey, without frightening him with the ridiculous theories from Anne. The theories which were insanely absurd but which both she and Carl seemed to be heeding, like it was some sort of superstition. Like they didn't want to tempt fate.

"Why don't you take her somewhere else tomorrow?"

"Like where?"

"I don't know but I'm sure she's seen enough of the pubs at home. Maybe treat her to a week away or something."

Tommy stopped walking and turned around to face her.

"What's got into you? She can't just take a week off!"

"You won't know unless you ask!"

"I'm not going to ask her that! It's way too soon. I'd look desperate!"

" I just think it would be nice to get a change of scenery, that's all."

"Why are you acting so weird? You really think there's something wrong with me, don't you?"

"No, I don't."

"I'll think about it" he agreed finally as he turned to start walking again. Maybe a long weekend would be nice. Amy gets Monday's off anyway.

Kelly marched behind wondering how quickly she could start him at the Spa in Harrogate.

As soon as they got back Kelly put some pizza's in the oven while Tommy went upstairs to pack.

As he folded his few clothes into his rucksack, he couldn't get Becky's face out of his mind. She was more real than any dream he had ever had and, as he moved around the room in silence his mind went back to the nights alone in his room as a child. The nights he had listened to the tv outside and the quiet exchange between his dad and Kelly as they tried not to wake him.

He also remembered the nights he pretended to whisper to Becky, but he had a memory of it in a different bedroom. It felt like much earlier than when Sophie came into his life.

He sat down on the bed and tried to put the memories into some sort of order. The bedroom was smaller and the tv wasn't downstairs. It was right outside because it wasn't a house at all, it was a flat.

He dropped his bag on the floor and tried to catch his breath. Why on earth would he have been pretending to whisper to Becky years before Sophie woke up?!

He left his rucksack half packed and went into Kelly's room where her handbag was lying on the bed. He opened it and took out the business card of Anne. He needed to speak to Anne himself! He turned the card over to her address in York.

He took a photo of it with his phone and returned the card.

York seemed like a good place to take Amy for a few days.

Chapter 17

"I'm working this weekend." Amy called to Niki who seemed to be sleeping off a hangover after her outburst the previous day.

She had, once again, found it necessary to reiterate her dislike of Tommy and his inherited insanity.

She had obviously been filling in time after making dinner and leaving it to warm. The gin bottle was on the worktop and the bottle of tonic was almost empty. It wasn't unusual to have a drink on a Friday night but not this early and certainly not two days in a row. It was totally out of character and seemed to have been triggered by her meeting with Tommy on Thursday morning.

By the time Amy had taken the bus home from Scarborough her mum was already in bed having declared a migraine, but the two empty wine bottles and the stench from her room told a different story.

There was definitely something about Tommy, that had got her in a state, and there was no way Amy was going to admit that she had met up with him on Thursday afternoon, only minutes after she'd left him!

Now Friday night seemed to be, gin night, and she had ranted on for a good five minutes about Tommy's reputation and his disregard for women before finally waving her finger at Amy again as she swayed unsteadily.

"And another thing." Niki yelled before staggering towards the stairs.

Amy never found out what the other thing was, as her mother pulled herself up the stairs by the banister.

"Where's dad?"

"Gone to the rugby! He'd tell you the same if he were here! Your dinner's in the oven, I'm going for a lie down."

There was a bang as she missed the top step and then a few more footsteps, as she made her way to the bathroom.

Amy had never seen her mother like this before. There was no way she could tell her anything about Tommy yet. She shuddered as she imagined her mother's reaction if she knew that the demon of Filey had taken her daughter's virginity! She might just hunt him down and kill him with her bare hands!

Amy had got up early on Saturday, in the hope that she could get away from work early. Tommy had booked a hotel and had nothing else to do all day, so if she managed to get away at three, she could dump her car somewhere and get Tommy to collect her. They could be at the hotel early evening.

"I'll see you Monday night then!" Amy called again.

"She's gone back to sleep love." Pete called.

Amy hurried down the path. Threw her suitcase on the backseat and started the engine. She had escaped and, in a few hours, she would be with Tommy again.

She clicked on her seatbelt and beamed from ear to ear.

At four thirty that afternoon, she parked her car down a side-street and transferred her case into Tommy's mini.

"Not exactly the car you picked me up in last time." She grinned.

"No, I thought I'd bring the posh one today."

"Yes, I can see that!"

"You could say I borrowed the other one. It was my mum's."

"And this one is…?"

"Oh, this one is all mine. It's her idea of keeping me alive."

"Looks more likely to kill you, if you ask me."

"She thinks I would kill myself trying to impress my friends and this is her solution."

Amy frowned so he continued.

"Its pretty hard to show off in a rust bucket that goes from naught to fifty in three days."

"Clever lady. Well I'm glad she's kept you alive so far. Is my car even safe here?"

"It's a housing estate! It's hardly going to alert the police is it? You getting in, or what?"

She got into the passenger seat and gave him a quick kiss on the cheek.

He revved the engine, slammed it into gear and lurched away with a screech of tyres.

"Just for the record," she said nonchalantly, "I'm not impressed."

"Thank God for that," he said as he slowed the car down to an acceptable speed, "I almost shit myself!"

Amy laughed out loud and put her hand on his knee affectionately. She loved being with this boy.

"Does this woman even know we're coming?" she asked, suddenly sounding serious.

"Yep. Called her yesterday, she's expecting us at ten am tomorrow. Do you think you can get that gorgeous body out of bed for then?"

"Cheek! I'll have done a four-mile run and had a shower by then!"

"You've brought your running shoes?"

"You bet I have, never go anywhere without them. You have to look after your body you know. You only get one."

There were a hundred sleazy remarks he could have responded with but instead he just put his hand over hers and smiled. He loved being with this girl.

As soon as they got into the room and dropped their bags, he pulled her into his arms, and she relaxed against him instantly.

"Are we allowed to talk this time?"

"Yes, if you like. Didn't you like the silence?"

"I loved it! Just wondered if it was a rule of yours or something?"

"I don't think something can become a rule unless you've done it more than once."

"Are you saying you've never made another guy stay silent."

"I've never made another guy, full stop." She retorted.

"You mean….?" He raised his eyebrows.

"Yep. Doesn't matter does it?"

He pulled her closer. "Matter? I think its bloody amazing."

"I thought it might scare you off!"

"Only if I was planning a casual affair I suppose."

"Well what makes you think I'm not?"

"Are you?"

"Not likely!" she pushed him onto the bed and landed on top of him.

"Aren't we getting dressed for dinner?" he gasped between the hold her mouth had over his.

"You never heard of room service?" she panted as she pulled his tee-shirt over his head.

"Shouldn't we be thinking about precautions?"

She laughed "I've been on the pill to regulate my periods for quite some time, we're good to go"

This time the lovemaking was different. Lighter somehow. They chatted and played and explored and experimented with a kind of friendliness he had never felt with a girl. He didn't understand it, but he liked it. It felt natural and cheerful, almost jovial with interludes of something almost touching on sacred.

They had planted the root deep, and now the flowers seemed to be growing from that root in a delightful and beautiful way.

As she sat astride him, her hands raking through her flaxen mane with pleasure he watched her face. The ecstatic expression as she rocked gently, with him gripped firmly inside her, was having an unbelievable affect on him. She was barely moving but her body was holding him tightly as she took him higher and higher. He wanted to thrust hard into her but he couldn't bear for this to change, so instead he just lay looking at her closed eyes, her partly bitten lip as his hands cupping her small perfectly shaped breasts, until wave after wave of orgasm hit him over and over again.

He had just experienced the best sex of his life.

As he lay prostrate on the bed, she was already reaching for the room service menu.

"I'm starving, are you?"

"I don't know what I am," he murmured, "but I don't think starving is the first word that comes to mind."

As she lay down beside him with the menu in her hand, he caught a glimpse of them both in the mirror and his eyes were drawn instantly back to it. They made a remarkable couple. Her hair was the same shade of blonde as his own and her complexion was the same peachy white, interrupted with vivid blue eyes. He smiled. They would make beautiful babies together.

After they had eaten club sandwiches with chips, followed by banoffee pie they lay watching a late night film until they could barely keep their eyes open.

As they lay down to sleep, she turned away from him and settled in the nook of his body. His arm folded around her waist and within seconds they were asleep.

The next morning, he woke up on his back. The hand that had been holding her was dangling on the floor. He panicked and sat up. Beside him, she seemed hardly to have moved at all. Still facing away from him, breathing softly.

"Not been for a run then?" he teased.

"What time is it?"

"Half eight."

"What? I never sleep past six!"

"Well you did today."

"You must have worn me out." She said as she flopped back onto the pillow.

"I'll get breakfast sent up. Tea? Toast? Cereal? Fruit?"

"All of the above." She mumbled from under the pillow she had buried her head beneath.

"It'll be here in thirty minutes, time for a quick shower." He called after putting the phone down and whisking a towel from the hook.

He dropped the towel on the floor, switched on the drencher and stood under the deafening flow. He didn't hear the shower door open, but he felt her naked body behind him as her hands snaked around his stomach.

She cupped her hand under the soap dispenser and lathered her hands as she remained behind him. Her soapy hands massaged his stomach is small circles, circles edging downwards towards his already erect penis. As her slippery hands massaged and stroked him, his legs began to shake, they could hardly bear his weight. Within seconds he ejaculated into the flow of the shower.

"Come on, get out the way, a girl needs to get washed." She laughed as she tried to push him sideways so she could stand under the water.

"You're unbelievable!" he was still supporting himself with his arms on the wall.

"Unbelievable. Hmm, I like that." She said approvingly as she tipped her head back to wet her hair.

He stood to the side for a moment and watched her. Her blonde hair turned the same light brown shade under the water as his did. Kelly used to tell him it was like magic painting as the water changed it, but he had never seen it with his own eyes before As he watched the water gradually colouring each section from white to brown he knew exactly what she meant. It was incredible how alike they were.

Half an hour later they were in the car on the way to Anne's.

"What exactly do you think she's going to be able to tell you that she didn't tell your mum?" Amy asked with the last slice of cold toast half eaten in her hand.

"I don't know. It's not that I think she can tell me anything new, it's more that I'm not sure that what she did tell got passed on to me."

"You think your mum and dad lied?"

"Not so much lied as held something back, I think. I need to act like they told me everything but that could be a bit tricky!"

Anne answered the door with a smile. She had definitely made an effort. Her hair was clean and almost styled, her dress, although drab, looked freshly ironed and went some way to disguising her round shape.

Tommy had only met her half a dozen times before, but he remembered her well. She was still as motherly and as friendly as before. She had been one of the few people around at that time that he found comforting.

"Come in, come in!" she gushed, ushering them briskly into the living room, as though they were long lost friends.

Tommy was taken aback. She had certainly prepared for this visit. Three chairs had been arranged around a dining table onto which several folders had been neatly piled. Alongside the folders were several textbooks, writing pads and selection of pens.

Teacups were already in place and a huge plate of chocolate biscuits and cup cakes took pride of place in the centre.

"So where would you like me to start?" she said excitedly as she poured the tea and sat down.

"I'm not really sure," Tommy replied, "everything you know about my mother's illness I suppose.

"Ah!," she frowned, "that's if it was an illness. I assume your parents told you all about my unproved theory?"

"Yes." Tommy said positively, not really knowing anything of an unproved theory.

"Well the thing is, the Solar cycle is called the eleven year cycle but in reality it can be anything from ten to twelve years"

"Solar cycle?" Amy interjected, "What's that got to do with insanity?"

Anne looked at Tommy, "You haven't brought her up to speed I see?"

"No. Sorry. Perhaps you could give her a quick recap?"

Anne rubbed her hands together excitedly while Tommy and Amy exchanged nervous glances.

Tommy didn't know any more about this than she did, and it was obvious Kelly and Carl had chosen not to enlighten him. It was the perfect way of getting her to go over it but, as Tommy sipped his tea, he was becoming more and more suspicious of the woman he had found so comforting, only a few minutes before.

Amy sat with eyes like saucers as she soaked up the theory of some natural phenomenon along the stretch of coast of her hometown.

Tommy was feeling anything but intrigued. The only thought in his mind was that this woman seemed to be offering some plausible explanation that might prove his sanity, and yet his own mother had kept it from him. He felt betrayed. More than betrayed! He was starting to believe she wanted him to think he was ill! Now it started to make sense that she had been trying to keep him away from home. Away from Filey. She had lied to him. She had never lied to him before.

Amy was leaning forward in her chair as though desperate not to miss a single syllable of Anne's investigation.

"So, you think the magnetic surges can affect the electronic impulses in the brain of some people?"

"Exactly!" Anne said as she threw herself back in her chair in appreciation of this competent student.

"So, the hallucinations?"

Anne smacked her lips as though she were preparing to deliver a monumental revelation.

Tommy was staring at the biscuits and wondering if Kelly might be suffering from Munchausen syndrome. That she might be trying to make him dependent on her, to keep him for herself, but that didn't explain why his dad went along with it.

Anne was just warming up.

"Everything we see, or feel is just electrical impulses making connections in the brain. That's why drugs that effect the brain can create hallucinations, memory loss, déjà vu. In fact déjà vu is a good example. The brain is seeing something for the first time, but it makes an error of communication and tells your brain it's a memory. It's incredible!"

Amy was munching biscuits eagerly and washing them down with tea while Tommy stared blankly.

"Tommy? Are you listening? It's probably perfectly explainable. Not insanity and not some weird visitation to another world!"

Tommy was listening but was far from overjoyed at the way this was going. As he tried to forget his parents plot against him and take in the theory, he realised that, if she was right, it proved something else. Whatever slant he put on it the conclusion was the same. It was a guilty verdict. He had sent Sophie to her death. There was no happy place where she lived with John and her children.

"So, what exactly do you think is different about that stretch of coastline?" Amy asked without noticing Tommy's anguished expression.

"I've a few ideas but nothing really conclusive. Maybe its just a natural hot spot."

"So, all Tommy needs to do is to stay away from there? Or at least to stay away when the cycle is going through its restart?"

"Well that's just my first theory." She poured more tea as though announcing the commencement of act two.

"I don't buy that." Tommy finally spoke. Quietly and calmly but decisively.

"Why do you say that?" Anne smiled as though she might be onto something with Tommy.

"You are saying that all my hallucinations are invented by my own brain that can no longer separate sight from imagination."

"Well, that rather over-simplifies it but yes."

"Well the other day I was sure I remembered being a child and talking to Sophie's daughter Becky."

"Yes, but Sophie had been ranting about her phantom family constantly, hadn't she? I'm not surprised you had nightmares about it."

"No. Not then," Tommy went on, "It was before that. It was back in the old flat. Sophie was still in her coma."

Anne stared at Tommy. Amy stared at Anne. Tommy turned white.

"And that brings me to my second theory." Anne said calmly.

Chapter 18

Amy was standing behind Tommy with her arms draped around his shoulders comfortingly as Anne went out of the room and returned with another folder and a fresh pot of tea.

"This theory is far more unbelievable, and I've tried a thousand times to discard it, but there's always something. Some little thing that places it firmly back on the table."

"We're listening." Amy said softly as she continued to stroke Tommy's shoulders from behind.

"I'm going to ask you to just open your minds for a few minutes and to consider this, no matter how unlikely or bizarre it sounds."

"Tommy?" Amy prompted.

"I'm listening."

"Imagine there's a kind of 'backup copy' of the life we live. I don't know how to explain it accurately, a mirror image almost?"

"Ok." Amy said. Partly to reassure Anne that someone was actually listening, but also because she had quite a hunger for what might be coming next.

"Well imagine if certain people, like Sophie, for instance are affected by this hot spot in a more colossal way. Imagine if they manage to slip from one copy to the other?"

"That's some theory!" Amy laughed. "I mean, I do believe there are other forces out there, I always have but you are talking of a dual existence or something?"

Anne cocked her head and raised her brows.

"That's totally ridiculous!" Amy was becoming annoyed.

"Just bear with me a second," Anne continued, "imagine if some people like Sophie moved over and started to make changes there, throwing everything out of kilter.

Tommy was thinking about the phone numbers that had disappeared along with his car. As terrifying as the theory was, he felt strangely comforted that, for the first time since this started, there was a person who seemed to have some concept of it.

"Look. I believe in ghosts and spirits," Amy said condescendingly, "but this? This is just total tosh."

"I told you it wasn't an easy concept to process, but there have been lots of things similar to what Tommy just said. Things that have led me along this road so many times, but I've never been able to find anything that would hold up as proof."

Amy had already shut off. This was a mad woman and this was a dead end but as her interest waned, Tommy's started to grow.

"What about what I just told you then?" Tommy suddenly joined in. What Anne was saying fitted in so accurately with everything he had experienced, and he wasn't going to pass it off as nonsense just yet.

Amy had now gone firmly in the opposite direction.

"This is ludicrous. I think we ought to leave Tommy."

"No, not yet. What exactly do you think would prove this theory of yours?"

"Just one thing that couldn't possibly have come from the person's own mind. Something that couldn't have been already known."

"Well what about my memories in the flat? That happened long before Sophie woke up. Long before she started telling everyone about her other family?"

"I hear what you're saying and I'm not disbelieving you, but I don't think the vague recollections of a small child would give my theory a great deal of credibility in the scientific world do you?"

Amy had gone quiet. She knew the hypocrisy of her own words. Words spoken by someone who already collected photographs of ghosts and orbs from another world. Another parallel world. The world of the dead!

"There's a few other things." Tommy said quietly as though afraid of being heard by ears other than those around the table.

"Like?" Anne asked.

"Well when I was in one of my episodes, the girl I met was called Vicky. It wasn't until I went home with her and saw Sophie that I realised who she was. They called her Tori. How would I have known that?"

"Wait a minute. Kelly didn't say anything about you meeting Sophie!"

Tommy sighed, "No. It hadn't happened then."

Anne shuffled excitedly. This could be exactly what she'd been waiting for! Imagine if she could prove the sceptics wrong after they ended her career and humiliated her, calling her deranged and unfit to be a psychologist!

"Anything else.?"

"Well, there is something else, but I hadn't thought of it as strange until today."

Tommy stopped for a moment as though undecided. Amy gave him a gentle nudge.

"Go on Tommy."

"Well, after what you've just said about the solar cycle," he stopped as though building up courage to continue, "I find it quite unsettling that this Becky was studying astrophysics. Doesn't that seem like a bit of a coincidence?"

Amy could see her own hands shaking. This was far more unnerving than any of the séances she'd been to. She wanted to leave.

Anne grinned and pulled over her notepad.

"Excellent! Anything else?"

"Nothing else like that but there was just one other strange thing."

Anne was transfixed on whatever might come out of his mouth next.

"When I was there, well no-one recognised me, and even my possessions seemed to disappear! My car and credit card. It was like I didn't exist there."

Anne thought for a while.

"No idea why that would be, never heard of that before. But you recognised other people?"

"Yes, Kelly and Jake but they didn't know me either. They had a son of their own."

Amy could see the emotion on his face when he spoke of Kelly's other son. His heartbreak seemed stronger than his trepidation.

Anne continued scribbling.

"We need to get you back there!"

"Not likely!" Tommy snapped.

"Don't you see this could be a breakthrough like this century has never seen. It would be on a par with the discovery of gravity or electricity. We have a moral obligation to pursue this Tommy."

"We? There's no 'we' here. This is your investigation not mine!"

"You can't shirk your responsibly on this Tommy, you just can't. I've known only a handful of people who have the ability you have, all of them happened during the start of a new solar cycle and all of them along this coast!"

"So, go and pester one of the others!" Amy chipped in, "Tommy has been through enough!"

Tommy looked over at Amy in gratitude, and then back at Anne whose excitement was turning quickly to alarm.

"It has to be you Tommy. It has to be."

"Why?" Amy butted in again, "Why does it have to be him?"

Anne stared at Amy menacingly. It was more of a threat than a stare.

Amy stared back, she was not afraid of the fat little woman with her tall stories and short temper.

Tommy could feel the atmosphere between them becoming uncomfortably acrimonious.

"Let's just calm down and let Anne tell us, shall we?"

"She doesn't need to," Amy's eyes were still challenging Anne's, "It's because the others are all dead isn't it?"

Tommy physically jumped.

"I'm right aren't I? You've somehow managed to drive them all to killing themselves? Like Sophie?"

Anne rose to her full five foot two and glared at Amy.

Tommy knew that if anyone had driven Sophie to suicide it certainly hadn't been Anne. He tried to defuse the situation.

"Let's just go back over it and see if there's anything we missed." It was a feeble attempt to restore a constructive discussion.

"Can I use the toilet please?" Amy asked defeatedly.

"Upstairs, first on the right." Anne replied with equal politeness.

Once in the privacy of the bathroom Amy opened her phone and searched for any further information about Anne Hathers. She scrolled through the suggestions of facebook and other social media groups. Three pages down she found reference to an article published several years earlier.

Her dismissal from her post for inappropriate behaviour and eventually to the trial in which she was acquitted for aiding and abetting a suicide. She took a screenshot of the page and clicked out of it. She didn't know what they were talking about downstairs, but she knew they needed to leave. They were in the house of a mad woman!

She returned calmly to the table and smiled weakly.

"I'm really not feeling well. Can we leave now Tommy? Maybe come back later in the week?"

Tommy looked at her. She did look rather hot and sweaty.

"Yes, of course. Sorry Anne. I'll get in touch tomorrow. You've been a big help so far."

Anne's eyes narrowed. She didn't trust Amy one bit.

Tommy got up to leave and Amy was already at the front door. She turned the knob, but the door was locked.

"You seem to have removed the key from the front door." She laughed unconvincingly.

"I just need you to stay a while longer," she explained, "there's a lot more of my research you still haven't seen!"

Tommy frowned at Amy and her eyes widened. He realised something was very wrong here.

"Key please Mrs Hathers?"

"You need to understand first!"

"Key please!" He repeated more firmly.

"If you go now, you won't come back, I know you won't! I've seen that look before and this time I won't be fooled!"

She was standing firmly between him and Amy and immediately Tommy saw red.

He pushed past her, knocking her firmly into the table and took Amy by the hand.

"We are leaving now!"

Anne stood in the doorway between the hall and the living room with her hands on her hips like some castle guard.

"You're not leaving until.."

She was cut off mid-sentence as Tommy took hold of the hair on the top of her head and pulled her forward into the opposite wall. As her head hit the brick wall, he pulled Amy back into the living room and slammed the door to trap her in the hallway.

"Bring me that chair!" he yelled to Amy as he held onto the door handle.

Amy hurriedly dragged over the chair which he jammed firmly under the handle.

"Come on, window!" he tugged her by the arm while his other hand was already lifting the latch.

He gave Amy a leg up onto the windowsill and as she jumped onto the pavement he leapt through and landed beside her.

They ran to the car and didn't speak a word until the doors were slammed shut, the engine started and the wheels screeching away.

"What the fuck just happened?!" Amy shrieked as they sped away with hearts pounding.

"No idea!" Tommy yelled back, "but I know we're not going back there again. The woman is totally un-hinged!"

"Should we call the police?" Amy panted.

Tommy answered without even considering it.

"No, the last thing we need is the police poking their noses in. We might all end up in a padded cell!"

Chapter 19

Back at the hotel they went straight back to the privacy of their room to try to make sense of the morning ordeal.

Immediately Amy opened up her phone and showed him the screenshot she had taken in Anne's bathroom.

"I think I need a strong drink!" Tommy declared as he plonked himself down on the bed.

"Me too. I'll order some sandwiches and a bottle of wine, my nerves are shot!"

Amy picked up the room service menu for the third time.

"You should know that bloody thing by heart!" he teased.

"Well I think we should stay in this room for a bit. To be honest, we're not safe to be let out, are we?"

Tommy laughed and then so did she. They laughed hysterically as they remembered Anne's tantrum and her wild theories.

"We've been held prisoner by a psychopath!" Amy squealed, hardly able to breathe.

Tommy couldn't say anything other than to draw breath between wheezes of laughter.

After twenty minutes of breathless hilarity they managed to calm down enough to wipe their eyes and accept the food and wine with some degree of sensibility.

Tommy poured the wine and handed one to Amy still holding one hand over his aching ribs.

They ate and drank in silence. Each was trying to process the sequence of events as they tried to separate fact from fiction, reality from speculation and truth from fabrication.

As Tommy shared the last of the wine between them, he found the courage to speak.

"I know she's clearly a tent short of a circus but some of the things she said were quite disturbing don't you think?"

Amy curled up beside him with her hand on his chest and kissed his nose affectionately.

"I think some of the things *you* said were more disturbing to be honest"

Tommy sighed, "Yes I guess that's what I meant really."

They lay in silence for a few more minutes and then Amy sat up purposefully.

"Like she said, it's the things that couldn't have come from your own mind that are strange."

"I know."

"So, all we have to do is to rationalise the things that seemed incredible."

"I've tried that. I do it most nights to be honest."

"Not with me you haven't! Let's take them one at a time."

"Go on then, if you must."

"The time you realised Vicky was actually Tori?"

"What about it?"

"Well did you know already that some people shorten Victoria to Tori?"

"Yes, I suppose so."

"And you obviously know Vicky is short for Victoria?"

"Yes."

"Then realistically, this perceived mystery could have been of your own making?"

"It's possible but not likely!"

"It's possible. Let's focus on what's possible not probable. The sub-conscious mind stores all sorts of information and spews it out randomly sometimes. Look at how crazy dreams can get!"

"I guess so."

"Also, the subject of Astro physics? You said Becky was studying this, yet you hadn't heard anything about Anne's theory on the solar cycle?"

"No. Never heard of it before."

"Maybe you overheard your dad and Kelly talking?"

"Nope!"

"You sure they didn't mention Anne's interest in it?"

"Nope!"

Amy picked up the empty bottle and then rang down for more wine as Tommy stared up at the ceiling scrolling through his phone.

"What you looking for?"

"Nothing really, just wondered if there was a chance that I'd taken any photos in some mystical world" he joked.

He flicked through the photo of Anne's old business card and then smiled.

"I think I did know! Before mum went to see Anne, we looked her up on social media and I remember a list of her qualifications. Astrophysics was one of them."

Amy hugged him tightly.

"So that means that the only thing we haven't found a plausible reason for is your recollection of talking to Becky in the old flat?"

Tommy seemed to have relaxed again as Amy went to the door and collected the new bottle of wine.

She filled both glasses and continued.

"So how sure are you? I mean, you remember whispering to Becky after Sophie filled your head with the names of her fantasy family and you remember being alone in your room at the flat. But how sure are you that they both happened at the same time?"

Tommy thought for a moment. He didn't feel so certain anymore, but that could have been the wine. He tried to remember but the more he tried to remember, the more vague it all seemed. One thing merged into another until it all felt like one long mixed up dream.

"Not very." He said at last.

She clinked her glass with his.

"I think it all came out of your own memory. Just like dreams and nightmares. And, as for all this about electrons and magnetism, I really don't know but I think maybe you would be wise to stay away from home for a while!"

They both took a large gulp of the wine as he threw her over onto her back and jumped on top of her.

"Afternoon film and an early night?" she winked.

The following morning, they went out for a walk after breakfast.

"I wish we could stay here longer." Amy sighed sliding her arm under his coat for warmth, as they walked along the riverbank.

"Well I could!" he laughed, giving her a shove, "It's you who has to be back at work in the morning."

"Oh yes," she shoved him back, "I forgot you are a man of leisure!"

"Well, I'm meant to be starting my new job soon but not really sure what it is as yet! I'm sure it won't involve falling asleep anywhere near Filey though."

He thought again about the information his mum and dad had kept from him. There was no wonder they didn't share any of the terrifying rubbish Anne was dishing out. Instantly they were forgiven. He smiled to himself. He knew his mum would never let him down.

"It sounds crazy now doesn't it?" Amy pulled him closer "Sleep does seem to be the trigger though, must be something about a relaxed mind?"

"I suppose I could just get myself a good supply of cocaine and stay awake until the sun has finished yawning and stretching or whatever it does!"

It helped that they could joke about it, but they each knew that the moment they were alone with their thoughts, it would be very different. They knew the events of this trip would start to torment them again, and that some of the words that had shocked them once would do so again.

"It's going to be difficult to meet up again if we have to keep trying to arrange secret dates isn't it?"

"Yes, I suppose it is," he agreed, "don't know what we can do about that though."

"Do you think Kelly could talk mum round? You know, assure her you're not a dangerous psychopath?"

Tommy would have loved for it to be that simple, but he knew Niki had seen a deplorable side to him. She had seen what he was capable of, and even though that devious boy seemed alien to Tommy now, he didn't blame her for wanting to protect her daughter from the fiend who had tricked his mother into throwing herself off the Brigg.

"Let's just see how things go." Was all he could offer.

"Is that code for 'maybe we won't last anyway'?"

Tommy hugged her close and kissed her hairy bobble hat.

"Absolutely not. I'm just a bit frazzled and out of ideas right now. If we have to keep meeting in secret for the rest of our lives that's fine by me!"

It was the most reassuring response he could give her, but the incredible thing about it, was that it was the absolute truth.

Later that day he dropped Amy back at her car and they both got out to say their goodbyes.

"I need to talk to my mum." Amy said decisively, "She's been totally unreasonable about you!"

Tommy panicked.

"No don't! Let's just leave it for now. If we have a big blow up right at the start, things will never be right for us."

She looked at her feet sulkily, so he gave her another shove.

"We might need a babysitter sometime down the line and I don't want your mum disowning us!"

She looked back up at him and smiled. She was pleased he cared about the relationship with her mum, but she was smiling mostly because he had eluded to them sharing a future together. That alone, was enough reason for now, to do as he asked.

She got into her car and started the engine and Tommy did the same. He followed her bumper to bumper until they reached the junction that would take them their separate ways.

As he turned left towards Kelly's condo and she turned right to go home, they both felt the wrench.

Amy watched him driving away from her in her rear-view mirror with a lump in her throat.

Tommy turned his rear-view mirror away, slammed into a lower gear and screeched away. After a few yards he had to slow down to wipe away the tears.

"I thought you might drop in at your Dad's tonight?" Kelly called from the kitchen when she heard Tommy drop his bag and close the door. "I was just going to call him and ask to speak to you!"

"Thought I'd give him time to cool down! You know what he's like."

Kelly knew exactly what Carl was like! He would be seething right now after the wild goose chase to locate Tommy.

She smiled as she imagined him waiting for the return of his wayward son.

"I've got some chicken in the wok, do you want me to throw some more in for you?"

"Yes please."

"How did your date go?"

Tommy didn't answer but walked into the kitchen and picked a chunk of chicken out of the wok.

Kelly slapped his hand with the spatula.

"That might not be cooked through yet, you idiot!"

He immediately stole another piece and grinned.

"How was your date?" she repeated.

"It was ok." He smiled.

"More than ok?"

"Yep, more than ok."

You know that if this is getting serious, you need to speak to Niki don't you.

"Yeah, but not yet eh? Let's see how it goes."

Kelly looked over at him as he munched contentedly on the chicken. She knew that look. He was as excited from this date as he used to be on Christmas Eve. This wasn't going to go away any time soon.

She threw in some more chicken from the fridge and handed him a beer.

As he disappeared into the huge lounge area and plonked himself on the white six-seater sofa she allowed her mind to wander a little.

She imagined meeting up with Niki at a café on weekday mornings with their grandchildren. She imagined how lovely it would be to be able to chat with Niki again and to share their news the way they used to on Friday nights. Spending Christmas mornings at some house yet to be purchased for Tommy and Amy. Helping their grandchildren unwrap presents while sipping eggnog.

She took in the plates of food, pushed Tommy's feet onto the floor and sat down beside him, handing him a plate and fork.

"I thought we might go into Harrogate later?"

Tommy shovelled in a forkful before speaking.

"Harrogate? It's already six o'clock. It's Monday night, why would you want to go into Harrogate?"

She stroked his hair the way she always did when she needed him on side.

"I've booked us a hotel tonight. I thought we might visit my Spa project tomorrow?" She was clearly uncomfortable about approaching the subject.

Tommy put down his fork for a moment to look at her.

"It's ok. I know why you are trying to get me away from here, especially at night."

Kelly looked shocked and embarrassed.

"What do you mean?"

"You can stop pretending mum. We went to see Anne."

Kelly's expression changed to that of a teenager who had just been caught out lying.

"I'm sorry I didn't tell you more Tommy. I just didn't want to.."

"You didn't want to frighten me. I get it. Well now I know and yes if you want to go into Harrogate that's fine. If you want to find me a reason to live away from here that's fine too but I don't want to lose Amy."

"There's no reason why you should. We can make up something to tell her and you can visit all the time."

"I don't need to make anything up. She was there. She heard everything Anne said, and I've told her everything I know."

Kelly looked suddenly hurt. She had always been the only person her son confided in.

"So, you took some of Anne's weird theories seriously?"

"I think the woman is deranged! Totally deranged but if you are asking if I think she had some plausible answers then yes, I think she might have. Enough for me to want to stay away for a bit at least."

"Go pack a few things love," she said soothingly, "let's go look at your new venture."

Tommy was still texting as he pulled on his seatbelt.

"Amy?" Kelly smiled as she started the engine.

"Might be." He smiled back.

As they drove along the seafront Tommy watched a group of college kids spill off the bus. That would have been him tonight. First day at college finished off by a trip into the exciting town of deserted Filey! He smiled as he watched them jostling along. They had obviously been in the college pub before deciding to explore their new surroundings.

One of them had the other in a head lock as he playfully pulled the poor boy along. The boy was seriously overweight and could barely keep his balance. His mop of salt and pepper hair was bouncing in the grip of his friend.

"Stop the car!" Tommy yelled as the jostling pair drew closer. He knew these boys. He had seen them before!

"Hey Jack! Harry!" He called through the window.

Both boys stopped and turned around.

"It's me! Tommy!"

Jack came forward to take a closer look and then squinted.

"Tommy?"

"Yes, you remember me from the registration day?"

Jack smiled tipsily.

"Well hello Tommy! Want to come for a drink?"

"Ignore him," Harry chipped in, "he'll talk to any fucker!"

"You do remember me though?"

"Well clearly we must have met since you know our names, but I have to say, your face doesn't ring any bells."

"Nope." Jack said as he fell against the door and pointed a finger in Tommy's face, and then slurred. "and I think I'd remember a face as blurred as yours."

Harry pulled him away as Kelly moved back into the flowing traffic.

"What just happened?" she said as they turned away from the seafront.

"I think I need to stay away from here mum." his pale complexion seemed tinged with green, "just get me away from here."

Chapter 20

That night only one of the two booked rooms was used.

Kelly refused to allow Tommy to sleep alone and insisted on sleeping on the sofa bed under the window of his room.

She woke him several times to check he was alright, and in the morning, she returned to her own room to shower and change but was back within twenty minutes.

As he got showered, she sat on the bed and ordered breakfast. It was a natural thing for both of them, to reach for the room service menu rather than to go to a hotel dining room. Carl always hated that about them. He said it was lazy and ant-social behaviour but his real issue with it was that Kelly could afford the extortionate prices and he couldn't. Tommy did it all the more.

"So, what do I need to know about this place that is likely to become my future?"

"Just go in with an open mind Tommy. Look for what you could make it, not what it is now."

Tommy could feel that this was not going to be up to Kelly's usual standard. She was gifting him something he was going to have to put heart and soul into.

They left their belongings at the hotel and drove a few miles out of the town. The countryside was stunning but when Kelly turned the car down a tree lined driveway towards a large tired looking house, he shot her a puzzled glance.

"It looks more like the rambling home of some rich old spinster."

"Yes. It might not be a college, but it is definitely a place of learning." she nodded confidently, "come on, I'll show you round."

"Morning Kelly!" A smartly dressed girl called from behind a mahogany counter as they walked into the warmth of an airy reception area.

"So, this is your new project?" he smiled as he started to warm to the idea of actually owning something.

"Yes, It's not really off the ground yet but I was intending that eventually it might be my flagship."

"There's a lot to do if you want this old place to outshine the others!"

"Yep. There is!" She said as she pushed open an office door and pulled out a huge leather chair at a mahogany desk for Tommy to sit down.

"Try it out then."

Tommy sat in the chair and gave it a gentle spin. Outside he cast his eye over the enormous grounds with established trees which extended as far as he could see.

He was already thinking 'golf course' as he spun back and experienced a huge surge of power. He liked it. He could do this.

"I know it's not what you really wanted but I know you could build this into something great. Everything will all be yours one day anyway, so why not make a start?"

Tommy could feel she was treading carefully, trying not to bully him, trying not to assume anything but she needn't have bothered.

Tommy was streets ahead. He was already considering the idea or bringing Amy out here to live someday.

"Have I overstepped the mark?" Kelly asked submissively.

"I'd say you hit the bullseye." Tommy grinned as he spun around on his new throne.

"I suppose I better put together a training plan then." Kelly was already three steps ahead. Fate had handed her exactly what she'd been hoping for. Her son was going to follow in her footsteps, and she was already mentally clearing her diary for training, considering short term hotel bookings and longer term appartements.

"Just one thing," Tommy said quietly

"Yes?"

"I'd like to change my name to Palmer."

Kelly couldn't hold back the tears.

"Really?"

"Well it would seem sensible to change my name to the one on the building wouldn't it?" he grinned, suddenly wondering why he hadn't done it years ago. Why on earth had he kept Sophie surname for his entire life?

"Come here Tommy Palmer." She sobbed as she hugged his head.

"You know what mum?"

"What?"

"If Amy moved here with me her commute to work would hardly change!"

"You think I hadn't already checked that!" Kelly huffed as though he should have known.

"Gonna' be difficult for her to keep sneaking up here behind her mum's back though" Tommy added

"You want me to talk to her?"

"No!" That was the last thing Tommy wanted. He'd already broken his promise to Niki, and she might take revenge by enlightening both Kelly and Amy about his demonic history.

Kelly heard him but she didn't agree. She wanted to fix this for him just as she had fixed absolutely everything in his life.

With a few clicks Kelly had extended their stay in the hotel by two weeks. She had other appointments, but she wanted a foothold close to Tommy so she could introduce him to the basics of her company, mentor him, search for an apartment for him and also keep an eye on his mental health.

Tommy was texting Amy.

Kelly clicked on a few possible appartements for rent, printed an induction pack for Tommy, and rang through to reception for coffee.

Tommy was still texting Amy and arranging to meet her after work back in Filey then hoping to bring her back to his hotel in the evening.

"I expect you'll want to go back home later to have some time with Amy?"

"Yes, is that a problem?"

"Not at all, but make sure you stay at the hotel tonight. We start early around here you know! No special privileges for the boss's son."

"Point taken." Tommy said cheerily. He knew it was her way of reminding him not to stay over in Filey.

"Guess she could come over here and stay with me tonight."

"Of course." Kelly didn't mind what he did as long as he kept his eyes open whenever he was back home.

"I'm sure she'll come up with some excuse." He said confidently as he gave his chair another spin.

"Great. I'd like to meet the girl who has managed to grab your attention for two whole days on the trot!"

Kelly was curious. She hadn't set eyes on Niki's children for several years and even then, it had been an unplanned sighting in a supermarket. She recalled a slightly built little blonde girl with her unruly younger brother. The little girl had been quietly holding onto the trolly while the boy threw himself about screaming for something he had evidently been forbidden to have. It had been the noise of the boy's tantrum that had drawn her attention but when she realised it was Niki she had hurried off in the other direction.

The unspoken rift between the former friends was as undeniable as it was inexplicable.

That evening Kelly was sat at the hotel dinner table when her son entered with a stunningly beautiful blonde on his arm. The girl was smiling at her long before she approached the table and within ten minutes of conversation Kelly was thinking that this was just too good to be true.

She had always expected trouble from Tommy. Carl warned her often enough about spoiling him and how he would one day bring home some wayward drug addict or one of the wealthy middle-aged widows from a cruise, but this girl was delightful. Well mannered, well educated, sharp witted and attentive. She could see exactly why Tommy was smitten.

As they chatted over a bottle of merlot Kelly took a moment to watch them as they chatted happily. They were, without doubt, one of the most beautiful couples she had ever seen with their pale pink complexions, blue eyes and silky blonde hair.

She needed to smooth the path for them. She needed to make sure nothing spoiled this for Tommy. Niki was her old friend, and she knew she could fix this.

After dinner she went back to her room and called the old number she had for Niki, without any expectation that she would answer.

"Hello?"

"Niki?"

"Yes, who is this?"

"Sorry, I got a new number. It's Kelly."

"Kelly?"

"Yes. Long-time no-see eh?"

"You could say that. I assume this is about Tommy?"

"Tommy? Why would you think that?"

"Well, it would be a bit of a coincidence if you had suddenly decided to look up an old friend just after your son paid me a visit. I suppose he told you he came here last week, asking about Sophie?

Kelly was trying to think on her feet. She knew nothing about this. She assumed he'd met Amy in some pub or club.

"Yes. He was just curious, and I think I was being a bit vague, so he came to you. Sorry about that."

"No. It's fine. I know how kids can be, but I told him to stay away from Amy. They seemed to be getting a bit pally."

"Oh right." This wasn't a good start.

"So why are you calling? Is something wrong?"

"No. It just got me thinking about old times, you know how it is. We all get wrapped up in our own lives and when he mentioned you I got a bit nostalgic about the old days and how close we used to be."

"Yes. I guess we all just moved on that's all."

Kelly could feel Niki wasn't going to be as receptive as she'd hoped.

"Well in the spirit of old times sake I wondered if you would like to come over for a meal sometime"

"Oh. I don't know. We don't go out much."

"Come on Niki. Where's that fun girl I used to know?"

Niki also felt a touch of nostalgia. She hadn't really had any good friends since. Not like the bond she'd had with Kelly and Sophie.

"When were you thinking of?"

"Saturday lunch? my place at twelve? I'll ask Carl."

Niki didn't reply but Kelly could still hear her breathing.

"Port and Lemon?" Kelly enticingly, "or is that too old-fashioned now?"

"The classics never go out of fashion!" she exclaimed, amusingly.

"So?"

"So, I'll tell Pete he's going." She conceded.

It was an obvious reference to the way they used to refer to Pete as being under the thumb.

"Great" Kelly punched the air when she ended the call.

"She had her plan in place. She was going to fix this for Tommy and Amy. Everything was going to be fine."

Niki punched the sofa as the call ended. She'd allowed herself to be manipulated by Kelly just as she always had. Now she was heading back to contact with the boy she had washed her hands of and his malignant insanity.

She was however, looking forward to seeing the condo that most women seemed to talk about. She was also a little excited at the prospect of having the famous Kelly Palmer as one of her friends.

Kelly was already arranging for caterers to deliver an impressive lunch on Saturday, and to make sure there was an adequate supply of champagne, wine, beer, liqueurs and obviously a very expensive vintage port.

She knew Niki had reservations about Tommy and she knew she wanted to distance herself and her family from the terrible memories, but she also knew that people can be seduced in many ways. Pete always had a severe lust for wealth and she was sure that the idea of his daughter getting her feet under the Palmer table would be practically irresistible.

Fickle though it may seem, Kelly was in no doubt that when it came to gentle persuasion, hard cash was the greatest seductress of all.

She sat on the four-poster bed with her crystal glass in her hand and looked around the magnificent hotel suite with its tall ceiling, gold pelmets and heavy velvet drapes.

What parent could walk into Kelly's world and not want a slice of it for their daughter?

Two rooms down the corridor, Amy and Tommy were resting in each other's arms after making love.

"Sometimes I sense that you feel some sort of loyalty to your first mum?" Amy said softly, "to Sophie. Almost regret or something?"

Tommy was taken aback and thankful that her head was on his chest, where she wouldn't notice his expression.

"What makes you think that?"

"I don't know. It's like there's a sort of agitated sorrow in your voice when you speak of her."

Tommy hadn't realised he's shown any emotion at all when he mentioned Sophie, but obviously, she'd picked up on something.

"Guilt I suppose." He hadn't decided how far he was prepared to go with that opener.

"Guilt? It's not like you pushed her off the cliff is it?" She looked up grinning "Unless there's something you haven't told me?"

She was obviously joking but it was enough to cause him to back off a bit.

"Very funny! I guess I just wasn't a very adoring son."

"Well it sounds like she wasn't exactly mother of the year either, from what mum said?"

"No she wasn't, but back then I had no idea what she was up against. If her episodes or hallucinations or visitations or whatever you choose to call them were as real as mine, then how could she possibly accept a boy she'd never met as her son?!"

"Don't be so hard on yourself," Amy sat up, startled by the sudden abruptness in his voice, "I doubt she even noticed your lack of affection for her since her attention seemed to be focussed elsewhere, and you were just a child who wanted his real mum back weren't you?"

"How do you know all this?"

"I asked my mum all about the story of the mad boy, when she warned me away from you."

"Sounds like she doesn't blame me for any of it then?"

"No. Of course she doesn't blame you! That doesn't mean she thinks you are a sane boy from untainted stock though!" She laughed.

Tommy wished that his pedigree was the only issue. If it was only his sanity in question rather than his evil doings, he might be in with a chance of winning Niki over.

"Well, let's just say I do feel guilty about how I treated her. It all feels much worse since…."

"Since what? Since you met her again?"

"Believe me," Tommy sighed, "I know exactly how weird that sounds but yes, since I met her again. I wish I'd just said sorry or something."

"Why didn't you?"

"I don't know" he lied.

Inside he was screaming to tell her everything. He wanted to scream the truth! He wanted to say.

"Because she thought I was trying to help her so why would I be sorry?" He wanted to offload all of it. Years of wondering if she'd realised that his plan had been to kill her. If there might have been a moment of clarity. A single moment when she realised that she had been tricked. When she stopped breathing and there was just nothing. No family.

He knew it was unlikely. She'd either died or found them and either way, she would never have known what he did. Nevertheless, the notion had haunted him for years and, terrifying as it was, he hoped his recent meeting with her, and her other family, was reality.

Amy was frowning as she watched his face reacting to the thoughts in his head.

"Perhaps you should make your peace with her?"

"I'm not going to try to find her again if that's what you mean!"

"No, I don't mean that. I mean we could buy some flowers and take them to the Brigg. Say a few words or something? Tell her you're sorry for not welcoming her back? I've got this Saturday off if you want to go then?"

Tommy squeezed her hard.

"How did I ever live without you, beautiful lady?"

"It's a total mystery to me." She laughed as she kissed him hard and then slid on top of him.

"Not again?" he teased.

She licked a finger and seductively moistened a nipple.

"Oh, go on then."

Who was he to argue with a golden goddess!

Back down the corridor Kelly settled down to sleep with a smile on her face.

By Saturday night Tommy's new relationship would have the unconditional blessing of Niki and Pete.

What possible reason could either of them have to object to a match as perfect as this for Amy?

Chapter 21

On Saturday morning Kelly swung her Ferrari into the parking area of her condo with Tommy sitting silently beside her. They both got changed with an equal amount of solitude as they prepared for their respective rendezvous.

Kelly had decided not to disclose the exact nature of her plan for the day. She wanted to keep the surprise of winning over Amy's parents for later when they could all join up for evening drinks.

Tommy was a little surprised that Kelly didn't seem too hurt by his plan to lay a shrine to Sophie. He was also surprised that she had offered to lend him her car, which was something she hardly ever allowed. Partly because he would be driving it on third party insurance, but mainly because he acted like an idiot whenever he got behind that wheel.

Kelly was just grateful to get him out of the house for a few hours regardless of what sentiment he wanted to extend to Sophie or how carelessly he treated her car. Today he was out with Amy though, she knew he would at least drive safely.

He flipped the keys in the air and caught them again cockily on his way out.

"Have a great day son." Kelly called from the kitchen where she was sneakily arranging the worktop space in preparation for the caterers.

"Don't be too lonely without me!" he called back as he slipped into his walking shoes, grabbed a rain jacket and made his way along the glass corridor separating the house from the pool and onto the viewing platform.

"How could it not be a great day?" he thought, as he took a second to peer out over the sea, to the horizon.

At last his life was going in the right direction. He was starting his journey to take over Kelly's empire, he had a date with Amy, and he had the keys to a shiny red Ferrari. Life doesn't get any better than this!

Autumn was in the air but that didn't deter him from slipping on his jacket and pressing the remote to remove the car roof. He jumped in without opening the door, started the engine and turned the radio up to full volume. The whole neighbourhood would know Tommy Taylor was on the road this morning as he blasted along the narrow seafront road with his elbow on the open window and his thick blonde hair dancing merrily in the backdraft. He grinned. Before too long he would be Tommy Palmer!

By eleven thirty he was sitting in a café with Amy holding hands over the table and gazing at her face.

"I wish you would stop staring at me! It's creepy!"

"Suppose I just can't believe my luck." He grinned.

"You're such an idiot. You sweet talking bastard!" she laughed

"You have no idea, do you?" he sighed, picking up one of her hands.

She frowned for a second, anticipating some smart punch line but his face was totally serious.

"Yes ,I do." She said finally, "I know exactly what this is."

"Ok then, now that the love thing is settled, lets order some lunch!" the comedy had returned, and she hit him hard with the menu.

At the condo Kelly had set out her huge dining table with four places. Her best cutlery and the crockery that had cost more than some would spend on a new car, were already in situ.

The caterers turned up exactly on time and Carl arrived, as expected at eleven forty-five.

"My God, is the queen coming?" Carl gasped as she led him into the dining room.

Carl had only visited Kelly's home a couple of times before. He passed it regularly and always seemed to glance over but he had managed somehow to keep his exposure to it down to a minimum.

He didn't begrudge her the success she was enjoying, far from it. He knew, without any doubt, that what she had could never make up for the years of sacrifice she had made for him. He knew she would have given all of this up in a heartbeat to have had a child of her own. The sibling she always craved for Tommy, and the love she craved from Carl.

He knew he could never repair the damage he'd done. The years of keeping her hanging on a thread, always hoping. The years of devotion she had given which he had accepted thoughtlessly and selfishly while he yearned for Sophie. He knew that finally trying to commit to her only after discovering Sophie's treacherous disloyalty had been the final fatal blow that closed her heart.

Kelly didn't love men anymore, she played with them. She didn't trust them or even want to. She toyed with them because she wanted to punish them. All of them. She wanted to punish the men who tried to love her, them because she couldn't punish Carl. She wanted mostly to punish them for not *being* Carl.

She no longer wanted him, he knew that, because he had tried a hundred times before settling for Sonya, but still, he knew that he was to blame for her childless life and her numerous toy-boys.

He looked back along the glass corridor, over her indoor pool and out to the horizon. It wasn't a bad way to cheer up a broken heart, that was for sure, and no matter how many times he gave himself the same lecture, he was still gripped with envy and jealousy every time he saw this place.

He hated that she was providing Tommy with all the things he couldn't give. That was her payback and it was devastatingly absolute.

"I'm feeling a bit nervous." She confessed as she handed him a gin and tonic.

"It's just Niki and Pete," he replied casually, "Try to remember that."

She returned to her glass-topped bar and poured one for herself.

She had her hair in an intricate 'updo' that would have been fit for a bride.

"Your hair looks nice." Carl said, in an attempt to fill the awkward silence.

"One of my girls popped round earlier to fix it for me." She smiled politely as though they had just met. As though there were no history between them, but as he watched her walk away to sit down, he remembered every moment of that history.

Her outline had not changed an inch. She was wearing a pale rose silk catsuit that gently touched every contour of her hour-glass figure. The zipper at the front was high enough to conceal her cleavage but low enough to show the curve of her breasts that eluded to one. She still walked with the confidence of a catwalk model, with her head high and as he watched her lower herself elegantly onto a chair, he wished he could just touch her skin for a moment.

Outside came the noise of tyres on the gravel of her private carpark area. Two car doors slammed, followed by footsteps up the steps.

"Oh my God Pete, just look at this place!"

Kelly blushed slightly at Niki's outburst.

Pete shook Carl's hand firmly.

"Nice to see you again mate."

"You too. Fancy a beer?"

Kelly frowned at Carl's audacity at assuming the role of host, but she decided to let it go.

They sat at the dining table and Kelly brought in the exquisite buffet while they chatted about old times and Pete nibbled on things he didn't even recognise.

Finally, over coffee, it was Niki who decided to cut to the chase.

"So why are we really here?"

It was the moment that Carl would always remember as the game changer. The pivotal moment in which their lives would be changed forever.

Carl and Kelly exchanged a glance. Niki saw it.

"I'm not stupid Kelly," she continued, "we haven't heard from you for years and suddenly Tommy turns up at our door and now this. Something is going on!"

Kelly took a deep breath before speaking softly to her old friends.

"It's about Tommy and Amy."

"Tommy and Amy? There is no Tommy and Amy! What are you talking about?"

Carl took over the conversation.

"Tommy thinks you believe he's unstable, mentally I mean. He thinks you don't want him getting friendly with Amy, in case he's inherited some madness. Some sort of condition from Sophie."

"He's damn right I don't want him getting friendly with Amy!"

She wanted so badly to tell them what he did but she had made a bargain and it was more important that Tommy stayed away than the satisfaction she would get from finally telling his parents what a conniving little shit he was.

Kelly and Carl were knocked speechless at the venomous retort.

Pete simply stared at his wife with some unidentified morsel of food sitting in his open mouth.

No-one spoke.

Down on the seafront Tommy and Amy were walking along the clifftop, with the large bouquet of red roses Tommy had bought from a florist in Scarborough.

Amy held his hand tightly. It had been a lovely morning. She loved that Tommy had taken up her idea of making peace with his late mother. It made her feel valued.

She had loved their trip into Scarborough that morning when they had bought matching hiking boots in the tiny store that smelled of leather and canvas. Mostly she had loved the way he nudged her when they had walked by a jewellery shop and whispered.

"If you want a surprise, you'd need to give me a hint on what you like."

She hadn't taken him seriously. She didn't dare to take him seriously but as she walked beside him along the clifftop with her hand firmly in his, she knew it had been no joke on his part.

Finally, Tommy stopped walking and moved towards the edge of the cliff.

"This is it," he said calmly, "this is the spot."

Amy moved a little closer to the edge and peered over. It was a two hundred foot drop down onto a gravel beach. Her legs turned to jelly, and she had to take a step back.

"It wasn't like this then," Tommy added, "It was evening time in January, the tide was in. Not the same at midday in September you know?"

It didn't matter to Amy. Tide or no tide, she still felt nauseous at the idea that anyone could find the courage to do it. She wasn't even sure water would make any difference. If anything, she thought that it might make the whole prospect even more terrifying.

She watched Tommy's face as he lay down the roses and made some sort of silent prayer to his biological mother, and for the first time since she had heard the story, she was beginning to grasp the horror and the magnitude of it. Of the unimaginable trauma Tommy had suffered as a small boy.

Kelly was pouring the coffee and trying to think of something constructive to break the silence, but Carl suddenly shoved his size elevens right into it.

"Well, let's just say it's a bit late for that." He blurted carelessly.

Niki's face turned purple.

"What do you mean?!"

Kelly tried to repair the damage as she shot Carl a reprimanding scowl.

"We brought you here because we heard that the two of them had become closer Nik, and Tommy thought you needed some reassurance about him."

"Closer? What do you mean closer?!"

Pete put his hand over Niki's in an effort to calm her down.

"It's fine love. Let's just listen to what they have to say about Tommy and then, if we need to, we will talk to Amy"

"I asked how close?" Niki was rising to her feet, "how close Kelly?"

Kelly sighed and looked towards Pete for alliance, but Niki was already marching round the table towards her.

She leaned over until her face was only an inch from Kelly's illuminated foundation.

"Where is he?!"

"Niki, sit down." Carl said politely, as the enormity of his recklessness was beginning to resonate.

"Are they together now?! Are they? Are they?!"

Kelly put her head in her hands for a moment. The damage was already done. There was no use in lying.

"They were going for a walk on the beach this afternoon. Tommy wanted to lay some flowers down on the Brigg for Sophie."

"Oh, I bet he did!" she growled as she jumped up and headed for the door, "come on Pete, we're leaving!"

Pete rose up obediently, shrugging an apology to his host as he hurried to catch her up.

As they ran down the steps toward their car, with their coats flying behind them, Kelly turned to Carl in horror.

"She's going after them!" she screamed causing him to drop his coffee cup on the table, "Come on, we'll have to take your car, Tommy's got mine!"

Tommy and Amy had walked a way along the Brigg and were walking back slowly, arms around each other, enjoying the last rays of the September sun. Out near the water line, a man was throwing a ball into the waves for his dog and a child with bare feet, was jumping in the puddles left by the tide. Amy remembered doing that herself, determined to paddle, refusing to accept that the summer was finally over.

Tommy turned to Amy for an affectionate peck and then frowned at the sight of four adults fifty yards away, hurtling towards them screaming with arms akimbo.

He instinctively pushed Amy behind him while he assessed the situation.

His grip on Amy tightened as the woman in front came into focus.

"My God, that's your mum!"

Amy pushed him aside and stepped forward.

"Mum! What on earth's wrong?" Amy's eyes were quickly scanning the faces of the others as she checked for who might be missing.

"Is it Dean? What's happened?"

Niki ignored her daughter completely as she strode forward and squared up to Tommy.

"We had a deal Tommy! Remember?"

"Deal? What deal?" Amy snapped.

Tommy shuffled uncomfortably. He was going to try to defuse this, but the feeling of dread was already creeping over him.

"You were to stay away from my daughter, and in return I was to keep your evil little secret!"

Amy turned to Tommy for reassurance.

"It's ok Amy." He soothed as he squeezed her hand.

"What the fuck are you talking about Nik?" Pete snapped as he tried to bodily remove her from Tommy's face.

"Ah! You see there are things you don't know about little Tommy here, aren't there Tommy?"

Niki was still in mid conversation when she fell sideways under the impact of Kelly's thrust.

"Get out of my son's face Nik! If you have anything to say just say it!"

It was the centre stage Niki wanted. Everyone was listening. It was the moment she had dreamed of for years. Of finally having a reason to expose Tommy for what he was.

"This little brat. This spoilt evil little brat murdered Sophie! Go on Tommy, tell them how you managed to kill your own mother."

Carl was stunned. He looked from one person to another as he tried to make sense of it.

"You see," she snarled, "he gathered together all her bits of paper, things about her fantasies and then he pretended he had heard it all from her imaginary daughter! How clever was that for a young boy eh? She jumped off the fuckin Brigg because he'd convinced her they were all out there somewhere, waiting for her. You should be flattered Kelly, he did it for you! All for you!"

Kelly and Carl both starred at Niki and then straight at Tommy.

Carl was the first to speak.

"Is this true Tommy?"

Tommy let go of Amy's hand and stepped forward towards his father.

"Dad, I didn't know what she would…"

Carl lurched at Tommy, knocking him to the ground and in a split second, Kelly grabbed him from behind.

"Get off him Carl!" she had one arm around his throat from behind and the other had his mop of brown grey hair in her fist.

"He was a bloody child! What did he know?! Get off him!"

Carl was choking, he couldn't speak. Kelly rolled him sideways and pulled Tommy back to his feet.

As Carl was trying to get his breath, Kelly gave him a thunderous kick in the stomach.

"How dare you attack our son?! And for what? You still defending that bitch who didn't give a shit about you, are you? You're pathetic Carl, fuckin pathetic."

Even Niki had taken a step away. She had never seen rage like this before, it was almost inhuman.

Everyone stood back as Kelly stood her ground in front of Tommy, narrowing her eyes as she glanced at each in turn. Challenging any of them to try to get through her. She may have been nothing more than a petite woman in a pink silk jumpsuit but at that moment she was something else entirely. She was a tigress protecting her cub and she was prepared to die in the process if necessary.

Everyone remained still, still and silent until her rage subsided, her breathing quietened and her body relaxed.

She then turned back to Tommy.

"You two go. I'll meet you at the condo."

Tommy brushed himself down and reached for Amy's hand. For a moment she hesitated. She looked over at Niki. Niki was defying her to disobey. She blinked slowly and then took Tommy's hand.

As the couple started to walk away, Niki's heart was pounding. She had played her hand and it hadn't worked. Kelly had ruined it with her obsessive protection for her son.

As she watched the couple walk away almost cradled in each other's arms she had a choice to make.

She had played her hand, but she was still holding one card. She was holding the trump card that would win her the game, but she knew the absolute cost of playing it.

She watched them walk along the cliff until they were almost out of earshot and then she filled her lungs.

"He's your brother!"

Both figures stopped instantly.

She couldn't remember seeing them turn around, she only remembered seeing them stop.

She could feel Pete's stare. She met it defiantly. Carl was moving towards her. Kelly was frowning as though she couldn't understand the implication. All eyes were on her. This was not the centre stage she wanted.

Silence fell for the second time as the six figures stood motionless on the Brigg.

In the silence, she could feel her secret bleeding slowly into the minds of every one of them. It was changing everything. It was re-writing history. Changing everything they thought they knew, everything they had ever felt, everything they had believed.

The silence was broken by a sound that chilled her soul. She had never heard such a sound before. It was more like a howl from the depths of hell and it was coming from Pete.

He fell to his knees for a matter of only a few seconds and then he fell silent.

Carl was still watching him when he suddenly reared up like a phoenix and lurched forward. Carl hit the ground from the force of the blow as he heard the crack of Pete's fist hit the side of his head.

He was still trying to get up when the punch from Tommy knocked him back down.

Niki was screaming at Pete and Amy was wrestling to restrain Tommy.

Kelly did nothing.

She just watched while her son avenged her. She was beyond feeling any hurt from Carl, he had betrayed her a thousand times in a thousand ways and this new revelation had no impact, but as Tommy threw another punch she relished the moment for what it was.

All hell had broken loose but as she watched the fists fly, saw the figures reel, and heard the savage cries she knew this was the moment of reckoning.

Carl had slept with Niki while she'd been the idiot who was probably, at that very moment, caring for the child he'd made with Sophie, but even that couldn't hurt her now. Her heart was frozen to Carl and he could inflict no more pain on her but this time it wasn't her who was suffering from his egotistical actions.

As she watched Tommy throw another punch, she was far from indifferent. She was enraged that his inability to keep it in his pants had ruined Tommy's future, and for that alone she wanted to kill him.

Tommy stood up as Carl lay squirming on the grass. He looked at Amy. She was crying. He kissed her hand and then backed away.

"Tommy."

He couldn't bare to hear her voice.

Kelly could see the pain in his face and walked over to put her arm around him.

"Leave me alone!" he was crying and shaking at the same time.

"Leave me alone, all of you!"

"I'm sorry Tommy." Niki said softly.

"Sorry?!" he screamed, "You're fuckin sorry?! I've been sleeping with my own sister you stupid bitch!"

As Carl tried to get up, Pete gave him another shove and stormed away.

"I can't deal with this! Find some other mug to put you up tonight Nik."

"Dad!" Amy sobbed.

"Well that's just it, isn't it? Apparently, I'm not!"

Pete strode off towards his car, towards his new life with his disappointment of a son and without the one shining star in his whole pathetic world. Without his little princess.

Tommy paid no attention to Pete's departure or of his cutting words to Amy. He couldn't absorb any more. He couldn't think anymore.

He banged his head with the heel of his hand several times as he backed away from them all. Away from his madness and hallucinations, away from his fear of ever going to sleep again, away from his incestuous love for his own sister.

"Tommy, keep still" It was Kelly's voice

Tommy was still backing away. He was only inches from the edge.

"Tommy. Come here love. You're near the edge."

Tommy hit his head again.

Kelly saw his foot slip over the edge, his body drop, his eyes as they disappeared, but then she heard his gasp.

They all ran to the edge. He was clinging to a clump of tall grass about six feet from the top.

"I'll get my rope from the car!" Carl shouted and was gone.

"There's no time!" Kelly screamed at him, but he was already racing toward the road.

Amy fell to her knees closer to the edge than she ever thought she'd dare.

"Your dad's coming with a rope Tommy. Just hold on a few seconds."

She was trying to hide the feeling of hopelessness in her heart as the roots of the clump started to become exposed.

"I'm going down!." Kelly screamed, to no-one in particular.

Niki and Amy exchanged a glance of disbelief.

"I can slide down onto that rock, right there, look! It's only an arms-length away from him. I can do this!"

Kelly sat on the edge and turned onto her stomach. Carl was already at the car with the rope in his hand. As she lowered her legs and slowly allowed herself to slither down the steep slope.

Amy and Niki instantly got on board. It was pure insanity, but it was the bravest act they had ever seen.

"A bit to your left Kell!" Niki called.

Kelly slowly made her decent to the outcrop of rock which was directly opposite her dangling son.

His desperate, terrified eyes met hers.

"It's going to be ok Tommy. Mum's here."

Tommy glared at her, the strands of grass in his hand were snapping one by one, he could feel them. Kelly could hear them. There was no time to wait for Carl.

She faced the cliff and reached out to her right.

"Can you reach my hand Tommy?"

Tommy tried to make a swing for it and several strands snapped instantly.

"Don't move!" Kelly soothed, "gently. Just gently reach for my hand."

Tommy extended his left arm to it's full reach. His hand touched Kelly's. He could feel her warm fingers curling around his hand softly and slowly they started to close, and then she was gone.

He closed his eyes and heard the sickening thud.

"Grab the rope!" Carl shouted, "don't look down son, grab the rope."

Tommy hadn't felt the rope drop onto his face from above. He didn't feel his hand curl instinctively around it, or his other hand release the last strands of grass.

He remembered the smell of the heather as he lay on the cliff top with people shouting and hugging and crying and stroking.

He remembered his dad trying to stop him from looking over the edge.

He remembered the broken doll in a pink silk jumpsuit lying on the beach with her leg grotesquely twisted beneath her. He remembered her left foot resting silently behind her ear over her right shoulder. He remembered the red halo of blood around her beautiful face.

He remembered the crowds and the constant hue of blue flashing lights.

He remembered being bundled into an ambulance wearing a blanket.

He remembered feeling an emptiness he had never felt before.

The emptiness that would never again be filled.

Chapter 22

An hour after being admitted, Tommy discharged himself from hospital after refusing the sedative that they were trying to give him for shock. A sedative meant sleep and he couldn't handle the prospect waking up in yet another nightmare. This nightmare was already more than he could bear. The most he could handle was to sit and stare at the wall. It didn't matter what wall and for that, the hospital was as good a place as any, but not when they were constantly trying to send him to sleep!

Amy had remained by his side while Niki and Carl sat in the waiting area. Carl needed to stay close to his son and Niki had nowhere else to go. Neither of them uttered a single word. There was too much to say and yet there was nothing worth saying.

By six in the evening they were all back at Carl's house sitting around the dining table, armed with untouched brandy, staring blankly into space.

The sorrow, the heartbreak, the chest beating, the remorse, the horror, the regrets and the remorse were all to be saved for some time in the future. Right now, there was room for only one emotion from Kelly's death and that was shock.

No-one knew what they should or could say to the others. No-one knew how anyone might react to anything.

Tommy's only thought was of Kelly. He remembered her vow to solve this or to die trying. He remembered every sacrifice she'd ever made for him. Every sleepless night when she'd gone into his room to comfort him while his dad slept on. Every school play she'd cancelled appointments to attend while his dad went out on a breakdown. Then he remembered the children she never had, the ones she's forsaken to stick with Carl and to be his mum. He never told her that he knew how much she'd sacrificed for him. He wished he could have at least told her. He wished he had screamed it at her as she fell so at least she would have known it.

He clenched his fists and screamed at the universe until his lungs felt like they were about to burst.

No-one spoke.

Silence was resumed and faces returned to blank and eyes returned to stares.

Eventually Niki was the one to break the numb silence.

"I'm sorry Tommy."

Tommy looked up as though surprised she wasn't still screaming at him as if he were the devil child. As soon as he realised the barrier of hatred had gone, he reached across the table and she took his hand.

"Do you think I'm insane?"

Niki stroked his hand as though he were an injured animal.

"I know you're not insane Tommy. I had my own unforgiveable reason for trying to keep you two apart."

Tommy withdrew his hand gently and shook his head.

"No. You're probably right. I'm not exactly the most level-headed person around right now."

Amy placed her hand on his lap under the table to reassure him.

Niki looked Tommy directly in the face.

"It was selfish of me to say what I did about you. I promised I would never tell because I knew you were just a child who wanted his mummy back. I broke that promise"

"I deserved it though, didn't I?"

Carl felt the rage beginning to rise again at the thought of Sophie being tricked into ending her life. He knew this was no time for another outburst, so he simply took a mouthful of brandy and kept silent.

"You gave her what she wanted Tommy. You gave her hope."

Tommy frowned at the woman who seemed to have turned from Hyde to Jekyll in an instant.

"You're not evil Tommy, and you are not insane. I know that for a fact."

"How could you know anything of the sort? You've no idea what's happened to me in the last two weeks!"

"I do Tommy and I know it's not insanity" She took his hand back in hers and held it tightly when he tried again to withdraw it.

"Listen Tommy. I never believed Sophie. I really thought she was having hallucinations or nightmares or psychotic episodes or something. Never once did I even allow myself to believe a single syllable she uttered, but I know something now. Something I didn't realise until we spoke in the café. Remember what you said?

"Some of it"

Tommy didn't care what he'd said in the café. It didn't matter anymore. Nothing mattered anymore. Kelly had gone.

"You told me that in this weird dream of yours, you couldn't find your father?"

Carl looked offended, as though his son had somehow erased him.

"What of it?" Tommy sighed without wanting the answer.

Afterwards, I drove home in a daze. I couldn't believe what you'd told me. I drank two bottles of wine. I kept trying to pass it off as a weird coincidence, but I know it wasn't.

Tommy allowed his attention to move for a moment from the shock of his mother's death to the horror of his other life.

"What coincidence?"

Niki took a deep breath.

Once again, her audience waited in bated breath for some mammoth revelation.

"You kept telling me that everything you experienced was from your imagination. From things you already knew?"

"Yes, they were. There were a few things that seemed unlikely, but we managed to find a logical explanation for every single one, even though a couple of them seemed to be stretching it a bit"

"We?"

"Yes, Amy and I." He said meekly.

Niki was past being annoyed at the illicit liaison.

"Well I really don't believe in any kind of hocus pocus as you know but when you told me about your father not being there, my blood ran cold."

"Why?" Tommy asked irritably, "What's relevant about that?"

Niki breathed audibly once again.

"Tommy, your mother told me a lot of detail about this other existence of hers and among it all she told me that when she left and ran away with John…"

She paused and looked sympathetically at Carl.

"What?" Tommy asked, "What did she tell you?"

"She told me that your father hanged himself in their old flat."

Tommy could feel his legs starting to shake. This made sickening, hideous, terrifying sense. He remembered thinking, the moment he saw Jake's wedding ring, that Kelly would never have married Jake. Not unless his dad was no longer within her reach.

He stared at Niki as he tried to control the activity in his legs.

"That might explain why Kelly and Jake were together, but it doesn't explain why neither Kelly nor Grandad knew me. I would have grown up around here. Neither of them knew me. Why wouldn't they know me!" he was getting close to hysterical.

"Niki! You're scaring him to death with all this rubbish!" Carl snapped angrily.

Niki's hands were shaking as uncontrollably as Tommy's legs.

Tommy asked again.

"Why did no-one know me Niki? Why?"

"Because Sophie told me that she was shocked to see you when she woke up. She was shocked because, in this other life she's discovered she was pregnant with your dad's baby."

"And?"

Niki started to cry.

"Well, as soon as she knew you didn't belong to John… I'm sorry Tommy. She said she had an abortion."

Tommy stared at her, as though she had just shot him.

"She aborted me?"

"I don't know what to make of it all Tommy" Niki said as she sat on her hands to try to control the shaking," but I do know that it's one hell of a co-incidence. It's not something you could have known about."

Tommy stood up and walked over to the window.

He recalled Sophie with her new life. He remembered every detail of it. All the years he had carried the guilt of what he did to her, and she aborted him!

He could hear his dad and Amy and Niki trying to talk to him, but it was no more than distance babbling.

He knew for certain that no dream could ever be that real. There was no doubt at all in his mind now.

He turned back to the whispering at the table and interrupted. "Come on Amy, we need to leave."

No-one argued but Carl threw an anxious glance at Niki.

Niki said nothing so Carl stood up as though trying to deter them.

"You have a lot of things to sort out Tommy. You've inherited a very big empire you know."

Tommy didn't answer but held his hand out to Amy.

Amy stood up and moved to his side.

"We need to leave," she said meekly, "Tommy is safer in Harrogate tonight, no matter what this thing is that's haunting him."

"I'll go pack a few things," Tommy said as he tugged Amy towards the stairs, "I'll come back and sort out the condo when I feel up to it."

As soon as they were out of earshot Carl whispered to Niki.

"They are brother and sister!"

"I think we all know that!"

"Well what are they doing?"

Niki put her hand on Carl's shoulder as she stood up.

"They are adults. Let them sort it out for themselves. I think they've had enough heartache, don't you?"

Carl poured another brandy

"I guess so, but you know they can't ever have children, don't you?"

"It might not come to that. Let's just leave them alone. We've all done enough damage."

Tommy returned with his rucksack.

"We'll come back tomorrow for more stuff, but I need to get on the road"

Carl and Niki hugged them both and as the door closed, they sat back down in silence for a while.

"You know what?" Niki smiled softly, "This kind of makes us a family."

Carl squeezed her hand, "I guess it does."

Niki picked up her drink and went over to the window to look up at the darkening sky.

"You know what else?" she didn't wait for a response, "The one thing Kelly feared was to fall in love?"

"I didn't know that!"

"Oh yes, she used to sit on her bar stool giggling and mocking us for wanting a love to die for. She called it dangerous. She was going to be the one to play it safe."

"Well she certainly did that in the end with all the casual affairs!" Carl added, slightly sarcastically.

Niki turned to face him.

"The hell she did! She'd had that kind of love all along!"

Carl frowned.

"The kind of love she feared the most. The love she would lay down her life for. You handed it to her the moment you put that baby boy in her arms."

Carl walked over and pulled her towards him for comfort. He knew she was right. The love Kelly felt for Tommy was far beyond anything he'd seen in a mother before. Tommy had been her world.

Niki held him close, she was shaking.

"You're shivering!" Carl said, taking off his jacket and wrapping it around her shoulders.

"Emotion and nerves I think." She replied as she stepped back to close it over her chest.

As she walked back to the table Carl pulled out her chair for her and kissed her affectionately on the top of the head.

Niki's heart missed a beat.

She had seen this behaviour from Carl before.

It was just like with Sophie.

Chapter 23

In the Harrogate hotel Amy and Tommy opened the door of their room and looked around.

Tommy picked up the new laptop Kelly had given him for his new job. He stroked his hand over the top of it affectionately. Inside it was his schedule for the next three weeks.

The visit to the supplier of state-of-the-art treadmills, the meeting with the cleaning contractors, the demonstration with the technology company who wanted to sell their suite of data collection tools from the customer's swipe cards. All the things he was going to do with his mum.

The laptop didn't know anything had changed. The laptop was happily keeping the schedule safely under that lid. He gently put it aside without disturbing it.

Amy was still standing at the door.

He walked towards her and held both her hands in his.

"I don't know what any of this means either." He whispered as his hands dropped from hers and he moved over to the window.

"I'm going for a walk. I'll be back in a few minutes."

"You'll freeze out there!" Amy protested as he left the room in a short-sleeved shirt.

Tommy didn't acknowledge her. He wouldn't feel the cold because he couldn't feel anything at all.

He walked out into the hotel grounds and looked up at the night sky. It was a beautiful electric blue, studded with stars. There was a huge ribbon of light cascading diagonally from way above his head right down to the horizon. It was as though the sun had found a slit in the dark cloak of the night through which it could peep. He gazed into it. That fissure of light breaking through the shield of darkness. For a moment he imagined it to be the entrance to his other world.

A doorway. A crevice through which he could slither in the way Anne had described. He couldn't take his eyes off it. It seemed to be beckoning him, daring him, mocking him.

He stood with one leg on a large bolder as the tears ran freely down his cheeks.

Somewhere Sophie was making supper while John sipped his whisky. Somewhere Vicky was telling them all about her first week at college and the absence of the boy she had brought home. He wondered what they all thought had happened to him. He was in their house and then he what? Just disappeared?

He remembered feeling like he was being dragged somewhere but to where? Perhaps Becky had stashed him somewhere. Perhaps he was sleeping the days away, just like Sophie or maybe she was looking for somewhere to hide his body. He shuddered.

His macabre thoughts slowed down the tears until the next surge hit him.

He thought of Kelly. Somewhere Kelly would be putting her son to bed. Her own son. Her real son. Not the one she had inherited from the woman who didn't want him, and the man who treated her like shit.

He started to sob. The ribbon of light that he'd been imagining to be some sort of door in the universe, ceased to hold any allure for him.

The Kelly who lived in that place didn't know him. She had never held him or taken him to school. She'd never laughed with him, ruffled his hair or and drank cocktails with him on a cruise ship. The Kelly beyond that dark sky had never bundled him away to Scotland to protect him or hiked in the hills with him. She hadn't cooked supper on that tiny stove or slept on a mattress in the rustic lounge of that tiny cottage.

The Kelly beyond that light was happy. That Kelly had never loved him. She had no memories of him, but it didn't matter because he remembered every single moment. He remembered it all for both of them.

He blew a kiss into the starry night sky and slowly returned to the hotel.

Amy was sitting on the bed waiting. As soon as the door opened, she rushed and folded her arms around him, and he sobbed again into her hair.

"Let's just get a shower and try to get some sleep?" she said decisively.

"Sounds good. I'm bushed!"

They showered separately for the first time, and then lay side by side in the huge bed, staring at the ceiling.

Eventually her hand searched for his and he squeezed it tightly.

"Try not to think about it." She whispered.

Tommy had replayed the horrific event in his head a hundred times already. The sound of that sickening thud as Kelly's body hit the beach. The touch of her hand as she tried to curl her small hand around his. Her sheer determination to refuse to believe she couldn't save him, that somehow her mental strength would compensate for her small frame. It was madness to think she would ever be able to hold his weight, but he'd gone along with it.

He closed his eyes tightly and tried to remember what was going through his mind in that moment. Why he didn't try to stop her. Was it because she was his mum and he trusted her? Or was it that he was just so desperate, he allowed her to take the risk.

He banged his fists angrily on the bed.

Amy's hand returned to his after being thrust aside with the impact.

"It's not your fault." She tried to reassure him.

Tommy was staring back at the ceiling.

"How is it you always know what I'm thinking?"

Amy hesitated before she replied.

"Perhaps it's in our blood."

Tommy turned on his side to look at her.

"How could something this cruel have happened?"

She wasn't sure if he was talking about Kelly or their love.

"I don't know."

"I thought it would change everything instantly, you know. I thought that knowing what we know would dissolve all the feelings I have and replace them with disgust"

"It doesn't though, does it?"

"Nope. It doesn't."

She stroked his brow gently as she nestled back down beside him.

"You know that our birth certificates show different fathers?" she said, still staring, still stroking.

"What of it?"

"Well that means that legally we haven't done anything wrong."

"Yep, but now we know, don't we?"

"Yes, we do, but the rest of the world doesn't"

"What are you saying?" His tone suddenly changed to somewhere between horror and hope.

"I'm just clarifying the situation, that's all."

He sat up and looked down at her. There was the hint of a smile at the corner of her mouth.

"Are you suggesting?"

She shrugged.

He frowned.

"Could you honestly revert to being my brother?" she asked, "could you watch me date and then marry some other man?"

Even the words made his stomach churn.

"Not a chance."

"I know that I couldn't watch you date another girl. I just couldn't"

"So, what does that mean?" he asked defeatedly.

"I think it means we either get out of each other's lives completely, forever, or..."

"Or what?"

She slid her hand onto his chest and then kissed him gently on the lips.

"Or this."

Tommy slid his hand over her stomach and pulled her close, as her arms folded around him.

Chapter 24

On Christmas Eve 2029 Amy was attempting to make eggnog, while Tommy was messing with the programmer on the tree lights again.

"Freddie! Will you please give your sister her stocking back?"

Little Kelly was crying again.

Freddie reluctantly handed back the stocking.

"When will Grandma and Grandad be here? I'm fed up of waiting!" he moaned as his baby sister took her stocking back triumphantly.

Both children had the same striking blonde hair as their parents. That was the beauty of having enough money to find the perfect sperm doner.

Their huge house had been tastefully renovated but it's two-acre garden had been left untouched with its orchard and natural meadow area. Amy liked the children to be closer to nature with swings made from ropes hanging from trees and a wooden homemade tree house.

"They're here now!" Amy called gratefully, as she heard the tyres on the circular gravel drive.

The house was only a few miles from the Flagship Spa Tommy had created in his mother's honour. He knew she would have loved it. He had worked relentlessly on it after her death.

It had been the distraction that he desperately needed, but it had been more than that. He wanted to do her proud. He had opened that laptop and kept every damn appointment!

Unaccompanied, untrained but determined. He had made his mark and made it well. The company now bore the affectionate name of Kelly Palmer & Son.

"I hope your car's fully charged son, as I've just pinched your charge point" Carl announced as he dumped a bag of gifts in the hallway.

"Mine doesn't need a charger any more dad! I keep telling you that. It's self-charging!" Tommy shook his head in disbelief that he'd forgotten again and then frowned back at the Christmas light console.

Not a single light on the enormous tree was lit.

"I still can't get used to these bloody upside- down houses either," Carl continued, "bedrooms should be upstairs and living rooms down!"

Tommy shook his head again and then smiled as the lights sprang into action.

"Oh my God, what is that Amy?" Niki squealed as she entered the kitchen and peered at the curdled liquid in the bowl.

Amy clenched her fists and growled.

"I can never make this bloody stuff!"

"You got more eggs love?"

"Not enough." Amy said defeatedly as she poured it down the sink, the same as every other year.

Tommy came in to wash his hands, stared at the congealed yellow gunk then proceeded to relocate the numerous pans of peeled vegetables and the huge raw Turkey that was still defrosting.

"I don't know why you don't just buy eggnog! In fact, I don't know why you do all this retro stuff. Why can't we just get a drone Christmas dinner delivery like any other family with our resources?"

"You say that every year!" Amy retorted, "It's traditional and it's more fun. I like the smell of a turkey roasting on Christmas morning"

"Yeah, well I like the taste of eggnog and look how well that went!" he teased as he flicked a blob of the congealed gunk in her face.

Niki took off her coat and rolled up her sleeves while Carl followed Tommy back into the lounge, where Freddie was trying to teach his little sister how to play dominoes.

"But I don't wike that one, I wike this one!" Kelly said as she clutched the double six in her tiny hand.

"Let her keep it." Carl said to Freddie who was starting to turn red with rage. "and you come to daddy Kelly. That's a great domino and we need to play it right away!"

She climbed up on Tommy's knee and opened her tiny palm to allow him to take the treasured domino.

Carl gave Tommy's shoulder a squeeze as he passed by to sit down.

"Do you ever wish the kids were your own?" He asked quietly.

"They are my own!" Tommy retorted.

"You know what I mean."

"Well if you're asking if I wish they had my genes then no I don't. At least I know they haven't a chance of inheriting anything sinister, don't I?"

"Yes, you have a point there," Carl agreed before continuing, "but do you find it more difficult to bond with them? You know, not being of the same blood so to speak."

Tommy laughed out loud.

"When it comes to bonding and loving a child that's not strictly your own, well, I think I had the best role model ever don't you? I mean, I was taught by the master of it!"

Carl blushed. Tommy still had the same love for Kelly as he always had, and it hurt to hear him reiterate it.

He knew the connection Tommy had with her was still colossal compared to the one between father and son. The one that Carl had been working on relentlessly and devotedly since her death.

He smiled at Tommy and nodded his acceptance. It didn't matter how hard Carl tried to make up for lost time. He had left just about all the parenting to Kelly and he deserved the reminder of it.

"Looks like the drinks are here!" He announced cheerily as he nudged Tommy to open the door for Niki who was standing with a tray as she tried to push the heavy wooden door.

She poured the mulled wine it into the Christmas cups and handed them out along with orange juice for the children.

"Merry Christmas everyone!" Tommy said as they all raised their glasses.

"Not exactly eggnogg though is it?" Amy said apologetically.

"It's the thought that counts." Niki added quickly.

"Yeah and she should have thought of buying some in!" Tommy ridiculed.

Tommy took his drink and made his way out onto the balcony with its cream limestone steps leading down into the garden. The night sky reminded him of another sky many years ago.

A dark blue starry sky with a slither of light across it, almost like the sun was still trying to filter through a crack.

Amy came up behind him, kissed him gently on the cheek and then went back inside. She knew exactly what he was thinking. She always had.

He continued to peer at the streak of light as though trying to peep into what lie beyond. He closed his eyes to try to feel it. To sense it or to imagine it.

His eyes were still closed when Carl walked up beside him.

"Is it happening again?" he asked calmly.

Carl knew it was approaching. He kept track of the solar cycle religiously and he already knew that the dormant sun was about to start its new cycle. Soon, sun spots would start to emerge into the otherwise silent space.

"Yep," he replied, "The minimum is over. She's waking up again."

He patted Tommy on the shoulder.

He knew his son was thinking of Kelly. Every ounce of energy he had put into growing her empire into the giant it was today, had been for her. For her legacy. To make her proud.

He also knew that Tommy believed she was still out there.

"You need to leave it alone son."

"I know."

"You will then, won't you?"

"I don't know."

"You can't be thinking of returning to Filey?"

"I need to one day, dad."

"No, you don't! Just sell the condo and get someone else to clear it out! It's been left like a shrine long enough!"

Tommy turned to face his father without trying to mask his tears.

"Dad. I can't leave this alone forever. You know I can't. I keep thinking that maybe if I had explained everything to her and Jake that day."

"You keep thinking what? That she would suddenly remember you or something?"

"Maybe. Or there might just be some glimmer of recognition. I know Kelly and I know she would have tried to understand it. I don't know why I just ran away"

"Tommy. You have a family to think of. You can't start off this bloody madness all over again."

Tommy sighed.

"I tried to grieve for Kelly. You know I did. I tried to be normal, like to wish for that one last conversation, for one last moment with her but I couldn't. I couldn't because I know I could do it in person one day. Maybe if I just stayed in the old condo for a few nights. Just to see if anything happens? I can't grieve for someone who I know I might meet again can I?"

"She's gone son. Whatever this is, it's best left alone.

"No! Even if it's not this time, I will go back. I'll return to Filey at the start of a solar cycle just to prove it one way or another. I've probably only got three chances to do it if I'm going to find her still alive!"

"Tommy…"

"Please go back inside dad. I just need a moment. I'll be in soon."

Carl returned to the huddle of squabbling domino players.

"Is he alright?" Amy asked

Carl raised his eyebrows.

"I'll go and check on him if he doesn't come in soon." Amy said reassuringly as she prised another domino from her daughter's sticky fist, placed it on the table and then went out for more mulled wine.

As she poured the wine, she looked out onto the balcony but couldn't see Tommy.

Quickly she put down the bottle and rushed out. He was no longer standing out there staring blankly at the sky but as she scanned the garden, she managed to catch a glimpse of the taillights of his car.

Carl rushed to her side.

"He probably just needed a moment to himself." She smiled, but Carl felt the familiar panic raging through his soul once again.

"I'm going after him!"

Niki tried to calm him down.

"Don't be ridiculous, you've been drinking, and your car's not charged!"

"I need to go after him!" Carl was becoming hysterical.

"Go back inside Carl and calm down!" Niki said as she pushed him towards the sliding doors, "You're frightening the kids."

Carl returned to the lounge and picked up his dominoes.

Amy returned to the kitchen to baste the turkey and saw Tommy's phone sitting on the worktop.

Niki pulled little Kelly onto her knee and tickled her into releasing another domino.

The family tried to carry on as though it was any other Christmas Eve. The carols were playing, the stockings were hung, and the mince pie and carrot were ready on Santa's platter.

All heads turned as the latch clicked and Tommy stood in the open doorway with two bottles in his hand.

"Eggnog!" He announced triumphantly.

He could see the relief on the three faces that were gratefully smiling back at him and felt guilty for causing them all to worry.

He had just needed some time to think. He had needed some time to remember and he had needed some time to swing by his office at the Spa and check that the old sports bag he had thrown into a cupboard so many years ago, was still there.

Amy brought out fresh glasses and filled them with the traditional eggnog she loved, and as she handed one to Tommy she leaned over and whispered in his ear.

"Thank you."

Tommy smiled and kissed her cheek.

He raised his glass to everyone as he tried to dispel the feeling of guilt.

As he took a sip and watched Amy scoop little Kelly up in her arms on this lovely Christmas Eve, he hated that it was tainted by the compelling thoughts in his head.

He held his glass in one hand but the other was deep in his trouser pocket, toying affectionately with the old keys to Kelly's condo.

Printed in Great Britain
by Amazon